THE LAST PRIEST OF TINTAGEL

PAMELA TAYLOR

Black Rose Writing | Texas

ISBN: 978-1-68513-683-3
LIBRARY OF CONGRESS CONTROL NUMBER: 2025940386
PUBLISHED BY BLACK ROSE WRITING
www.blackrosewriting.com

Printed in the United States of America
Suggested Retail Price (SRP) $21.95

The Last Priest of Tintagel is printed in Garamond Premier Pro

*As a planet-friendly publisher, Black Rose Writing does its best to eliminate unnecessary waste to reduce paper usage and energy costs, while never compromising the reading experience. As a result, the final word count vs. page count may not meet common expectations.

To Ellie and Adrian, David, Judith, and Miranda
You helped bring this story to life

In the driving rain, the weary priest makes his way to the chapel, as he has done every day for years. Today, in November 1361, he resolves that he won't spend another winter on this lonely windswept headland.

— From the placard at the ruins of the medieval chapel at Tintagel

THE LAST
PRIEST OF
TINTAGEL

I

Oxford, England, 1326

Piran sat alone in the tavern staring into the half-empty mug of ale on the table in front of him. It was his third mug of the evening – an indulgence he never permitted himself. But if he was going to be sent home tomorrow, did it really matter if he was profligate with his rapidly dwindling funds tonight?

Ned, his best friend, had suggested he come along with the others this evening. "It'll take your mind off your problems, Piran." Groups of students from St. Edmund Hall went out drinking every night, and Ned joined them two or three times a week. Except for the occasional Saturday, Piran declined, claiming he needed to prepare for the following day's discourse or complete some treatise he was writing at the master's request. A plausible excuse that allowed him to avoid having to admit he really couldn't afford such extravagance.

But tonight, in another uncharacteristic moment, he'd agreed. "You go on ahead," he told the others. "I'll catch you up."

"Be sure you do," Ned admonished. "You need more fun in your life, mate. Things won't look so dire after an evening's revels."

"I'll be along straightaway. Just need to add the last sentence to this letter to my *kerens*." No matter how much he spoke Latin in his studies or English with his friends, he found it impossible to think of his parents in anything but his native Cornish. He wasn't sure he'd even be sending the letter, but leaving a task unfinished just didn't sit right.

On his way to join his mates at The Stag, he'd passed the open door of The Boar and paused to look inside. It was relatively quiet, and despite Ned's encouragement, Piran really wasn't in the mood for the raucous high spirits at The Stag – and especially not for the jeers and insults that would be hurled his way if de Villiers and his cronies were there. So he walked up to the bar, laid down a farthing, and asked for a mug of ale. Every conversation went silent as every eye in the room turned his way.

The landlord slowly appraised this would-be customer from his brow to his boots and back again, ending with a piercing gaze into Piran's eyes. "Best ye take note ye're in a townie bar, young man. There'll be no roistering or fighting on these premises, ye understand? I run a sober establishment here."

Piran hoped his expression showed only benign compliance and gave no hint of his amusement at the man's utter oblivion to the irony of his last remark. Best not to leave any doubt though. "All I want is a place to sit quietly with my thoughts and my ale. I trust my money's good here?"

The landlord eyed the farthing for a long moment then reached for it with one hand and the ale pitcher with the other, stopping his pour when there was still a good inch between the top of the liquid and the rim of the mug. Piran had seen this gin a hundred times before at The Stag, where the students were so engrossed in their merriment that they took no notice of the short pours and the landlord managed a full extra measure – and thus an extra farthing's profit – out of every pitcher. When the man placed the mug on the bar in front of him, Piran waited patiently – as did the rest of the patrons, hoping, no doubt, that this student who'd dared invade their space would raise some boisterous, self-righteous complaint about being cheated and get thrown out for his troubles. But the only sound came from the hearth, where a log burned through and the severed parts crashed onto the grate.

At long last, the landlord retrieved the pitcher and topped up the mug. With nothing more than a nod of his head, Piran took the mug, found a table not big enough for more than one or two people, sat down, and took his first swallow. The table was close to the hearth, which was fortunate because warmth was as big a priority as ale this February evening. Piran was tired of being cold. He'd been warned by the prior of Launceston, who'd helped him perfect his Latin, that there were no fireplaces in the Halls of Oxford lest some drunken student in excessive high spirits start a conflagration that would spread to nearby Halls or even set the entire town ablaze. Which, of course, made the taverns with their roaring fires even more attractive of a winter's evening. Which, naturally, meant the precautions taken by the university were more than justified. Piran had wondered more than once what it would take to break that cycle so he didn't have to try to grasp his quill with frozen fingers for five months out of the year.

While he sat alone at his table, the other patrons slowly returned to their own pursuits, casting an anxious – or perhaps just curious – glance his way now and again. But as time went on and no one came to join him, even the glances stopped. Now, two hours and two mugs later, he took another swallow, but the ale still stubbornly refused to shed any light on either the cause of his current troubles or a way out of them. His gut told him that sanctimonious bastard de Villiers was somehow responsible. But his gut was no more forthcoming than the ale about exactly how.

Piran's university career had been progressing splendidly. Thanks to the letter from Launceston's prior, Master Bertran had agreed to add Piran to his roll. Despite the master's initial severity, Piran's dedication to his work soon won him the occasional word of praise. And when, in the middle of his second year, he was deemed sufficiently proficient in the arts to begin his theology course – his whole purpose for coming to Oxford, after all – he threw himself into his studies with a zeal none of his fellow students even tried to match. Now in his fourth year, he'd been overjoyed when the master had taken him aside after mass on the third Sunday of Advent. "Continue as you are, Chegwin, and I shall be pleased to award your degree in July."

But something changed when lectures resumed after Twelfth Night. Words of praise gave way to accusations of laziness and admonitions to redouble his efforts. And then, yesterday afternoon, the letter arrived. He took it from his pocket and read it yet again by the glow of the fire.

Mister Chegwin,

You will present yourself at my lodgings at precisely noon on the day after tomorrow. There, we will discuss your recent shortcomings, and I shall determine if you will be given a chance to redeem yourself or if you no longer have a future at this university.

Bertran

With a sigh, Piran returned the missive to his pocket. Was his dream – nay, his very purpose in life – to be thwarted when it was so close to being realized – so nearly within his grasp? He hung his head and muttered to his mug, "But I haven't done anything wrong."

A man at the nearest table turned his way. "You in trouble, son? Not on the run from the sheriff, are you? On account of Simon . . ." He inclined his head toward the landlord at the bar. "He wouldn't take kindly to that."

"It's nothing like that," Piran replied. "Just my studies."

"Well, in that case, it be no business o' mine."

Piran downed what was left in his mug and was headed to the bar to make his evening's expenditures a full penny when Ned walked through the door. "God's bones, Piran. What are you doing here? I've been looking all over for you. Don't you know this is a townie establishment?"

Once again, all eyes turned to the newcomer, and the landlord glared at Piran. "Ye forgotten what I told ye?"

Piran set his empty mug on the bar, ignoring the question, and turned to find Ned standing right behind him. "Come on, Ned. Let's go home."

As they walked out the door, the landlord called after them. "Don't ye be bringing your roistering friends back here, ye hear me?"

They hadn't gone five steps when Ned announced, "De Villiers was looking for you tonight. Overweening whoreson was more insufferable than ever, if you can believe it. Buying drinks for everyone. Spending money like he was some kind of rich lord spreading around his largesse."

"I doubt he wanted to buy me a drink. More likely, just wanted to flaunt it in my face that he'd buy drinks for anyone but a Cornishman."

"You're probably right about that. But why were you drinking alone in a townie bar?"

"Never mind, Ned. Let's just go home."

II

Avignon, France, Four months earlier

No matter how many times Archdeacon de Grandison walked these corridors on his way to the papal apartments, he never failed to marvel at the transformation of this place from its previous purpose as a comfortable but typical episcopal palace to a grandeur that rivaled even the Lateran Palace in Rome. When the long-deadlocked and highly partisan Conclave of 1314-1316 had finally managed to settle on Jacques Duèze as the next Pope, the Italian faction had convinced themselves he would return the Holy See to Rome, and no one believed he would live long enough to do much of any consequence. So far, he was proving them wrong on both counts. At the age of seventy-six, he was still in robust good health with no signs of diminishing intellect and had steadfastly refused to leave France, instead enhancing the papal presence in Avignon. The transformation of his residence had happened over time, of course, and de Grandison had witnessed much of it with his own eyes as he'd served the Pope as nuncio, among other roles, for the past seven years.

Those whose job it was to limit access to the Holy Father knew the archdeacon well and allowed him to move unimpeded throughout the palace. The guard outside the entrance to the private quarters jumped to open the door as de Grandison approached. "He's expecting you, Archdeacon. You'll find him in his study."

When de Grandison reached the study, he found the door open and the man known to the world as Pope John XXII gazing out the window toward the river. Not wanting to startle the older man, he knocked quietly on the door frame.

"Is an open door not an invitation to come inside?" the Pope said without turning away from whatever held his attention in the distance.

"It's not my habit to presume, Holy Father."

"Indeed it is not." The pontiff turned to face his guest. "Do come in, Archdeacon."

De Grandison crossed the room, dropped to one knee, and kissed the papal ring. "*Sancte Pater.*"

"*Salve, fili mi.*"

The formalities attended to, de Grandison rose and the two men embraced like the great friends they had become over the years. Reverting to French – the first language for both of them – the pontiff continued, "I've been eager for your return, John. We've much to discuss." He gestured toward comfortable chairs arranged in front of the hearth, where the remains of a fire smoldered. "Do take a seat. I must be getting old, my friend. It's only mid-October and yet I'm happy for a small fire to break the chill in this room of a morning."

"You look just the same to me, Jacques. You've already outlived three kings and half the college of cardinals. I don't think God's planning to send for you anytime soon."

Duèze chuckled. "I need more men like you around me, John. Laughter is good for the soul."

"Surely there are some among your court worthy of your approval."

"I put them in three categories: the bored, who are therefore boring; the ruthlessly ambitious, who are always scheming; and the drooling sycophants."

It was de Grandison's turn to laugh. "No wonder God doesn't send for you. He's probably worried which category you'd put *Him* in."

"Put my curiosity out of its misery, John. What news from your latest mission to the court of England? Is Edward satisfied that our efforts have resolved the issues between him and Charles?"

"I'm not sure satisfied is the word I'd use. What he is at the moment is impatient. His son performed the agreed homage a couple of months ago yet Charles still hasn't returned the Gascon lands. And Edward wants the boy back in England, but Isabella refuses."

"Perhaps I can intervene with Charles, but that seems less likely with his sister. I'm given to understand she doesn't want their son exposed to the influence of the Despensers, and a mother defending her cub is one of the most ruthless creatures on earth."

"She's made her reasons abundantly clear to Edward as well, but a father – and particularly a king – who wants his son and heir in his own court rather than that of a man he distrusts can be pretty intractable as well."

"Tell me, John . . . is what they say about Edward true?"

"That he's a sodomite and that's why he keeps the Despensers around?" Duèze nodded. "Well, as to the former, I can't say with absolute certainty. What I *can* say to both questions is that Edward is incredibly naïve. He's grateful for the Despensers taking the burden of administration from him, so he turns a blind eye to what he assumes are minor indiscretions and treats the nobles' complaints as the exaggerations of men who resent someone else having a modicum of power. From what I've been able to learn – including from my own family – the complaints are legitimate, and Edward is making a big mistake by failing to take notice. Isabella, on the other hand, sees clearly what her husband does not."

"And the other thing?" Duèze prompted.

Is he searching for a way to bring Edward to heel? De Grandison wondered. *To reconcile him with Isabella and remove her leverage over her brother relative to the Gascon territory?* Whatever his friend's motives, he owed him nothing less than complete honesty. "It's a difficult question, Jacques. Perhaps, perhaps not. Edward's naïveté tends to make him injudicious in his speech. He uses the same language to speak of love for a brother as for a wife or mistress. So when he uses those same words in reference to Hugh – or to Piers Gaveston in the past – can one really know if the love he professes is brotherly or otherwise?"

"I'm inclined to the view that rumors don't persist as these have without some basis." Duèze paused, as if in thought. "But I'm equally disinclined to excommunicate a man without provable evidence. I suppose we shall just have to let the discord between husband and wife play itself out as God sees fit." He sat up straighter and flexed his shoulders, as if trying to shake off something unpleasant. "Enough of that for now. What say you to a stroll about the garden before the sun gets any lower? You can regale me with your more enjoyable exploits since you were last here."

That evening, over a simple but tasty supper, John brought the conversation around to the topic that always interested him after the completion of an assignment. "Where are you sending me next, Jacques? What dragon needs slaying this time?"

Duèze threw his head back and laughed so heartily an attendant came scurrying into the dining room. "Are you alright, Holy Father?"

"Better than alright, Alphonse. Enjoying myself more than I have in months. Now return to whatever it is that you do."

"One of the sycophants?" de Grandison asked when the man was out of earshot.

"One of the boring. A self-appointed worrier over my welfare. I can scarcely rise from my bed of a morning without him fretting about my health or my mood or how taxing the coming day might be. He means well, of course, but it's more tiresome than you could possibly imagine." Duèze downed what was left in his goblet and reached for the wine pitcher to pour a refill. "Really, John. You as my personal Saint George? There's an image I'll not soon forget."

"My sword is at your command, oh great king of Silene." De Grandison raised his goblet to his friend then completed the gesture by taking a sip of wine. "Legends aside, Jacques, I know you well enough to be in no doubt that you already have a plan for what's next for me."

Duèze smiled and then, it seemed to John, his expression turned briefly sad before brightening once more. "I do indeed. And one that will be most advantageous to you. Sadly, it will mean you'll be away from these premises far longer than I would like."

"Am I permitted to know what it might be?"

"All in due course, my friend, but I'm certain you'll be pleased. That said, it will be important that you be in England when the moment arises, and I fear that means you should go sooner than later. Charles has so far resisted Isabella's entreaties to become involved in her dispute with her husband. A wise move, to my way of thinking. But we both know Isabella is her father's daughter. Once she sets her mind to something . . ."

Duèze let the thought hang in the air while he took a swallow of wine then rose from the table. "Pour yourself a refill and let's retire to the comfort of my sitting room." De Grandison did as he was bid then followed his host to the room next door where the fire was lit and a dozen candelabras bathed the room in warm light.

"As I was saying," the pope continued, lowering himself into a chair amply supplied with cushions for the comfort of his aging bones, "if Isabella succeeds in changing Charles's mind, that could mean war between France and England. And it would not be in our best interests for you to be stranded on the wrong side of the Channel. To that end, I've secured you a position at Oxford as *magister regens* for as long as it may suit my purposes."

"And what of my duties as Archdeacon?"

"You'll continue to manage them as you have while serving as my emissary. The university will grant you that latitude. But if I may suggest . . . it would not go amiss for you to begin preparing someone to succeed you."

Why all the secrecy? de Grandison wondered, but he wouldn't ask even though Jacques was being far more inscrutable than usual. *I suppose I'll find out soon enough. And he's always had my best interests at heart.* "And when do I return to England?" he asked aloud.

"You needn't take up your post until the beginning of the new year. Stay here for a time. Spend the Christmas season. I'll be bereft of your company long before I'm ready, so allow me to enjoy it for as long as I can. In the meantime, maybe we'll learn what Isabella's up to."

"It was being whispered around Edward's court that she's taken up with Roger Mortimer."

"And my sources say she's considering an alliance with the Count of Hainault. Even thinking of betrothing her son to the count's second daughter."

"Edward would be livid if she undertook such a thing without his permission."

They continued thus until the fire was reduced to embers and the candles had begun to snuff themselves out in puddles of their own wax, old friends enjoying a welcome respite from the responsibilities of their calling.

Oxford, England, Feast Day of St. Julian, 1326

"De Seton told me you were back, John, and I've been remiss in not inviting you here sooner. Please . . . take a seat." Master Bertran welcomed de Grandison into the room he used as a study and gestured toward a pair of chairs near the hearth. "It's been a long time since we shared a room at Broadgates Hall when we both thought we wanted to be lawyers. And look at us now. You at the beck and call of the Pope, and me trying to pour knowledge into heads, some as receptive as sponges and others that seem as impervious as stone."

"Well, for some reason he chooses not to divulge, the Holy Father seems to think I need experience of your profession." De Grandison took the chair opposite his host. "It will be good to have a friend to consult about those problem students."

"Which, I'm ashamed to admit, is precisely why I wanted to talk with you."

"I've done something wrong already? Certainly not by intent, I assure you."

"Quite the contrary. I have one of those problem students and am at a complete loss for what to do about him. I was hoping a fresh mind might have some ideas."

"Not certain I can offer much advice, but I'm happy to listen."

"It's a most peculiar situation, John. This young man has been one of the most promising intellects I've ever accepted onto my rolls. More than just a sponge – eager to explore difficult topics, thoughtful and cogent in oral discourse, and showing sparks of brilliance in his writing. So promising, in fact, that it's been my intention to encourage him to become a fellow of one of the colleges and pursue a doctorate. Despite the fact that he's been singularly focused on becoming a priest, I've been hoping to persuade him along a different path – or at least to convince him to postpone entry into the priesthood until he can do so with credentials that would accelerate his advancement in the Church."

"He sounds like the sort we could use more of in our calling," said de Grandison.

"He is. Or rather, he was. Since lectures resumed at the start of the year, he's undergone some sort of transformation. His writing has become . . . uninspired . . . at times, even naïve or simplistic. And that's when he even completes an assignment at all. He still speaks well in oral discourse, but his confidence is waning . . . increasingly so with each time I'm forced to reprimand him about a deficient or missing treatise. It's really quite puzzling."

"I assume you've considered the possibility that, with his degree in sight, he's taken to spending his evenings in the tavern rather than at his studies."

"That would be my conclusion for anyone else, but not Chegwin. In three and a half years, he's never once been reported to me for excess of any sort. Neither drinking nor brawling nor any of the boisterousness we both know these young men get up to when they taste freedom for the first time. I have it on good authority he's only seen in the taverns one night each week and even then, he limits his drink to a single mug of ale. Something else has gone wrong, John, and I've been utterly unable to lay my finger on the cause."

"So what would you like me to do, Hugh?"

"Put simply, discover the problem so we can get him back on the right course. To let such a mind go to waste through my neglect would be . . . dare I say sacrilegious?"

"Perhaps if I could see his writings . . . both the flawed ones and some of the earlier ones. Maybe even some from other students so I'd have something for comparison."

"I anticipated your request. That stack on the corner of my writing table is yours to peruse. But, John, would you also consider taking him under your wing for a time? What if he's simply gotten bored with me and is no longer challenged to do his best?"

"Surely you don't think that's likely."

"It would be the utmost hubris on my part to deny the possibility."

"If you think it might help."

"Well, I'm certain it can't hurt. What if he's simply afraid to discuss with *me* whatever's troubling him lest I become disappointed in him after the praise I've given in the past? He's always struck me as one with a strong desire not to let down those who've supported him."

De Grandison threw up his hands in a gesture of acquiescence. "Very well. When can I meet this herebefore gem of academic glory?"

"I've summoned him here at noon tomorrow. Perhaps you could arrive a quarter hour earlier."

"Well, as it seems I'm not otherwise obligated . . ."

"I'm grateful, John. In all my years as a master, I've never seen a case like this. It's usually quite the opposite. They see the time looming when they should be expecting to receive their degree and develop an almost palpable fear they might fall short. In fact, I have one such now – a Mister de Villiers – who has suddenly gone from wastrel to diligent student – almost as if it were some sort of religious conversion."

De Grandison chuckled and rose from his chair. "Until tomorrow then." Taking the stack of papers from the table and making for the door, he added, "It seems I have some reading to do."

III

Despite the ale – or perhaps because of it – Piran slept fitfully, his dreams a strange hotchpotch of the impossible. His *mamm* in tears after being berated by the landlord at The Boar. Except that the landlord looked like de Villiers, and he kept shouting at Piran's *mamm* that Cornish women were the worst kind of puterelles. Himself as a young boy, following his *tas* around the baron's estate counting deer – with Master Bertran following behind berating him for his faulty Latin grammar. An image from a stained glass window of Jesus saving the fishermen in a storm. Except that Jesus was holding his hand out to Piran, but as soon as Piran took it, he dropped it, sank into the sea, and flailed around to find his savior's hand again. And all the while, he knew he was dreaming but couldn't bring himself enough awake to shake it off. When he finally woke fully with the sunrise, he was as tired as if he'd never slept at all.

He needed to clear his mind and calm his thoughts before meeting with the master and he couldn't do that here in the Hall, so he dressed quickly, threw on his cloak, and headed for the one place he'd be certain to find some peace. The sun had barely begun to warm the wintry air as he made his way west along the High Street before turning left on Grope Lane, which was utterly deserted at this hour of the day, though that would change, Piran knew, after sundown. When the lane ran out, he followed the well-trodden path past Merton College, eventually coming to St. Frideswide's Priory.

He'd first wandered into the priory church while exploring the town not long after arriving in Oxford for the first time. It was the most beautiful place he had ever seen. The elaborately carved wooden ceiling from the entrance to the crossing gave way to even more elaborate pendant vaulting in stone above the choir and the altar. Rounded arches in thick walls near the entrance held beautiful stained glass. But farther down the nave, the old Romanesque architecture was superseded by the Gothic, with pointed arches and beautiful stone tracery adorning even larger, more colorful windows.

During his journey from Cornwall, Piran had begun to question himself. Why was he leaving everything behind – his home, his family, all the people and places he loved so well – to embark on an entirely new life? But inside the priory church, all doubt vanished. Somehow, within the majesty of this place, he felt a peace deep in his soul unlike anything he'd experienced before. There was a presence here – something so much greater than himself that he felt he could draw strength and comfort from it. And if he could bring this peace and comfort – this grace from God, as he understood it – to people who would never in their lives see anything so magnificent, then that would be a life well lived.

At the east end of the north aisle, he'd come upon a narrow chapel almost entirely filled by a shrine. One of the monks found him there on his knees in prayer. "Is someone dear to you in need of healing, my son?" he asked quietly.

Piran crossed himself and rose to his feet. "No, brother. At least, not to my knowledge. I just wanted to pray to this saint to bless my family, who are far away. I also asked him to intercede with St. Piran on my family's behalf."

"Her," said the monk. "These are the relics of St. Frideswide, to whom our priory is dedicated. Look here." He pointed to the carvings along the top of the shrine. "Just here on the corner, among the foliage. This is her image. She had the gift of healing in her lifetime and is even now known for restoring the faithful to health."

"I'm sorry, sir. I . . . I didn't know. I meant no disrespect."

The monk's smile was warm . . . almost fatherly. "I'm Brother Ansfrid. You've come to Oxford to study, I presume."

"I mean to become a priest."

"Then you must apply yourself diligently and not be swayed by the lusty pursuits of so many young men who come here as students."

"I doubt I can afford lusty pursuits. My family is of limited means."

"That is often not a deterrent, I fear. But should you find yourself tempted, know that you are welcome to come here instead."

From that day on, St. Frideswide's had become Piran's refuge. It was here he'd come to shake off the humiliation after his first encounter with de Villiers. It was about two months into Piran's first year that he'd begun to realize he could spare a farthing now and then to join Ned and Robin and James, the others who shared their four-person room, for a night at the tavern. They'd been enjoying a pleasant mug of ale at the Swindlestock when the hum of conversation suddenly waned as a group of five students strode through the door. One sported a pheasant feather on his cap, though the remainder of his clothing didn't speak of great wealth. Nevertheless, the other four seemed to defer to him as he marched up to the bar and ordered ale for his entire entourage.

Ned put his head down and spoke quietly to Piran. "Ignore him. There's a large empty table on the other side of the room. If we pay him no mind, maybe he'll just take his mates there and leave us alone."

The tactic worked for a time, but then the group started making their way around the room, going from table to table where they were either welcomed or shunned. Neither reaction seemed to faze feather-cap, who acted as if everyone should be pleased that he deigned to grace them with his company. And then he came up behind Robin, his four acolytes in tow. "Ned Fletcher," he greeted the table.

"Martin," Ned replied.

"Martinus to you, Fletcher. Haven't you learned that yet?" Ned didn't bother to reply, but the self-styled Martinus didn't seem to care as he'd set his gaze on Piran. "And who might you be? I don't think I've seen you here before."

Without looking up from his ale, Piran replied, "Piran. I don't come often."

"Piran?" Feather-cap turned to his acolytes. "What kind of a name is that?"

"I'm named for a saint," Piran said quietly.

"Then you must have another name to go with it."

"Leave him be, Martin," said Ned.

"You stay out of this, Fletcher. I like to know the names of men I meet so I can greet them when we see each other in the street. Come now, Piran, I'll go first. Martinus de Villiers, at your service."

"Piran Chegwin."

"Chegwin?" De Villiers's expression turned dark and his tone menacing. "Chegwin, you say?"

"Aye," Piran replied quietly.

Now de Villiers raised his voice to address the entire room. "Chegwin? A Cornish pig in our midst? We really can't have that, now, can we?"

"Really, Martin?" Ned rose to Piran's defense. "He's a university student just like you and me. What does it matter where he comes from?"

"I told you, Fletcher." De Villiers looked down his nose at Ned. "It's Martinus. And it matters because he's Cornish."

"I'm from the West Country too," said Ned.

"Dorset," De Villiers retorted.

"Lyme Regis is almost in Devonshire."

"And neither one is Cornwall. God's bones, man, they're not even English. Don't even speak the same language as us. And they don't belong in an English university, much less in *my* tavern."

Piran had had enough. He rose from his chair and turned to confront his accuser. "Yes, I speak Cornish. I also speak English as well as you." Then he switched to Latin. "And I've no doubt my Latin is far better than yours."

De Villiers turned to his acolytes. "You heard him. The Cornish pig just insulted me. What are we going to do about that?" The acolytes edged closer.

Ned, Robin, and James were now all on their feet. If there was going to be a brawl, it wasn't going to be five against one. "I think it's you who insulted Piran," Ned paused briefly before adding "Martinus" with a snarl.

"And it isn't *your* tavern," Robin chimed in.

"Wherever I choose to drink is *my* tavern."

"Then choose to drink elsewhere," said Ned.

Piran was growing increasingly anxious. Master Bertran had warned him about tavern brawls that turned into knife fights in the streets and made it abundantly clear that he wouldn't hesitate to strike a student off his roll for such behavior. Conversation in the bar had ceased and every eye was on the two groups facing off over the small table near the hearth.

Then de Villiers did something utterly unexpected. Turning to his acolytes, he handed his mug to one of them. "It seems I'm dry, Wainwright. Fetch me another ale." But even as Wainwright headed to the bar, the tableau remained frozen, the audience fixated, wondering what might happen next.

When Wainwright returned, de Villiers took the mug then scanned the room, obviously wanting to be sure everyone was watching. He took a step closer to Piran, downed a swallow of ale, and then threw the remaining contents of the mug in Piran's face. "No Cornish pigs," he declared and slammed his mug down on the table. When he repeated the words and the gesture, the acolytes took up the chant.

"Let's get out of here, Ned." Piran grabbed his friend's arm and tugged him toward the door. Robin and James lingered, as if they wanted to stay and fight, but as the rest of the room joined in the chanting, all four of them fled into the cold night air.

"We can't just let him get away with that, Ned," said Robin.

"And what do you propose we do? He's got everyone in the place riled up now. I, for one, don't like those odds."

As he took off down the High Street leaving his mates behind, Piran heard James say, "Maybe we should go to the Stag." In Grope Lane, Piran elbowed his way among the men bargaining for the services of the women who plied their trade there, earning himself several epithets and one order to "Find yer own woman, whorseson; this'un's mine." Catching his toe on a loose cobble, he almost stumbled into a couple having it on against a wall near the end of the street, but they took no notice. When he finally reached the priory church, he was grateful to find the door open and, inside, a soft glow from candles burning somewhere near the crossing. He made his way toward the glow and found a monk lighting fresh candles at the entrance to the choir stalls. "What brings you here at this hour, my son?"

"One of your brothers once told me I could always seek sanctuary in these precincts."

The monk turned his attention from the candles toward the new arrival. "I did indeed." A great sense of relief washed over Piran as he recognized Brother Ansfrid. "And the fact that you smell strongly of ale tells me you've recently come from a tavern. That your clothing is soaked tells me it wasn't a pleasant experience for you. Come."

They sat in the choir stalls and, without really intending to do so, Piran found himself pouring out the whole story.

"It's in the nature of far too many men, young Piran, to scorn what they choose not to understand. I think perhaps that's a lesson you'll not soon forget. Such men are often obdurate . . . unwilling to be persuaded. You may believe you were humiliated, but in fact you showed great courage by not rising to the bait. I commend you for that."

Since that night more than three years ago, Piran had sought the solace of the priory church on numerous occasions. Sometimes it was to work through a matter that was troubling him, as when he'd been worried near the end of his second year that his family might not have the money for him to continue. Sometimes it was to calm himself, as when he'd had a particularly nasty encounter with de Villiers and his mates, who seemed always to travel as a pack wherever Martinus wanted to go. Sometimes it was just to enjoy the beauty and serenity of the place and to contemplate what kind of priest he wanted to be once his studies were complete and he could be ordained.

Today, he needed to think. Master Bertran would be expecting some sort of explanation. But an explanation for what? *How can a man explain what he doesn't understand himself?* Despite his certainty that de Villiers was somehow implicated in whatever was afoot, he couldn't cast blame without proof. And then another, even more disturbing thought crossed his mind. *What if I'm not even allowed to speak? What if the master has already made up his mind and his only words will be of dismissal?*

He made his way to St. Frideswide's shrine. Perhaps she would understand his needs. Perhaps she could heal his worried mind. She was the patron of Oxford. Surely that meant all of Oxford and not just those suffering a physical ailment. In any event, she was all he had, and he fell to his knees in prayer.

IV

Feeling like a condemned man walking to his own doom, Piran showed up outside Master Bertran's lodgings well before the appointed hour. To be late would be to pile yet another offense on top of those he was supposed to have already committed. All he could do now was to wait and try to hope.

The moment the bells at St. Fridewside's began to toll midday, he rapped strongly on the master's door, then took two steps backward to wait at a polite distance as he counted the bells. He had reached ten and was considering that he might need to knock again when the door finally swung open, revealing the master himself. "Chegwin. Punctual as usual."

Piran doffed his cap and offered a little bow of the head. "Master."

"Do come in, Chegwin."

Piran stepped inside with a confidence he didn't really feel, but he knew hesitation would not win the master's approval. He stood, cap in hand, with his back pressed against the wall while Bertran closed the door. Without a further word, the master led the way down the corridor, opened the second door on the right, and entered the room.

Piran assumed he was meant to follow and found himself in what was obviously Bertran's study. Across the room, in front of three tall, narrow windows was a large writing table with elaborate carving on the legs. Its surface held several neat stacks of papers, presumably student work, and on one side, a large open book that the master must have been consulting – *perhaps for his next lecture*, Piran mused. To the right, a small sideboard held a pitcher and four elaborately decorated goblets while the remainder of the wall was filled with shelves stacked with books and boxes of scrolls. To the left, several chairs were arranged before a fireplace with a carved surround where a nice fire warmed the room.

To Piran's great surprise, one of the chairs was occupied by a priest. A man with large, brown eyes in a clean-shaven face and wavy brown hair combed straight back from his forehead and trimmed neatly at the length of his ear lobes. The fine fabric of his cassock said this was no ordinary priest. Bertran took the chair next to the priest and gestured to one on the opposite side of the fireplace. "Take a seat, Chegwin." Now quite uneasy – utterly uncertain what this new development might mean – Piran hesitantly did as he was bid.

"This, Mister Chegwin," Bertran continued, nodding his head toward the priest, "is Archdeacon de Grandison, lately in service to the Pope and now, at the Holy Father's express request, assigned to us here as a *magister regens*."

Piran rose from his seat, half bowed his head, half genuflected, and muttered, "Father … uh … Archdeacon." Sitting back down, he added, "I'm sorry, sirs, I don't know the proper form of address."

"Archdeacon should suffice," said Bertran.

"Actually," de Grandison now spoke, "given my current role, I believe the proper address is 'Master,' is it not?" He glanced at Bertran, who merely smiled. "Of course, Mister … Chegwin, is it? I've no objection to 'Father' if you find that more comfortable."

"Yes, Master … Father."

De Grandison smiled. A smile that came from the depths of his eyes and seemed to Piran the kindest expression he had seen in all his time at university. But even that apparent kindness was not enough to break through his anxiety over what was about to happen.

Bertran got straight to the point. "You know why you're here, Chegwin."

Piran desperately wanted to protest "But I *don't*, Master. I *truly* have no idea." But he held his tongue.

"You know I've become increasingly disappointed with your work," Bertran continued, "and yet I've seen no indication of any effort on your part to return to your previously high standards. I've contemplated the possible reasons for your failure at some length and have decided, with some reluctance, that it's best for me to remove you from my roll."

Though he'd known this was a possibility – though he knew he should accept the master's decision with whatever composure he could muster – the blow was so overwhelming Piran couldn't prevent his shoulders slumping forward and his despair rising to the surface. He was vaguely aware of someone in the room talking, but the only thing he could do was stare at his shoes and struggle to get his emotions under control. *How could this be happening? How could he explain it to his family who had sacrificed so much for him? To the Launceston prior who had believed in him and encouraged him to pursue his dream? To the baron – his father's employer – who had given him the money for this final year? How could he even make sense of it for himself? All he'd ever wanted – ripped away for no reason that he could understand. Could this really be God's will? Not the God he thought he knew. Not the God whose love and comfort and grace he so wanted to share with others.*

At long last, he became aware of the utter silence in the room and knew he could no longer avoid the inevitable. Raising his head, he looked blankly at Master Bertran and murmured, "Yes, Master. Whatever your decision. I'll be on my way then, if I may?"

Bertran stroked his chin. "Chegwin, have you heard anything I just said?"

"I heard I'm to be struck from your roll, sir, so that means the end of my time here."

"Get a grip on yourself, Chegwin. Bring us some wine, de Grandison. I believe the lad needs fortification."

The priest went to the sideboard and returned with the pitcher and three goblets, filling each and handing the first one to Piran. "Drink ..." He paused. "I don't believe my friend Bertran told me your Christian name."

"It's Piran, Father."

"For the patron of Cornwall?"

"Aye, Father."

"Then drink, Piran. But slowly. Bertran and I will join you." He took a goblet for himself and handed the other one to his host.

Piran took a tentative swallow. The wine was good. But he couldn't let it go to his head. And that could happen all too easily after last night's ale and no food yet today.

"Now, let me repeat what you seem not to have heard, Chegwin," Bertran resumed after taking a healthy swallow from his own goblet. "The conclusion I have reached, with some reluctance, is that I may have taught you all I'm capable of – that the reason we find ourselves at the current impasse is that you could benefit from a new perspective. That's why I'm removing you from my roll – so that de Grandison can add you to his. With your avowed desire to enter the priesthood, perhaps it's time for you to be guided on that path by someone of the same persuasion."

Piran took another swallow of wine, not so much because he was thirsty as to give himself time to take in what he'd just heard. "So . . ." He hesitated, still uncertain. "So I'm not to be sent home?"

"Not at the moment, no."

"Thank you, Master. Father. I'm truly grateful. I won't disappoint you. Either of you. I promise. I can't begin to express my gratitude, sir." Piran's relief was such that he couldn't seem to stop talking.

De Grandison's kind smile returned. "Then perhaps, Mister Chegwin . . . Piran . . . we should begin our work together over a good midday meal and become acquainted. Master Bertran has had more than three years to come to know you. That means I have quite a bit of catching up to do. May I suggest the Swindlestock?" He rose and addressed his host. "If you'll excuse us, Bertran?"

"By all means, my friend."

Piran's head was spinning. Somehow he managed to get to his feet, offer a final acknowledgment to his master – well, his previous master now – and follow de Grandison out into the lane. Once they were alone and headed for the High Street, Piran knew he had to speak up. "Father, I'm sorry, but . . ." He stopped in his tracks.

De Grandison turned to face him. "Sorry already, Piran?"

"I'm sorry, Father, but I can't afford to eat at a tavern. I've already paid for my meals at St. Edmund, and I've nothing extra."

"Then you'll be my guest. I may not be the heir, but that doesn't mean I don't benefit from my family's position. Now shall we? I'm really quite hungry."

For the first time in two days, Piran smiled. He could feel hope returning. And even though they'd only just barely said hello, he knew he liked this man.

At the entrance to the Swindlestock, Piran hesitated. "Something else wrong, Chegwin?" his companion asked.

"Sorry, Father. Only, I had a bad experience here not long after I first arrived in Oxford, and I haven't been inside since."

"Then it's high time you replace that bad experience with a good one."

"Archdeacon!" the landlord called out as soon as they stepped inside. "You picked a *fine* day to grace these premises. We have that pheasant potage you're so fond of."

"Then we'll have two bowls, Arnold, a big chunk of paindemaine for each of us, and two large mugs of ale."

"You heard him, wench," Arnold admonished the barmaid. "Get to it." She scurried away to fetch the food while he filled two mugs to the brim. "And you'll have my best table by the fire. Diggory . . . Hutch . . . you lads have warmed your backsides long enough. Find yourselves another table so the archdeacon can have his meal in comfort." While the backside-warmers fled to the other side of the room, the landlord carried the two mugs of ale to the table without spilling a single drop. Then with a broad sweep of one hand, he said, "Your table, Archdeacon. And let me have your cloaks. I'll hang 'em on pegs behind the bar so's nothing gets spilled on 'em."

No sooner were they seated than the barmaid reappeared with steaming bowls of potage and half a loaf of bread. Piran was in a daze. How had this landlord – known for his short temper and short pours – become such an obsequious host? It was all down to the archdeacon, of course. Piran was of no more import than the stool he was sitting on. *Nobody would even know I was here if I weren't with de Grandison.* He tore a chunk off the loaf of bread and picked up his spoon. *Might as well enjoy it while I can. Might be the only time I'll ever be so lucky.*

Halfway through the bowl of potage, Piran suddenly realized he was gulping his food – his dining companion had enjoyed no more than a few spoonfuls. De Grandison must have noticed as well. "Rather better than what they serve in the Halls, eh, Piran?"

"More like what I imagine food in heaven must be like. What they serve in the Halls is . . . well, the best I can say for it is that keeps a man alive."

De Grandison laughed aloud. "Then enjoy. And have another bowl if you'd like."

No sooner had Piran raised the spoon to his mouth again than the door opened and de Villiers and his acolytes strode in. They appeared to be headed for the bar when de Villiers suddenly stopped, leaving the acolytes stumbling all over themselves as they tried to avoid running into their leader. Turning on his heel, de Villiers announced loudly enough for everyone to hear, "I've changed my mind. I think I'd rather drink at The Stag this afternoon." He began to make his way toward the door, but chose a path through the tables that brought him alongside the one where Piran sat. "Cornish pig," he murmured under his breath, then quickened his pace and made a flamboyant exit with the acolytes rushing to keep up.

De Grandison took no obvious note of what was happening, but once the door closed behind the pack he asked, without looking up from his meal, "Acquaintance of yours?"

"I wish he wasn't."

"Seems he doesn't like Cornishmen."

"Me least of all."

"I admire the way you simply ignored him."

"I've learned it's what gets under his skin the most. He wants a fight." Piran took a swallow of ale. "We both know I'm no match for him. It makes him really angry when I don't rise to his bait. But at least I get to keep my pride and my bones intact."

De Grandison took the last bit of bread and wiped his bowl clean before popping the bread into his mouth. "Does this fellow have a name?"

"Martin de Villiers. At least, he was christened Martin, but he insists everyone call him Martinus. Talk among the other students is that he thinks calling himself Martinus will help him advance his career in the Church once he gets ordained."

"Oh, dear." De Grandison chuckled. "What a rude surprise awaits him. But nothing less than such arrogance deserves." He emptied his mug and pushed his dishes to the side of the table. "Alright, Piran, let's start working out how we're going to address Master Bertran's concerns so that you get your degree in July."

"With respect, Father, I should really go now. I'm supposed to be in the master's lecture when the bells toll for Nones, and I don't want to disappoint him further."

"Never mind that lecture, Piran. I'll see that you don't miss anything. And besides, you're on my roll now, and I have no intention of striking you off before we get to the bottom of whatever it is that's gone wrong in your studies. Why don't you start by telling me why you want to be a priest."

V

"We've got a problem, Martinus." Wainwright burst through the door, interrupting de Villiers as he held court with the other acolytes in the room that he rented on the second story of a private home on Brasenose Lane. Though his family wasn't noble, they had sufficient means to allow him the luxury of a room of his own rather than the cramped, four-to-a-room quarters most students endured and enough spending money to enjoy his time at university.

No less than he deserved, to Martin's way of thinking. As the third son, he'd been short-changed his entire life. John, the eldest, was groomed to take over the family's wine trade, his health fretted over, every little sniffle a cause for concern, a search for his bride carefully undertaken, his future always the first topic of conversation. Peter, the next, was their mother's favorite, and she persuaded her father to give him the small freehold farm that would have been her inheritance eventually. Martin always felt like an afterthought, especially when his father told him bluntly that his only choice was to become a priest.

"I'll pay for your studies, but then you'll be on your own," his father declared. "Nothing more from me or from your mother – or from any of this family."

"But what if I don't want to be a priest? What if I don't want to spend my life in some tiny village in some parish no one's ever heard of?" Martin had tried to protest.

"You'll become a priest and that's final. I'll have none of your whining, boy. And don't think you can go complaining to your mother. You can go to Oxford, where I've secured you a place, or you can walk out of this house now and never look back."

So he'd chosen Oxford, thinking that would at least buy him some time to figure something else out. But shortly after he'd arrived at the university, he came to the realization that there was more to the Church than just parish priests. There was a whole aristocracy one could aspire to. And that, he decided, was where he would set his sights. He bought himself a fine cap with a pheasant feather and set out to show the world he was anything but an afterthought. The first time he gazed at himself in the mirror wearing the cap, a smug smile slowly appeared on his face. He would rise to the heights of that aristocracy. And nothing – and nobody – would stand in his way. The smile turned to a leer. God help anyone who tried.

It had been a stroke of luck that the four students who occupied the much smaller room across the corridor from Martin in Brasnose Lane were so awed by his apparent superiority that they chose to follow him around like lost puppies. Every man of substance, rising in the world, needed an entourage, and the foursome suited Martin quite nicely. He might even find some of them useful when doing his assignments became too tiresome.

Now, stopping in mid-sentence, he turned what he hoped was a look of pure disdain on the intruder. "You always have a problem, Wainwright. What is it this time?"

"It's not *my* problem – it's yours." Wainwright joined the other three sitting in a row on the bed while Martin occupied the only chair in the room. "Bertran has struck Chegwin off his roll."

De Villiers's annoyed expression changed at once to a broad grin. "That's no problem, Wainwright. That's what we've been trying to make happen, isn't it? Cause for celebration, don't you think, men?"

While the others attempted to reflect de Villiers's elation back to him, Wainwright shook his head. "You didn't let me finish, Martinus."

"What's to finish? We've won! The Cornish pig will be gone on the next coach that comes through."

"Not so fast, Martinus. Chegwin's going nowhere."

The grin became a glower. "What makes you say that?"

"Because I know. I saw the pig hanging around outside Bertran's lodgings yesterday and thought maybe something was up, so when I went there today to scribe for the master while he dictated his thoughts on the latest completed assignments, I kept my ears open. He said yours was promising, by the way – that if you continued in this vein, you might just get your degree after all."

"Forget about my treatise. What about Chegwin?"

"That's exactly what I asked when the master finished dictating without mentioning St. Piran."

"And?" De Villiers was getting impatient, but Wainwright seemed to be enjoying a rare chance to be the center of attention.

"He said . . ." Wainwright paused, straightened his spine, lifted his chin, and looked down his nose. "He said 'You needn't concern yourself with him, Mister Wainwright, as he is no longer on my roll. He is now under the supervision of the new teaching master, Grandson.'" His imitation of Bertran complete. Wainwright wrinkled his nose. "That's a funny name, don't you think – Grandson? Whose grandson is he?"

"It's de Grandison, you idiot," Martin said through clenched teeth. "Do I have to tell you *everything*?"

Wainwright shrugged, apparently unconcerned by Martin's rebuke. "Alright, de Grandison then. Anyway, your problem is, I won't be able do what you want any longer if Master Bertran isn't overseeing Chegwin's work."

De Villliers rubbed the back of his neck then rose from his chair and began pacing – five steps past the acolytes perched on the bed, seven steps back toward the door, another pass in front of the acolytes, once again to the door. Four heads on swivels followed his every move. On the next pass, he suddenly stopped and faced them, startling them all into leaning backward as if he were about to strike someone. "What we have here, gentlemen, is merely a setback. What we need is a new plan. And if I'm not mistaken, what a new teaching master needs is a scribe to assist with his record-keeping." He surveyed the four candidates in front of him, looking closely at each in turn.

"Can't be me, Martinus," said Wainwright.

"Of course it can't, you idiot. That would be too obvious. Besides, I still need a spy in Bertran's domain, so you'll stay where you are." He scanned the other three again, rubbing his chin as if contemplating a momentous decision. "Hawthorn, it's you."

"Not me, Martinus, please," Hawthorn whined. "I barely have time to do my own work, much less work for someone else."

"It's you, Hawthorn. You have the best hand, so you're the most likely to be accepted as a scribe. And if you can't finish you work, just copy someone else's." Then as an afterthought, he added, "But make a few changes so you don't get caught. Having you thrown out on your ear wouldn't suit my purposes."

Hawthorn hung his head in defeat. "It's not so bad, Hawthorn," Wainwright tried to console his friend. "In fact, it's kind of nice spending some time in a master's study with a warm fire."

De Villiers struck a pose, hands on his hips. "That's it, then. It's decided. We'll get rid of the Cornish pig yet. Come, gentlemen." He marched to the door and grabbed his cloak from the nearby peg. "Drinks at the Swindlestock, I think. Our little enterprise won't be defeated so easily."

Piran sat patiently in de Grandison's study while the archdeacon read his work – a homily appropriate for Whitsunday that he'd been asked to write as if he were preparing to deliver it to his parishioners. Patient in his demeanor, at least. Inside was utter turmoil. His future hung in the balance. If he was still found wanting . . .

At long last, de Grandison laid the pages on the small table beside his chair. "You can put your mind at rest, Chegwin." Piran couldn't suppress an audible sigh of relief, which brought a smile to de Grandison's eyes. "Your theme – that the Holy Spirit helps us to live in harmony despite our differences – is a worthy one. The way you've presented it shows deep insight. But more than that, you've succeeded in inviting your listeners to examine their own hearts without in any way casting them as evil or lacking. It seems to me, Piran, you have the makings of a very fine priest."

"Then I can dare to hope, Father, that I'll receive my degree after all?"

De Grandison didn't answer directly. "The other thing this shows me . . ." He gestured to the pages on the table. ". . . is that Bertran was right to be concerned." Piran's face fell. "Don't despair, lad," de Grandison rushed to add. "What I mean is, we need to find the reason for the poorly prepared treatises. I've read all your work, and until the beginning of this year, it showed great promise and then . . ." He went to his writing table and fetched the pile of papers Bertran had provided. Proffering one to Piran, he continued. "This one for instance. Do you recall it?"

"Aye, Father. An analysis of St. Augustine's views on a Just War."

"The theory well articulated and the analysis relative to Edward I's war on the Scots thoughtfully presented." Handing the next document to Piran, he said, "Now this one . . . look it over and tell me what you think."

Piran quickly scanned the two sheets of paper. "Father, I've never seen these pages before in my life. I don't know whose writings these are, but they're not mine. I never wrote this – or anything like it."

The archdeacon sat up straighter in his chair and studied his student carefully. The young man seemed thoroughly perplexed, shaking his head as he read the words once again. De Grandison handed over the entire stack of pages. "Here . . . have a look at all of these and pick out the ones you don't recognize."

Examining every page, Piran kept shaking his head, only now and again pulling out a page to set aside. Finished, he handed over six pages. "It's easier to pick out the ones I do recognize, Father. These. All from last autumn. The rest . . ."

De Grandison furrowed his brow. "Chegwin, I don't want to doubt you, but I have to be absolutely certain. Are you suggesting Master Bertran has substituted someone else's work for yours?"

"I'm not suggesting anything, Father. I'm only saying I never wrote these. Can't you see the difference in how they're written? I don't mean the letters on the page; I mean the thoughts expressed."

"Calm yourself, Piran. This is exactly what Bertran and I both saw, but what neither of us can understand is why. If you didn't write them, then who did?"

"I don't know, Father. And I don't know how they came to Master Bertran with my name on them."

"Then it seems we have some work to do to figure this out. Give me the rest. I intend to lock all these in a strongbox so no one can tamper with them. In the meantime, I have an idea how we can begin to work out what's afoot. I want you to continue to attend both Bertran's lectures and mine. For each treatise you're assigned to write in both courses, I want you to make two copies. One, you'll turn in as you usually do, with those of all the other students. The other, you'll bring straight to me and trust it to no one's hands but mine. Then we'll see what happens."

"But, Father, I'm down to my last two shillings. I can't afford the extra paper and ink."

"Then you'll have some from my own supply. Just don't tell anyone where you got it. And don't let anyone else in on what you're doing lest whoever's behind this discover the trap we've set."

A week later, de Grandison and Bertran dined together in the latter's lodgings. "I hope you like partridge, John," said Bertran as he carved the bird and put a substantial portion on his friend's plate. "Mistress Morlond fancies it her very best dish and insists on serving it to my guests." Filling his own plate, he sat down and picked up his knife. "In truth it's not bad at all, but I rarely tell her so."

"Treating your housekeeper like one of your students, then?" De Grandison sampled a morsel of the partridge. "This is really quite delicious. You shouldn't be so sparing with your compliments, Hugh, lest someone woo her away." He sipped his wine. "Like me for instance."

It wasn't long before the conversation turned to young Chegwin. "So you're telling me, John, that someone's tampering with the papers that are being submitted to me?"

"It seems that way. Chegwin was quite sincere in his insistence that most of the work you'd seen this year was not his. I'm inclined to believe him."

"Well, he's never given me cause to doubt his honesty."

"In any event, my little trap should uncover the truth either way."

"Heaven forfend I have a cheater on my rolls, but if I do, he should be purged straightaway."

"What can you tell me about someone called Martin de Villiers?"

"That pompous fool?" Bertran rolled his eyes to the ceiling. "Acts like anyone should be honored just to be in his presence. And those four simpletons that follow him around all the time just feed his need for attention. At least one of the simpletons is *somewhat* useful – scribes for me and has proven adequate to the task."

"What's de Villiers studying?"

"Theology. Certain a brilliant career in the Church awaits him. I'm sure if you asked him, he'd say he expects to be a bishop mere months after receiving his degree. Too sanctimonious and self-righteous for my liking though."

"God deliver us from more of *those*." The archdeacon shook his head in dismay and reached for the wine pitcher to refill his goblet. "Were you aware he has a particular contempt for Cornishmen?"

"More so than his contempt for mankind in general?"

De Grandison chuckled. "If what I observed at the Swindlestock the day you introduced me to Chegwin is any indication, quite a bit more."

"That's curious. We don't have all that many lads from Cornwall. Most of the St. Edmund Hall lot are Bristol-born, though there are always quite a number from Dorset and Devon. Of course, the ones from Devon who stay on tend to become fellows of Exeter College." It was Bertran's turn to refill his goblet. "Now that you mention it, we had one lad from Bodmin who left unexpectedly a couple of years ago. Never offered a satisfactory explanation for why he was going – just that he couldn't continue here. I thought it odd at the time because he was doing well and wasn't short of funds. But then time moves on and one doesn't dwell on such things." He paused when Mistress Morlond brought in the final course of the meal – apple tart and the Little Rollright cheese he fancied.

De Grandison took advantage of the break in the conversation. "If this apple tart is even half as tasty as your partridge, Mistress Morlond, then I shall have to persuade Hugh to invite me to dine more often."

The housekeeper beamed and blushed and bobbed a little curtsey. "You're too kind, Father. But I'd be pleased to cook for you anytime."

When she'd left, de Grandison couldn't resist teasing his friend. "You need to compliment her more often, Hugh. Then maybe she'd be pleased to cook for you as well."

Bertran replied by spooning a mound of apple tart into his mouth. Finally finished chewing, he returned to their previous conversation. "You think de Villiers could actually be behind this?"

"I'm certainly not ruling it out. And I intend to keep an eye on him. Perhaps you should do likewise."

VI

Two weeks later, Hawthorn barged into de Villiers's room without knocking. "I always knew you were hedge-born, Hawthorn," Martin sneered, laying down his quill, "but really . . . have you absolutely no manners at *all*?"

"You won't care when you hear my news, Martinus."

Observing some kind of peculiar protocol, Hawthorn now waited for an invitation to speak further. De Villiers just stared. The acolyte continued waiting. Finally, an obviously irritated Martinus said, "Well, are you going to tell me or is your only purpose today to try my patience?"

"I finally convinced that new master to hire me."

"Tell me you haven't been whining at him like a begging child."

"You think I'm stupid?" Hawthorn wisely didn't wait for an answer. "I just suggested he give me a try for a week and then he could make up his mind if I was worth it."

"So he hasn't actually taken you on."

"Well . . ." Hawthorn scrunched up his face for a moment, then brightened again. "But he will. I'll get this right, Martinus, I promise."

"See that you do. Now, go do all that work you claim you don't have time for, and leave me be."

Martin didn't pick up his quill again straightaway, instead moving to the small window to peer into the lane below. This was all too much like what he'd lived with at home. His father's favorites could do no wrong, while he, on the other hand . . . He remembered the time he'd almost gotten the best of them. His father had put him and Peter in charge of counting the money from the day's trading and writing up the account rolls. Martin hated writing – he hated anything that reminded him of his lessons with the local priest – so he'd volunteered to count the coins and let Peter be the scribe. He'd count out a certain number of coins into a stack and announce the amount to Peter. Then while Peter's attention was on the parchment, he'd scoop coins into their bag – well, all but one or two from each stack, which he slipped into his pocket without Peter noticing. He was sure their father would check the work and Peter would get blamed for sloppy records. He wasn't wrong – and Peter got a tongue-lashing unlike anything Martin had ever heard.

But while Martin celebrated the success of his little scheme, Peter had gone whining to John, and the two of them had found the little stash of money Martin had hidden under his pillow. When they showed the evidence to their father, the lashing Martin received had nothing to do with a tongue. He'd managed to succeed with his next scheme, which emboldened him for a time, but his father came down hard if John or Peter even hinted Martin was up to something.

Now that bastard archdeacon had taken Chegwin under his wing. Well, it wouldn't work this time. Martin's schemes were far more sophisticated now. *Why do anything yourself when you can get others to do it for you? And have them take the blame. Chegwin will be gone, I'll be blameless, and no one will be the wiser.* He let a smug smile cross his face.

This was going to work out to his satisfaction. Despite being on de Grandison's roll, Chegwin was still attending Bertran's lectures, so Wainwright remained useful. And if Hawthorn could manage not to botch things, they could discredit St. Piran from two different directions. *It's taking a little longer than I would have liked, but the Cornish pig will be gone long before anyone can award him a degree.* With that smug smile still on his face, de Villiers went back to his little table and resumed scribbling whatever inane notions came to his mind about Bertran's stupid assignment, due on Good Friday, to articulate what good Christians should understand from praying the Stations of the Cross. But it was a good opportunity to make Chegwin look the fool. Which meant the whoreson might be gone sooner than later.

"Time to spring your little trap, John," said Bertran as he and de Grandison left the lecture hall on the Wednesday after Easter. "I've received another treatise with Chegwin's name on it that is utterly deplorable for one so near to receiving his degree. Why don't you fetch your copy of his writing on the Stations of the Cross and come to my lodgings?"

"Give me an hour or so. I expect to find my scribe waiting for me and don't want to ignite his suspicion, so I'll take care of a reasonable amount of our usual business then send him on his way."

"Just come when you can," said Bertran as they parted ways.

Two hours later, Bertran shook his head in dismay as he compared the two documents arrayed on his writing table. "So it's true. Someone's substituting inferior work for Chegwin's. This . . ." He laid a hand on the document de Grandison had brought. "This is what I'd come to expect from the lad. That . . ." He gestured with his thumb toward the other one, not even deigning to look at it. ". . . is chaff."

"I'm curious, Hugh. What sort of work did you get from de Villiers for this assignment?"

"Something equally lame. The effort he put in earlier in the year must have turned out to be too much trouble; he's back to his old ways."

"Do you still have those earlier papers? I'd like to read them."

Before Bertran could answer, there was a knock on the door to the study. "*Deus*! I completely forgot. That will be Wainwright." Bertran quickly spread some other student documents on top of the two they'd been comparing then called, "Come in, Mister Wainwright."

The young man strode quickly to Bertran's writing table then looked puzzled at the disarray. "Where am I to work, Master?"

"I think we'll postpone this until tomorrow, Wainwright. The archdeacon and I have been discussing some of the submissions, and I'd like to finish that before preparing my assessments."

"Whatever you wish, Master." The young man took his time stepping away from the table, apparently in no hurry to leave.

"Before you go, Wainwright, fetch me the papers from January if you will."

"Of course." Wainwright went to the shelves by the sideboard and took a box from one of the lower ones, thumbing through the contents as he returned to the table and stared once again at the pages spread all over its surface.

"Just put it down anywhere," Bertran instructed. "I'll sort everything out when we've finished."

"Just so you know, sir, there seem to be some items missing from when we put them away earlier in the year."

"What's here will suffice, Wainwright. We'll worry about the rest later. Now leave us to finish. And be back at the appointed time tomorrow."

Wainwright took another glance around the room and then left without even acknowledging Bertran's instructions. When the door closed behind him, de Grandison commented, "Did you notice all those furtive glances at the pages on your table?"

"If you can call them furtive." Bertran chuckled. "Looked pretty blatant to me. Let me just be sure he's gone and not listening at the keyhole." Crossing the room, he opened the door and called, "Mistress Morlond?" The housekeeper appeared almost immediately. "Has Wainwright gone?"

"I let him out the front door myself, sir."

"Good. See that he doesn't come back inside before tomorrow."

"As you wish, sir."

"Oh, and would it be too much trouble for you if I asked John to stay for supper this evening?"

"Not at all, sir." Her tone brightened. "I'm always happy to cook for the archdeacon."

⊕ ⊕ ⊕ ⊕ ⊕

Wainwright made straight for de Villiers' room but had the good sense to knock. It took so long before he heard footsteps crossing toward the door that he thought perhaps Martin was out, but finally the door opened a crack and the man poked his head through. "Come back later, Wainwright," he hissed.

"We need to talk, Martinus."

"We can talk later. Right now, I'm otherwise occupied."

"It's important."

"So is what I'm doing. Now go away. I'll find you when I'm finished."

The head disappeared and the door slammed shut, leaving Wainwright fuming. He knew Martin would be angry, once he heard the news, that he hadn't been informed sooner. *Selfish bastard. Won't let us use his room for a bit of privacy with a wench, but God forfend we should interrupt **him**.*

In his own room, Wainwright found the other three sitting around doing nothing. "Come on, mates. Martin's having a swive, but there's no reason we should dally around for him. The Stag awaits." He didn't have to ask twice as the others gleefully bounded up and followed him down the stairs. He knew de Villiers would be furious that they hadn't waited for him, but right now, Wainwright didn't really care.

VII

"I think I've devised a way to catch them out," de Grandison announced when he and Bertran next dined together. Much to Mistress Morlond's delight, they'd made a Friday evening ritual of sharing a meal and their views on the week's events. Inevitably, the conversation came around to the apparent sabotage of Chegwin's future. "I'm convinced those January documents with de Villiers's name on them are Chegwin's work."

"As am I." Bertran nodded his head.

"We can prove what's been happening, but we can't yet prove who or how. That said, we both know Wainwright and Hawthorn are suspect, despite the fact we haven't been able to catch them doing anything wrong."

"I didn't say anything, but I wondered why you hired Hawthorn."

"When he came groveling for a job only a few days after Chegwin came under my supervision, I remembered his face from that brief encounter in the Swindlestock. If they'd had any sense, they'd have given me time to forget. In any event, I decided it might be useful to have him where I could watch him. And I hope what I've come up with trips one or the other of them up."

"I'm intrigued."

"I propose we suspend our regular lectures for three weeks and offer instead a combined series of lectures on Thomas Aquinas."

"You should teach that, John. You have a better view from within the Church."

"What I have in mind works better if we do it jointly."

They spent the rest of the evening laying their plans, and when they were satisfied, Bertran said, "You know, I'm beginning to think that year we studied Civil Law may not have been wasted after all."

De Grandison chuckled. "Nor my years observing the intrigue within the papal court."

"Wainwright and Hawthorn . . . you think they'll turn on de Villiers? They're utter thralls to him – have been since they arrived."

"I doubt their loyalty extends to being dismissed from the university while he escapes punishment. They'll almost certainly catch at any straw they think might save their own hides."

Two days later, de Grandison stood in front of the crowded lecture room and described what the next few weeks would hold. "You'll do well to pay careful attention throughout because at the conclusion of the course, you will each write a thesis on whether the inclusion of Aquinas in the Condemnation of 1277 was just or flawed. Those of you who normally attend Master Bertran's lectures will argue in favor of the condemnation. Those who attend mine will argue against. Those who attend both, see me in my lodgings this afternoon to get your assignment."

Piran loitered outside until he was sure any others had left before knocking on de Grandison's door. "'Bout time you showed up." The archdeacon's housekeeper was as sullen as ever when she let him in. "His holiness is waiting for you, so best you not dally."

"I'm sorry, Father. I—" Piran began as he stepped through the study door but de Grandison cut him off.

"Don't mind Mistress Chert, Piran. One of these days, she might actually find something that's to her liking, but I've yet to figure out when or what that might be. Please . . . take a seat. I was rather hoping you'd be the last to arrive." He spent the next half hour explaining the scheme he and

Bertran had hatched to finally reveal who was trying to sabotage Chegwin's career, ending with, "Your assignment, Piran, is actually to write no thesis at all. We're both in no doubt that something will show up with your name on it and where it shows up will tell us who to confront."

"But won't it look suspicious, Father, if everyone else is working on a thesis and I'm not?"

"You make a fair point, Piran. So choose whichever side you wish to argue, but only one copy this time and only directly into my hands. In fact, it might be useful for our eventual confrontation with the culprit to have your real work as evidence. But you'll need to be exceedingly circumspect about what you're preparing. We should keep them guessing about what I might have assigned you."

"That won't be a problem, Father. Or if anyone asks, maybe I can just encourage them to believe I'm actually writing whatever they think I've been assigned."

"Just be careful, Piran. Don't put yourself in any danger or the scheme at risk."

⊕ ⊕ ⊕ ⊕ ⊕

Three weeks later, just as sunlight was beginning to peek around the drawn draperies of his bedchamber, de Grandison was awakened by loud rapping on the door. "Wake up, Father," Mistress Chert called. "You've got a visitor . . . at this godforsaken hour no less."

The archdeacon roused himself on his pillows in an effort to shake off the dream he'd been in the midst of. "Who is it, Mistress Chert?"

"That student that's here all the time."

"Hawthorn?"

"No, the other one."

"Chegwin?"

"That one. I *had* to let him in. He was banging on the front door so loud he was going to wake the whole neighborhood, so what else was I to do?"

"It's alright, Mistress Chert. Just show him into my study and tell him I'll be there momentarily. Then you can go back to bed."

"No going back to bed once I'm awake, Father. Won't do no good. I'll never get back to sleep once I've been woke up so sharply."

"Very well. Then just do whatever you want." Unsure if she'd even heard him or if she was already going downstairs to shower their visitor with her early-morning crankiness, de Grandison sat up and swung his legs over the side of the bed. If Chegwin found it necessary to arrive so early, there might be something seriously amiss, so dressing properly would just have to wait. He threw a robe on over his nightshirt, stepped into his slippers, and headed down the staircase.

He found Piran in front of the cold hearth, cap in hand. "What's wrong, son, that brings you here at this hour?"

"Nothing, Father. It's just that I didn't want anyone to see me coming here. I was afraid it might make people suspicious." He held out the pages he'd been holding beneath his cap and de Grandison took them.

"Won't those you share a room with be suspicious of your being gone so early?" The archdeacon sat down in one of the chairs near the hearth and gestured for Piran to do likewise.

"They'll barely notice. It's not at all unusual for me to go out early to spend some time at the priory church before my day gets underway. It's peaceful there, and I can think without being interrupted."

"Is this what I think it is?" de Grandison held up the pages.

"Aye, Father. You said no one's hands but yours, and I didn't want to take a chance Hawthorn might be here when I delivered it."

De Grandison couldn't help but smile at his protégé's unwearied determination to prove himself worthy but then turned his attention to the pages in his hand. Five sheets of paper packed with small, dense writing on both sides, barely a quarter inch margin on any edge. Clearly the author was extremely frugal in his use of an expensive commodity. After reading four pages, he glanced up at Piran – whose anxiety was written on his face and in his hands that alternately folded and unfolded his cap – then resumed reading.

When he finally finished, he lay the pages in his lap then looked thoughtfully at the young man sitting opposite. "You're going to wear out that cap, Chegwin."

Piran looked down at his hands, apparently unaware of what they'd been doing. "I just . . . sorry, Father . . . I . . ."

"There's no need to fret, Piran. This is actually quite brilliant. It's well grounded in the theological arguments and makes a strong intellectual case for your choice. But best of all, I can say unequivocally that none of those who want to discredit you are clever enough to think of this approach. We *will* unmask them, Piran. You need only be patient for just a little longer."

"You . . . you really think it's good, Father?" The sparkle in Piran's eyes and the tone of his voice were those of an eager, first-year student wanting to be sure he'd just heard the master's words of praise correctly.

"It's better than good, Piran. And I can assure you Bertran will think so as well. Now, why don't you get on with your day and leave me to put this in the strongbox and get myself properly dressed."

Piran jumped to his feet. "Of course, Father. And I really am sorry about the early hour. I just thought it was best—"

De Grandison cut him off. "It's quite alright. Now off you go. And Piran?"

"Aye?"

"Do your best not to act too jubilant just yet. We wouldn't want to spoil our surprise."

Piran grinned then quickly composed his face as he reached for the door handle, causing the archdeacon to laugh aloud. Then he, too, composed himself. The scheme had to work; they couldn't fail this young man.

VIII

Two days later, Piran woke at the crack of dawn. In truth, it was not so much waking, since he'd never really slept – more taking note of the start of a new day. He'd tried to sleep, closing his eyes and willing sleep to come, but his mind wouldn't settle. There was simply too much at stake. And nothing he could do about it except to hope that those who sought to discredit him would try again.

Was it right to pray for someone to do wrong? Even if that wrong was in service of discovering the truth? If he couldn't even answer this question for himself, then how, as a priest, could he possibly hope to guide his flock through such a moral dilemma? Did this mean he wasn't cut out to be a priest? To admit that would be a terrible blow to who he believed himself to be – what he thought his life was for. But why was God putting all these obstacles in his path? Wouldn't a God who's supposed to see into the hearts of all men know how deeply he felt this calling? Was it a test of his faith – his dedication? Or was it a sign? A message that he should choose a different path – that there was a different purpose for his life. And why now? When his path had seemed so clear, his goal so nearly reached.

He had no answers – only questions that kept circling around, seeking to know but only creating more questions in his troubled mind and more turmoil in his soul. As he rose from his bed, taking care not to wake the others, he tried to push the questions away, telling himself the answers would come in the light of this day. He let himself out of the room as quietly as he could and set his steps toward the priory church in the hope that he could find the peace and grace there to accept whatever the day might bring.

Half an hour before midday, Master Bertran arrived back at his lodgings, having completed his lectures for the day. The afternoon had been set aside for something entirely different, and he couldn't suppress a twinge of – excitement? – anxiety? – curiosity? – he wasn't quite sure what – over how events might unfold.

Stepping through his front door, he called out, "Mistress Morlond – a word if you please," as he made his way into the study.

"Aye, Master?" She was there in an instant.

God's bones, woman, how is it you're never more than two steps away when I want something? You could scare a man to death showing up so fast. "Ah, good, there you are. I need you to do me a favor. I'm having my midday meal with Master de Seton at Balliol. When Wainwright arrives, tell him to bring that box on my writing table to de Seton's lodgings."

"Of course, Master. Anything else I should tell him?"

"Only that he should come straightaway. He'll be expected, so he'll be admitted without any questions." He started toward the door then thought of something else. "Oh, and make sure he doesn't take anything else from this room. Only that box. Nothing else."

"Of course, Master. And will you be dining at home this evening?"

"If everything goes well this afternoon, I'll even bring the archdeacon so you'll have someone to enjoy cooking for. If it doesn't, then he and I will likely be off at a tavern somewhere drowning our sorrow in vats of ale." The last thing Bertran saw as he left his study was the thoroughly perplexed expression on Mistress Morlond's face. He chuckled softly to himself as he left the house. *You really shouldn't taunt her like that, Hugh.* But in the next breath, he told himself, *But it's so much fun.*

Three lanes over, de Grandison was doing much the same thing. Except that in his case, he was writing instructions for Hawthorn. He was never sure if Mistress Chert would convey his instructions correctly or if her natural tendency to grumpiness would cause her to forget or omit something. His note finished, he called for her and folded his arms over his chest. She never came straightaway. And he never knew if she was in a far corner of the house and didn't hear or if she took some kind of perverse pleasure in making him wait. He'd almost decided he'd have to call a second time when she stuck her head around the doorframe.

"You want something, sir?"

"Yes, come here, Mistress Chert." He stood and walked to the other side of his writing table, where he'd placed the note next to a box of papers. She took her time getting there. "Now, when Mister Hawthorn arrives, bring him here and show him this note and this box. You don't have to tell him what to do – it's all there in the note. But he's only to take the box and the note. Is that clear?"

"As you say, Father. And if he don't come?"

"He'll come. You can be sure of that."

"And the other one? What if he comes?"

"The other one?" De Grandison was momentarily puzzled. "Oh, you mean Chegwin. He won't be here. You can be sure of that as well. Now, I'm dining with Master de Seton at Balliol. If anyone important comes looking for me, you can send them there."

"And just who might it be what's important?"

"Another master . . . the mayor . . . the sheriff . . . the Pope . . . I don't know." De Grandison sighed. This woman could be infuriating, but in truth, today it was his own impatience to get the afternoon's proceedings underway that was making him short-tempered. "I'm sorry, Mistress Chert." He tried to sound conciliatory. "Why don't we just say 'anyone but students' and leave it at that." Her silence, it seemed, was as close to an acceptance of his apology as he was going to get, so he headed for the door with a final, "Just remember what to do when Hawthorn arrives, alright?"

⊕ ⊕ ⊕ ⊕ ⊕

An hour past midday, the meal finished and the table cleared, Henry de Seton's housekeeper set two new places at the dining table. Not with eating utensils, goblets, and plates but with quills, ink pots, and a few sheets of paper.

As they dined, Bertran and de Grandison had laid out their expectations of what was about to take place. Bertran had been grateful when his friend, who was Master of Balliol College, agreed to be part of the proceedings. He needed everything to be witnessed by a very senior member of the university so that the miscreants could be in no doubt of the finality of the decision and that they had absolutely no recourse. He'd considered including the master of University College as well but in the end, decided that having too many people present might put Hawthorn and Wainwright on their guard.

Hawthorn arrived first. "I came as quick as I could, Father, like your note said," he addressed the archdeacon directly, ignoring the presence of anyone else and the fact that good manners would have him greet his host first.

"Just set your box on the table and take a seat there, Hawthorn," de Grandison replied.

Another quarter hour passed before Wainwright finally put in an appearance. "About time you arrived," Bertran chided his scribe, though he secretly hoped Wainwright had used the time for nefarious purposes. "Just take your seat opposite Hawthorn and we'll begin." He waited while Wainwright set down his box, took his seat, and squirmed around in his chair as if trying to get comfortable. When the squirming finally stopped, he continued, "If you're finally settled, Wainwright?"

"Yes, Master. Sorry, Master."

"Very well. I'm sure you're wondering why we're doing this here rather than each of us . . ." He gestured to de Grandison. ". . . assessing our own students' work privately. Master de Seton has expressed interest in our little experiment with combining our lectures and wanted to observe the results. Here's how we'll proceed. We'll alternate viewpoints, starting with

Wainwright and those arguing in favor of the condemnation. Wainwright, you'll take a treatise from the box and read it aloud, all but the student's name. That will save time as we won't have to wait for each of the three of us to read it separately. Once de Grandison and I have delivered our assessments, which you will duly record – and, naturally, Henry, you're welcome to comment as well – we will ask the name of the student. Hawthorn will then do the same from his own box."

The first two documents from each box were much as expected. As Wainwright reached for the next document in his box, Bertran thought he detected a subtle shift in the young man's demeanor. *Probably just your imagination, Hugh*, he told himself. *Be patient. They're no doubt trying to lull you into a routine before springing the surprise.*

Wainwright began reading. An utterly simplistic narrative that wandered aimlessly for three pages and boiled down to nothing more than if the Pope issued the condemnation, then it must be correct. During the reading, Bertran and de Grandison kept their eyes on Wainwright and their expressions blank. De Seton's expression, on the other hand, went very quickly from curiosity to consternation.

When Wainwright finished, de Seton didn't wait. "What is this, Hugh? Am I to believe this is really the work of a fourth-year student? My housekeeper could do better than that. *Deus*! My *horse* could do better than that."

Wainwright and Hawthorn couldn't prevent themselves from sharing a knowing glance across the table – something de Seton took no notice of but that didn't escape either Bertran or de Grandison.

"Not up to standards at all, I agree." Bertran kept his voice calm, his manner unthreatening – his turn to lull the scribes into complacency. "What say you, John?"

"Certainly not *my* standards. Tell me, Wainwright, whose lazy work is that?"

Wainwright made a great show of looking back at the last page of the document, as if he had to remind himself of the name. "Chegwin, sir. Piran Chegwin."

"That's interesting." De Grandison, too, kept his voice calm, as if everything were perfectly normal. "Quite interesting indeed. You see, Hugh . . . Henry. That's not the assignment I gave Chegwin."

Eyebrows raised, Bertran turned to his scribe. "Would you care to tell us, Wainwright, how that paper came to be in your box?"

"Like all the others, sir, I suppose. I just brought the box here like Mistress Morlond said I was to do."

"Would you care to try again, Wainwright?" This time, Bertran's voice had a stern edge. "You see, I checked that box before I came here, and not only did it contain the right number of documents but the names on them matched exactly with those in my lectures."

"I . . . I couldn't say, sir. Maybe someone went to your lodgings after you left and Mistress Morlond let them in."

"Tell me, John." Bertran changed tack. "What *did* you assign to Chegwin?"

"I let him make his own choice." De Grandison then pulled some pages from the sleeve of his cassock, unfolded them, and handed them to de Seton. "He brought me this two days ago and I must say, I find his choice rather astute. Tell me what you think, Henry."

While de Seton read, silence prevailed, broken only by the sound of Wainwright squirming in his seat. Hawthorn cowered, looking as if he'd like to disappear under the table. At long last, de Seton handed the pages back to the archdeacon. "Now *that's* what I expect of a fourth-year student. Even better than I'd expect, actually. As good as some of my fellows."

"My thoughts as well," said Bertran. "One of the best students I've ever had, though it seems he has his heart set on being ordained as soon as he receives his degree. Which, unfortunately, has been in question these last few months, but I think we've at last uncovered the cause." Then he rounded on Wainwright. "Haven't we, Mister Wainwright?"

"I . . . I don't know what you mean, Master."

"I mean those pages in front of you, which are obviously not Chegwin's work and which you slipped into the box on your way over here. I mean those treatises that were presented to me as Chegwin's earlier in the year and that were most certainly intended to discredit him. And as you are the only one who has access to my study other than myself, I'm left to the conclusion that you are responsible. So what do you have to say for yourself?"

"I . . . nothing, sir . . . I . . . it wasn't me, sir."

"Who else *could* it have been? I've let no one else into my study. Mistress Morlond certainly wouldn't do so without my explicit permission, and she's made no such request. There *is* no other explanation, Wainwright."

"It wasn't me, Master. Well . . . at least, it wasn't my idea."

"Shut up, Walter," Hawthorn hissed. "Don't you know what Martinus will do to us?"

"Oh, for Christ's sake, Hawthorn. Who cares about Martin? Can't you see it's what *they* can do to us . . ." Wainwright waved a hand at the three men at the end of the table. ". . . that matters?"

He rose from his seat and began pacing back and forth between the chair and the door to the corridor, getting closer to the door each time, until de Seton finally said, "You'll find that door locked, Mister Wainwright." Wainwright's shoulders slumped. His eyes downcast, he resumed his seat at the table.

"It may interest you to know, Wainwright," said de Grandison, "that we have absolute proof that Mister Chegwin did not write the treatises submitted in his name in January and February."

"We also have strong reason to believe," added Bertran, "that treatises purportedly from a different student were actually written by Mister Chegwin. So you see, Wainwright, why it appears you're on the hook for cheating, enabling someone to present another's work as their own, falsifying another's work, and concealing the scheme. Now, unless you want to be held entirely responsible for everything we've uncovered, I suggest you start telling the truth."

Silence reigned for quite some time as Wainwright studied his feet, apparently contemplating his dilemma. At long last, he sat up straight in his chair and turned his gaze to Bertran. "Very well. You want to know what's happened? I'll tell you."

"Walter, you can't." Hawthorn's tone was a peculiar mixture of misery and insistence. "Just think—"

Wainwright turned his head sharply to glare at his compatriot. "There is *no* way I'm taking the blame for this alone, Hawthorn, so you'd best get ready to tell your part as well." Hawthorn folded his arms across his chest and slouched down in his chair.

"Continue, please, Mister Wainwright," said Bertran.

"It was all de Villiers's idea. He doesn't think Cornishmen belong in an English university. So when he couldn't intimidate Chegwin into leaving – like he did with that milksop from Bodmin – he devised this plan to get Chegwin thrown out before he could receive his degree."

"De Villiers," said Bertran. "Can you be more specific?"

"Martin de Villiers. You should know him, sir. He's on your roll."

"I know him. And I suspected he was involved. But it was necessary that you tell me explicitly." Hawthorn slid lower in his chair, awareness of his own impending doom written on his face. "Now tell us the details of the plan. And I would caution you, Mister Wainwright – it would be wise not to omit anything."

"Martin thought that if Chegwin's work was sufficiently unsatisfactory, you'd strike him off your roll. He said he'd seen it before, where students got lazy or over-confident in their last term and spent too much time in the taverns and got dismissed as a result. So he ordered me to make sure whatever you got from Chegwin was poorer than that of a first-year student."

"And did you write these poor papers yourself?"

"Now and then, but mostly Martin wrote them and gave them to me to substitute for Chegwin's. But then he got these bees in his head that we could make *him* look better at the same time so you'd think he'd reformed and would never suspect what he was up to. The other thing he ordered me to do was copy Chegwin's real work but put *his* name on it. Of course, for all this to work, I had to destroy Chegwin's original treatise. And it was working too. Until you transferred him to the archdeacon. That's when Martin decided to expand the scheme."

"Is that where you come in, Hawthorn?" asked de Grandison.

When Hawthorn didn't reply, Wainwright rounded on him again. "*God's bollocks*, Hawthorn. If you don't answer, *I* will. Don't you understand Martin can't protect us?"

Hawthorn sat up a little straighter. "Yes, sir. I was to do the same thing Wainwright had been doing. Except you didn't make any assignments until . . . well, until this." He angled his head toward the box on the table. "Which means I haven't done anything wrong."

"I'll be the judge of that," said Bertran. "Is there anyone else involved in this scheme, Mister Wainwright?"

"Well," Wainwright hesitated.

"I'll remind you, Wainwright. You would be wise not to omit anything."

"Alright. Snape and Rogate knew about it. But they didn't actually *do* anything other than listen to Martin."

Bertran nodded and de Seton rang a small bell that had been sitting on the table in front of him. His housekeeper entered straightaway from the other door in the room, which, presumably, led to the kitchen. "You can send Hull to us now," said de Seton, and the housekeeper retreated from whence she'd come without a word.

Not long after, a key turned in a lock and the corridor door swung open to admit a young man who, judging from his age and attire, was most likely a fellow of the college. "Prompt as always, Hull," said de Seton. "Thank you. I need you to take a couple of other fellows and fetch three students here. Names of de Villiers, Rogate, and Snape. And where, Mister Wainwright, can these students be found?"

"Brasenose Lane, sir. At the corner of Turl Street. Top floor."

"Bring them straight here, Hull," de Seton continued. "And just so you get no arguments, you might want to emphasize how flattered they should be that I've sent a personal invitation for them to visit."

"As you wish, Master," said Hull.

"Bring them straight back to this room. Then when you return, fetch Mister Chegwin from St. Edmund Hall. But keep him company in my study until you see the others leave, then bring him to join us here."

"He'll be happy to come, Hull," said Bertran. "You'll have no need to flatter him."

"Anything else, sir?" Hull asked.

"Just get those three back here as quickly as you can."

Once Hull was gone, Bertran resumed. "Very well, Wainwright. We know what you did and why. What I want to know is how."

"How, sir?"

"How did you manage this under my nose?"

"It wasn't all that hard, sir. On the days when you were lecturing all day, I'd stop by your lodgings and offer to do things for Mistress Morlond. Bring in extra firewood. Go to the butcher or the baker for her so she didn't have to get out in the cold. That sort of thing. And then she'd let me do my work in your study – said I needed a warm place rather than those cold rooms in the Halls. That gave me the time and privacy to copy Chegwin's treatise to submit as Martin's and to put whatever Martin had given me in its place. Getting rid of Chegwin's original was a simple matter of tossing it on the fire and making sure it burned completely so no one would suspect anything."

"And the times when there was nothing from Chegwin?"

"Martin said we should do that now and again so it looked like Chegwin was getting really careless about even completing his assignments at all."

"Do you have any idea, Wainwright, how utterly appalling it is that you took advantage of Mistress Morlond's kind nature for such dastardly purposes?"

"Well, sir—"

"Don't answer that, Wainwright. You obviously don't. And it was largely rhetorical anyway. What I'd really like to know is what kind of power de Villiers holds over you to compel you to such egregious behavior."

The best Wainwright could manage was, "I don't know how to explain it, sir. He's just Martin."

Bertran rose and retrieved his box from its spot on the table beside Wainwright, with de Grandison following suit. "We'll assess the rest of these ourselves, Henry," he told de Seton, "unless you'd particularly like to read any of them."

"What I'd like is to meet this Chegwin and encourage him to stay on as a fellow here at Balliol."

"With his mind, he really should," said Bertran. "I'll add my encouragement to yours, as I'm sure John will as well. Just know the lad's dedication to becoming a priest is as strong as any I've ever seen."

Further conversation was interrupted when the corridor door suddenly swung open without a knock or any sort of warning. De Villiers strutted in, chin in the air, his cap with the pheasant feather at a jaunty angle on his head, a broad smile on his face. The remaining two acolytes followed two steps behind. As he took in the scene and realization dawned, his steps slowed, the chin sank, and the smile vanished. Stopping at the end of the table opposite de Seton, he doffed his cap. "Martinus de Villiers, Master de Seton. At your service."

"And those with you would be Snape and Rogate, I presume?" asked de Seton.

"You presume correctly, sir."

"Can they not speak for themselves?"

"I'm Snape, sir," said the one to de Villiers's left.

"Rogate, Master." The other gave a polite nod of his head.

"I invite you to be seated," said de Seton. De Villiers took the chair at the end of the table while the acolytes scrambled into the two vacant ones next to Hawthorn. "It seems we have them all present, Bertran. Pray continue."

"Martin de Villiers, we have today finished assembling irrefutable proof that you are responsible for a campaign to discredit one of your fellow students and that you've done so by cheating, by substituting inferior work, and by claiming another student's work as your own and that you've recruited both Wainwright and Hawthorn here as active participants in your scheme. As you know, any one of those things is cause for dismissal from the university. What do you have to say for yourself?"

The air of superiority returned. "That I've done nothing wrong, sir. I've copied no one's work, I've substituted no treatises, I've done nothing of which I'm accused."

"Perhaps you want to reconsider your answer, de Villiers. We have the whole story from Mister Wainwright. How you conceived the plan, how you instructed them what to do, how you personally prepared many of the inferior treatises, and how your personal animosity toward Mister Chegwin is the basis for the entire scheme. Do you wish to add lying to the list of your dishonorable actions?"

"Wainwright?" De Villiers's tone was one of pure derision. "You'd believe *him*? He's just cross with me because I won't let him use my private room to have it on with the strumpets he picks up in Grope Lane. He's just trying to get even with me, and I must say, he's picked a rather spectacular way to have his revenge."

"Mister de Villiers, I'll ask you one more time. Do you wish to add lying to your list of offenses? We have substantial proof of what has occurred. Wainwright and Hawthorn simply confirmed our conclusions about who was behind the scheme and provided the details on how it was carried out."

De Villiers crossed his arms over his chest and said nothing, apparently determined not to acknowledge anything of which he was accused. Bertran turned to the acolytes. "Snape, were you aware of what was going on?"

Martin glared at Snape, who cowered sideways in his chair. "You'd best answer, Snape," Hawthorn whispered. "They know everything."

"I . . . Martinus told all of us about it, sir. But I didn't do anything. I swear, sir, all I ever did was listen."

"Rogate?"

"I knew, sir. Martinus was proud of how he was going to get rid of the Cornish pig, so he talked about it a lot in our rooms. But I'm like Snape, sir. I never did nought but listen."

"Very well, then." It was clear from Bertran's voice and his posture that he was about to render a decision. "Martin de Villiers, for the offenses you've committed – including that of lying about your actions – you are dismissed from this university as from this moment and will never again be permitted to pursue studies here. Wainwright and Hawthorn, you are both also dismissed for your actions and for concealing the full truth of the scheme. Snape and Rogate, as you are guilty of not reporting what you knew to be afoot, you won't escape punishment. You are both banned from lectures for the remainder of this term. If you present appropriate statements of your reformed character, you may be permitted to resume your academic career in the future. Now, all five of you, leave us to get on with our honorable pursuits and don't let me hear anything further from any of you lest I engage the sheriff to see you're permanently removed from this town."

De Villiers rose, donned his cloak of superiority and marched toward the door. The acolytes, all despondent, lagged far behind. Once Bertran heard the sound of the front door closing, he sighed. "What a nasty business."

"But a necessary one, Hugh," said de Seton. "There's no place here for men of that ilk."

"Well, at least what follows will be far more pleasant. Where is Chegwin, I wonder?"

As he was asking the question, Hull walked in. "I couldn't find him anywhere, sir. Looked all over St. Edmund Hall, asked anyone I could find. I even went to the Swindlestock and the Stag to see if maybe he'd been there."

"I think I know where he might be," said de Grandison. "And if you agree, Hugh, it might be better if I go find him myself. I'll bring him to you in due course."

"I'm grateful, John. Go find the lad and give him the news."

✦ ✦ ✦ ✦ ✦

"He's been here all day, Archdeacon," said Brother Ansfrid. "Through all the holy offices and all the hours in between. I've been keeping an eye on him. Sometimes he's at prayer. Others just staring at the stained glass windows like he's seeking some sort of inspiration. Sometimes, like now, just sitting alone in the choir stalls. Usually, he wants to talk, but not today. When I asked what was troubling him, all he'd say was that his whole life was being decided and that he had no say in the matter."

"Thank you, Brother, for looking after him," said de Grandison. "And so you'll know, the news I bring will lift his spirits."

"That's comforting indeed. I'd best leave you to it."

De Grandison made his way down the nave and through the stalls to genuflect before the altar before returning to sit beside Piran. "It's all over, my son."

Piran didn't look up. "I think I'm afraid to know, Father."

"Your fear is understandable, but now you can set it aside. The whole plot has been exposed. All who sought to discredit you have been dismissed. Master Bertran is taking you back on his roll so he can confer your degree in July. And Master de Seton wants to invite you to continue your studies as a fellow at Balliol. All is well, Piran. Your future is secure."

Piran collapsed. His entire body shook and tears flowed from his eyes as the unbearable weight was lifted from his heart and his mind. De Grandison put an arm around his shoulders. "I'm sorry, Father," he somehow managed. "I know it's not manly to cry like this. I just can't help it."

"A man – especially a priest – must never be ashamed to acknowledge his emotions, Piran. If you've never had the experience of being brought to tears, then how will you truly be able to comfort a parishioner who finds himself in similar circumstances?"

Piran snuffled and wiped his nose on his sleeve then looked up at de Grandison. "Is that why God has put me through all this, Father?"

"That's a question only He can answer. But I know you'll be a better man and a better priest for having learned that sometimes others can look out for us as well – or even better – than we can look out for ourselves."

At long last, Piran managed a smile. "I'm grateful you were here to look out for me, Father. Grateful for Master Bertran too."

"Then let's go tell him. Another thing I can assure you is that he's just as grateful as you are to have this all behind us."

IX

It seemed the whole world heaved a sigh of relief once de Villiers and the others were gone. Lectures were no longer disrupted by the commotion of Martinus and the acolytes arriving in the hall just as the teaching master began speaking. In the taverns, conversation and merriment no longer paused each time the door opened as everyone looked to see if it was pheasant-feather-cap man come to rain his approval or disdain on everyone present. Piran threw himself into his studies with the kind of joy he'd experienced when he first stepped off the coach from Launceston and gazed in wonder at this new town that was the gateway to his future.

And now that joy was augmented by the pleasure of spending evenings with his mates at the tavern. When they parted ways after leaving Master Bertran's lodgings on the day Piran got his life back, de Grandison had pressed a small leather pouch into Piran's hand. "Make the most of your remaining weeks as a student, Chegwin. Enjoy the company of your mates. Get yourself some decent food. And while you're doing that, we'll work on finding the funds you need to continue your studies at Balliol." He paused briefly. "Assuming that's what you want to do."

"More than anything, Father, though I never imagined it could be possible. But I can't take your money." He tried to give back the pouch.

"I assure you, Piran, that small gift will *not* leave me destitute. And besides . . . what kind of priest would I be if I didn't try to help one whose need was greater than my own?"

Piran clutched the pouch tightly as he hurried back to his room, keenly aware from the weight that it contained more than just a few pennies, but he was utterly unprepared for what he found when he finally poured the contents into his hand. Twelve shillings. Almost half of what he normally had to make last for a full year. He could heed the archdeacon's advice and still have something left over to put toward another year of studies.

Thank God and all the saints his mates were out. He didn't want to have to explain this sudden windfall to them. Somehow it seemed like a very private matter. He quickly returned the coins to the pouch and added his own remaining six pennies.

But how *would* he explain his newfound means to the others? *Maybe they won't ask.* In his heart he knew this was unlikely – one of them was bound to comment, even if it was just an offhand remark. *Would it be a lie to explain it as the fruits of three years of frugality? After all, if Father didn't know I couldn't afford the taverns, he'd never have been so generous.* It was stretching the truth – a bit uncomfortably, if he was truthful with himself – but it was all he had if he wanted to protect what felt like an almost holy pact between himself and de Grandison.

That had been over three weeks ago, and tonight, he'd decided an appropriate use of the archdeacon's money would be to do something special for his mates, who'd stuck by him during those weeks when he was so self-absorbed he could barely give them the time of day. Knowing it would quickly become crowded on a Friday evening, they went to the Swindlestock early to be sure to get a good table. When Arnold tried to get away with a short pour on their first mugs of ale, Piran offered no complaint – just stood there, turning his penny over and over in his fingers and looking at the mugs. Finally, Arnold laughed and picked up his pitcher. "You're a smart one, you are, lad." As he finished filling the fourth mug, he winked at Ned. "Lucky for me they're not all so clever, right, Fletcher?" Piran placed his coin on the bar.

"He knows you by name?" Piran asked as they made their way to the best table in the place. Coming early had paid off. They'd be the envy of every student in Oxford for as long as they chose to stay.

"God's breeches, Piran. We've been coming here for nigh on four years now." Ned paused for a great gulp of ale. "Well, at least the three of us have. A good landlord learns the names of his best customers."

"Ned doesn't let him get away with short pours either," added Robin. "So I guess you can also say a good landlord learns the names of those he can't swindle."

Supper was lamb potage – rich and tasty and containing lots of the first broad beans of the season. Piran ordered a loaf of pandemaine to go with it, rationalizing the expense as being what the archdeacon himself would have done.

Their conversation inevitably turned toward what they'd be doing once they received their degrees. "Seems I really am going home to Ashill," said Robin. He'd told them some weeks back that the old parish priest there had gotten so feeble he couldn't say mass any longer, and the lord of the manor had petitioned Bishop Droxford to give the church to Robin. "I'm to go to Wells first to be ordained then back home. Church of the Blessed Virgin Mary."

"Well, at least you'll be settled," said Piran. "Master de Seton's holding a place for me at Balliol, but I still don't have all the money I'll need. Father says I shouldn't fret – that he and Bertran and de Seton are getting closer to finding a benefactor. But if they don't, I really have no idea what I'll do. The Launceston prior would welcome me into the brotherhood, but I've never wanted the monastic life."

"Guess that means you're going to be on your knees to Saint Matthew a lot over the next few weeks," said Robin.

"Not to mention your namesake." Ned laughed.

James raised his mug. "To Saint Matthew and Saint Piran." The rest followed suit and they drank the toast.

"Is toasting a saint sacrilegious?" Robin asked.

"As much help as I need?" said Piran. "Prayers . . . toasts . . . I'd go on a pilgrimage if I knew where to go."

"Except then you wouldn't be here to get your degree," said James.

"Alright, no pilgrimage then." Piran chuckled.

"At least not until after you buy me another mug of ale." Robin held his mug upside down to demonstrate his need.

With Midsummer's Day just three weeks away, it was well past Compline when darkness finally settled in. Since it was Friday night, there were no lectures to force them from their beds with tomorrow's cockcrow, so it was well past the onset of darkness before they decided to give up their prime spot in the tavern and make their way home. It being two days until the new moon, there was only starlight, but that hardly mattered. Their bellies were full and not even the wandering cat that darted across the pavement, almost causing Ned to trip, could dampen their spirits.

Until they turned into the lane that led to St. Edmund Hall. Ten feet ahead, four men blocked their path and as they turned to beat a retreat, two more stepped out of the shadows to cut off their escape. "Stay calm," Ned whispered. "We can talk our way out of this."

The first thought that went through Piran's mind was that Ned had more confidence than he should. The next, that he was glad the little pouch with all his money was on a leather thong around his neck and tucked inside his shirt so it wouldn't be easy to steal. And then he heard the voice – "The rest of you can go. It's the Cornish pig we want to carve up." – the voice he would never forget – and saw the glint of steel as de Villiers waved his hand.

Ned took a step forward, brandishing his own dagger. "We're not going anywhere, Martin. You want a fight, you fight us all."

Piran could feel the two men behind them edging closer, and Robin spun around, drawing a dagger to hold them at bay.

It wouldn't be a fair fight, six against four. *Six against three, really*, Piran thought. He'd never been in a fight before. Not even skirmishes as a lad. Every instinct in his body told him to run for his life. But there was nowhere to go. He could smell his own fear. Hear his own heartbeat. Taste the bile rising in his throat as his stomach churned and his gut roiled.

Suddenly, Piran found himself in the middle of a melée. Bodies moving all around him. Knives waving. Opponents circling each other, waiting to strike. Someone shoved him from behind and he stumbled forward.

Regaining his footing, he looked up to see he was headed straight toward an extended arm with a dagger pointed squarely at his midsection. He spun to his left and managed to avoid being impaled, but the blade caught his right arm, piercing his sleeve and slicing his flesh. Voices. Men hurling curses at one another one moment, dares the next. He caught a glimpse of someone – was it Ned? – turning sideways as a knife-wielder lunged at him and then slamming a fist into the attacker's face.

He grabbed his wounded arm and felt the wet patch on his clothing from the seeping blood. He'd lost track of Robin and James. He heard a knife clatter to the cobblestones behind him and turned to try to find it. At least with a weapon in hand, he could hold someone at bay even if he had no idea how – or even if – he'd be able to use it against a fellow human being. But it was hopeless in the dark, and some instinct told him he'd be an easy target if he got down on hands and knees to try to find it. A crunching sound followed by a yell told him another fist had found its mark, and he could only hope it wasn't one of his mates who was the victim.

He needed to get out of here, but he was surrounded by rapidly moving bodies and flailing arms and the occasional clash of steel against steel. And then, almost as if some unseen hand had swept the barriers aside, the way ahead was clear. He started forward, tentatively at first, and then it dawned on him that the way could be blocked in an instant, so he began to run.

He hadn't gone five steps when a leg kicked out from his right side, tripping him mid-stride, and he fell to the cobbles, landing hard on his left shoulder. The crack he heard sounded like a clap of thunder coming from inside his own body. The pain was excruciating. As he struggled to catch his breath, he became aware of a figure looming over him just as a boot connected sharply with his side, sending waves of pain throughout his body all over again. "You're *mine* now, *pig*," de Villiers spat out the words.

Piran tried to breathe deeply to calm himself but every intake of air felt like his chest was being ripped apart from the inside. Shallow breaths still hurt, but he could cope. He had to get up – not lie here at his tormentor's mercy – but his whole left side was useless. He tried to push himself up with his right hand, but that shifted his weight onto the left side, causing him to cry out from the pain. The best he could manage was trying to push with his feet, but he couldn't get good purchase on the uneven cobbles, some now wet with . . . he didn't want to think about what . . . so his progress was mere inches rather than the yards he needed.

All the while, the looming figure just stood there. "That's it, pig. Try to get away . . . just like the coward you are. Well, I don't tolerate pigs *or* cowards." And with that, de Villiers raised an arm.

Piran saw the dagger. The motion of the arm, beginning an arc that would almost certainly end in his chest or his gut. *Dear Lord, if this is how I'm to meet my end, make it swift. Forgive me all my sins and grant me entry into the glory of Heaven. Let the Holy Spirit bring comfort to my mamm and my tas . . .*

As he prayed, a shadow flew between him and his attacker. A scream. A thud that could only be a body falling to the ground. The voice: "Come on, men. Let's get out of here. We don't want to be anywhere near this place when the sheriff shows up." The sound of boots running away. And then silence. Was he alone here in the lane? Alone with the pain he could tolerate only if he didn't move? Would anyone find him before morning? Would he last that long?

Then two quiet footfalls. A gasp. The sound of retching, and something splashed onto his leg. The stench of bile and stale ale and onions and broth. *Do I dare speak?* **Can** *I even speak without ripping my lungs apart?* More footsteps, hurrying toward him. *Dear God in Heaven, please, no. Please not the attackers returning.*

And then a different voice. "Blessed Mary, what on earth has happened here?" *Could it be? Or am I delirious? Dreaming? Hearing what I wish I could here?* "You, there. Are you responsible for this?"

"No, Father. They ambushed us."

"Who?"

"De Villiers and his gang. We were headed home from the Swindlestock. What are *you* doing here, Father?"

He wasn't dreaming after all. Ned was here. Father de Grandison was here. He was safe. He took a deep breath to let out a sigh of relief and the pain washed over him, even worse than before, so he closed his eyes and let the darkness take him.

X

It felt strange to be back home, back to the small but comfortable cottage on the baron's estate, back to sleeping in the little attic room his *tas* had created when his *mamm* declared it was no longer fitting that he share a bed with his sisters. But it felt good to have his *mamm* taking care of him, even if, now and again, she insisted he drink one of her remedies. He'd learned as a child there was no point in resisting – it only prolonged the dread and the inevitable flow of her concoction past his tongue and down his gullet as he tried not to gag on the foul taste. So when she said "*Mar pleg, ow Piran, eva*" – please, my Piran, drink – he did his best.

He was so ashamed to have failed everyone who believed in him. "He what did this to you is the one what should be ashamed," his *tas* told him. "Isn't right to hate a man or do him harm just on account of where he was born. But you're safe now. He won't come looking for you here. And when you're better, mayhap the baron will give you a job taking care of his *marghti*. He's always liked you. You have a way with the horses and the stable boys. And you should find a wife. There be many a *teg mowes* hereabouts who'd think you a fine catch."

The Launceston prior had said much the same thing, though with no mention of horses or pretty girls. "There's no cause for shame, my son. Remember, Christ himself said 'Blessed are they who are persecuted for righteousness' sake.'" Piran wanted to protest that he hadn't been persecuted for righteousness but for Cornish-ness, but he couldn't quite form the words. "Christ went on to say," the prior himself went on, "that 'Whosoever shall smite thee on thy right cheek, turn to him the other also.'"

I've already done that, Prior – many times over. And this is what it got me. But still he couldn't seem to form the words.

"God has led you back home to us for now. But wherever you decide your destiny lies, my son, know that you would always have a place with us. The brothers would welcome you unconditionally."

He knew the prior was offering comfort. But he also knew he didn't want to withdraw from the world. His life lay in a different direction but the path to get there seemed hopelessly blocked by obstacles.

"Don't you fret, *ow baban*," his *mamm* whispered as she caressed his brow after he'd swallowed another cup of her dreadful medicine. Though he was a grown man, it was still comforting when she called him her baby and sang the lullaby he remembered from when he was just a wee one.

Hush-a-bye, my little crumb
The sheep are far from home
The hounds are to the far, far fields
And won't be home 'til noon.

And just like when he was a wee one, her sweet voice lulled him back to sleep like nothing else could.

When next he woke, the light seemed somehow brighter than he remembered from the tiny attic window. His eyelids were heavy and his mind felt shrouded in fog. When at long last he opened his eyes, the room he saw was indeed small, but not the one in Cornwall. A young boy sitting on a stool beside the door briefly made eye contact then scurried away. What was he doing there? And where was this place?

As the fog began to lift from his mind, he realized his chest was wrapped tightly in some sort of cloth, keeping him from taking anything other than shallow breaths. His left arm was folded over his chest and bound there, making it impossible to move that arm or shoulder. There was a bandage on his right arm as well, but it didn't inhibit motion in any way. He tried to shift in the bed but found it both difficult and painful so quickly abandoned the idea.

Footsteps beyond the door seemed to be hurrying toward the little room. More than one person, by the sound of it. Brother Ansfrid arrived first, followed soon after by two monks, each carrying a tray. One tray held numerous small bottles and a roll of cloth, the other a bowl with steam rising from it and a cup. The smell of broth filled the room. Brother Ansfrid brought the boy's stool to the bedside and sat while his companions set their trays on a table across the room, and the one who'd brought the steaming bowl disappeared without uttering a word. "Welcome back, Piran," said Ansfrid. "You've had quite an ordeal. But it's good that you're awake now."

"How . . . how long have I been asleep?"

"Brother Infirmerer gave you a sleeping draught. He wanted you to stay perfectly still for a few days for your broken bones to begin to heal."

"Is that why all this?" Piran pointed with his right hand to his bound left arm.

"It is indeed," said the monk who'd brought the tray of small bottles as he came to the bedside. "You have a broken cannel-bone and some broken ribs. There is no way to splint them, like we would for a leg, so the only thing we can do is prevent or limit movement until the bones grow back together. It will take some time, but if you follow my instructions, all will be well."

"And this?" Piran held up his right arm.

"A knife wound. Fortunately, it was not very deep. I stitched it up. In fact, I've come now to change the dressing and apply some more of this salve to ward off infection." He began unwrapping the coverings on Piran's arm.

"You still haven't answered my question, Brother Ansfrid," said Piran. "How long have I been here?"

"They brought you on Friday night. Today is Tuesday."

"And the others?"

"Your friends have come by every day to see how you were faring. I think they've been worried you might die." Seeing Piran's eyes grow wide with fear,

Ansfrid rushed to add. "You were never in any danger of that, my son. But it was obvious they didn't know the skills of our infirmerer. I've no doubt they'll be back today."

"Can I see them when they come?"

"Provided you don't exert yourself," said the infirmerer as he daubed something on the knife wound that made Piran flinch. "Yes, I know, it stings. But you will be grateful for the sting when the only lasting effect is a scar and not a missing arm."

"You've had another visitor as well," said Ansfrid.

"Oh?"

"The archdeacon's housekeeper has come every day. In fact, she was the only one who could coax you to drink Brother Infirmerer's tinctures, and each time, she stayed until you were safely asleep once again. The archdeacon asked to be informed as soon as you were awake, and I've already sent word."

Finished with the fresh dressing, the infirmerer walked to the opposite side of the bed. "Now, Ansfrid, with your assistance, we'll help him to sit up. He needs to eat if he's to regain his strength." The two monks locked hands under Piran's back and gently raised him upright. "Now swing your legs slowly over the side," the infirmerer instructed.

It hurt, but not as much as Piran had feared it might.

"You're not to do this on your own, my son," said the infirmerer. "Do you understand?"

"Aye. But what about when I need—"

The infirmerer anticipated the question. "The boy will be with you at all times. Just tell him, and he'll fetch two brothers to assist you straightaway."

Brother Ansfrid brought the food tray and placed it in Piran's lap. "Broth only for today, I'm afraid," Ansfrid said.

"In the cup is water from St. Frideswide's Well," said the infirmerer. Piran took a tentative sip from the cup, uncertain if this would be another foul-tasting remedy. But the water tasted sweet and fresh, and he drank it all down, suddenly realizing he was quite thirsty. The infirmerer chuckled.

"Yes, quench your thirst. But perhaps a bit more slowly next time so as not to assault your stomach. You've had some each time I administered the tincture, but now you must have some twice each day. And it might not go amiss to offer our saint a prayer of thanks for her healing waters."

"I won't forget, Brother."

XI

De Grandison put down his quill and reread the letter he'd just written.

May the blessings of God be upon you, Holy Father

With the fondest of greetings, as befits our friendship, and the hope that this missive finds you in your customary robust good health

It is quite fascinating to me how your assignments always seem to lead to something interesting. I will confess that my only expectation of my sojourn in Oxford was that I should bide my time while you maneuver the playing pieces into position for whatever it is you have in store for me but have not yet chosen to reveal. And yet, within just a few short weeks of my arrival, my path was crossed by a most intriguing young man – a Cornish theology student by the name of Chegwin who had run afoul of another student I can only describe as the villain of the piece, being possessed of an inordinate sense of his own self-importance combined with an unfounded disdain for all things Cornish. This particular villain may give you a laugh, Jacques, as he insists on being called Martinus, believing that going by the Latin form of his name will accelerate his advancement in the Church.

Unable to intimidate Chegwin by other means, this Martinus had engaged in a scheme to discredit his foe academically with the intent of having him dismissed from the university. Even though Chegwin's master and I devised a way to expose the scheme – and thus it was the schemers who found themselves dismissed – the story does not end there.

Resentful of his fate, Martinus then staged a physical attack on Chegwin and his mates, resulting in the death of one student and severe injuries to Chegwin himself. The attackers have succeeded in eluding all the sheriff's searches and so remain at large, their whereabouts a complete mystery.

But it is not my intent to dwell on the villain so much as the victim. As I have come to know young Chegwin during recent months, I am increasingly impressed by his considerable intellect. He quickly masters each concept of his theological training, but he also exhibits a keen facility for analysis and debate and an inquisitiveness not often seen in one so young – nor even, in far too many cases, in those of more mature years and experience in our calling. His contribution to the trap we set for the schemers was nothing short of brilliant, arguing both sides of the debate with equal conviction and then offering a creditable and well-reasoned argument for his own perspective on the matter. Though he professes that his only ambition is to be a caring parish priest – and I do not doubt for even a moment the sincerity of his sentiments – I am convinced that he is destined for quite a successful career in the Church provided he receives the opportunity.

Nonetheless, I find myself more than a little apprehensive about his future. Martinus is not the type to be dissuaded by his failures, but the sort for which each failure strengthens his resolve to succeed, no matter the cost. Though Chegwin has an assured place at Balliol for continuing his studies, I fear there may be no place in England safe for him until enough time has passed for his whereabouts to become sufficiently obscured that he cannot easily be found.

Thus it is that I take up my quill to make a request that you may consider quite presumptuous though I hope that, again in the spirit of our long friendship, you will grant me the kindness of giving it even a modicum of consideration. I can think of no safer place for this young man than in your service. He would do exceedingly well for Pierre des Près in the Chancery or, undoubtedly, in any role you might choose for him. I suspect he might also be quite adept as a student of canon law and thus able to serve you in ever more useful and important ways.

Of one thing, I'm quite certain. Once you have a chance to observe him, you will find him as interesting as I do. In fact, you might just have to invent a new category for him. Though it could be tempting, at first, to categorize him as a sycophant since he has a strong desire not to disappoint those who support him, that desire manifests itself not as fawning – or, as you once put it so eloquently, drooling – but as diligent pursuit of the task set for him, which I believe sets him apart.

Should you find it in your heart to give young Chegwin an opportunity to pursue his calling free from the fear of losing his life, then I will take him with me when I go to York in mid-July to consult with the archbishop before attending to my duties in Nottingham. There he can be ordained and then immediately take passage for Avignon. I have not yet spoken to him of either my concern for his well-being or the proposition I venture to make to you. Only if you agree will your name even be mentioned. And if my wish is not within your choice to grant, then I shall do my best to find another solution to safeguard this remarkable young man's future.

May the holy spirit watch over you and keep you safe, my dear friend.
Written at our lodgings in Oxford, the 6th day of June
John de Grandison

Satisfied, he folded the pages, inscribed the name of the recipient, and was pouring sealing wax when Mistress Chert barged into the room without knocking. "They just sent word, your holiness. The lad's awake."

De Grandison had long since abandoned any effort to convince her not to address him thus. The last time he'd reminded her the title was reserved for the Pope, she'd retorted, "As far as I'm concerned, if it's good enough for the Pope, then it's good enough for you, you being a holy man and all."

"You said I was to tell you straightaway," she added now, apparently her version of an apology for the breach of manners.

"I did indeed." He pressed the seal bearing his family crest into the puddle of warm wax. "And I'll be on my way momentarily."

"That you will. And you'll bring that lad back here where I can look after him . . . see he gets good food and does what he should to get better. What do a bunch of men know about how to take proper care of a body that's sick or injured? Oh, I'll grant you those monks know a thing or two about medicines and potions, but a woman knows better how to soothe a fevered brow."

Tempted as he was to smile at her earnestness, de Grandison restrained himself, knowing she might think he was mocking her, though that was far from the sentiment he intended. He'd been surprised when she had insisted on accompanying him to check on Chegwin the morning after the altercation. Even more surprised when they'd arrived to find the young man not fully aroused from sleep but resisting the infirmerer's attempts to administer medicine, and she sat down by the bed, took Piran's free hand in her own, and began singing softly. He had calmed almost immediately and then drunk the draught without complaint as she held the cup for him. *What terrible sadness*, the archdeacon wondered, *had once befallen this woman that she should hide such a tender heart behind the brusque – at times sullen, dismissive, or even disdainful – manner she now presented to the world?*

Every morning since, she had gone to the priory to check on the lad and make sure he took his medicines. And she had made it clear there was no room for debate – *she* would be the one to look after him just as soon as the infirmerer deemed it safe for him to be moved.

The wax now cooled enough that he could remove the seal, de Grandison returned it to the locked drawer where he kept it and tucked the key on its chain back inside his cassock. "You have my word, Mistress Chert, I'll have him brought here the moment it's acceptable to do so. In the meantime, there's something I need you to do. This letter needs to be sent straightaway." She picked it up, turned it over, and studied the address. Unsure if she could read, he went on. "It's to the Pope and it's quite urgent."

As if suddenly realizing she was handling a hot pot handle with no cloth for protection, she dropped the letter back onto the writing table and crossed herself three times. This time, de Grandison couldn't suppress a chuckle. "I can't be responsible for that, Father. I'm just a simple woman, and that… that's… sacred." She crossed herself again.

"I can think of no one who would handle it more responsibly." He retrieved the letter and held it out to her once again. "I ask only that you not be sparing when it comes to paying the messenger."

She took the letter, hesitantly at first, then grasped it in both hands and squared her shoulders. "I'll pay a messenger no more than he deserves."

"Then I recommend you find a very deserving one and pay him well. To deliver the message and wait for a reply. Young Chegwin's life may hang in the balance. That purse," he continued, gesturing toward a small leather pouch lying on the writing table, "contains extra coins so you don't have to deplete your housekeeping money."

At the mention of Chegwin's name, the housekeeper clutched the letter to her breast. "Whatever it takes for that sweet lad. Now off with you and see how he fares. I'll have this on its way before sundown."

⊕ ⊕ ⊕ ⊕ ⊕

De Grandison arrived at the priory to find Ned and Robin loitering in the cloister in whispered conversation. "Have you seen him already, Fletcher? How does he fare?"

"Thank heaven you've come, Father," said Robin. "We . . . well . . ."

"I'm ashamed to admit it, Father," Ned chimed in, "but we've been reluctant to go in on our own. We . . . we just don't know how to tell him about James."

"One thing at a time, men." The archdeacon stepped between them and placed a hand on each man's shoulder, propelling them forward. "Let's see what shape Chegwin's in first."

They found Brother Ansfrid and the infirmerer lowering Piran back into his bed. "Looks like he won't be going home with me today," de Grandison remarked.

"Your assessment is correct, Archdeacon," said the infirmerer. "But you can tell Mistress Chert that if our patient behaves himself and does exactly as he's told, his healing should have begun enough by the end of the week that we can give him into her care."

"That's precisely what she'll be pestering me to know the moment I walk back through the door to my lodgings."

The infirmerer smiled. "Tell her also she should continue her visits so she can learn how to help him without causing new injury."

"If I may offer a suggestion, Brother, with respect," De Grandison paused and the monk nodded assent. "You might find it more agreeable to simply let her observe your ministrations rather than trying to instruct her."

Now the infirmerer laughed aloud. "I've made that mistake already, Archdeacon, with a result that I'm sure you'll have no difficulty imagining."

"Indeed I wouldn't."

"Nonetheless," the infirmerer went on, "her sharp tongue could prove most useful in the coming weeks. It's quite common, once the bones have healed enough for the pain to subside, for the injured one – most especially if they're young – to decide to resume all their ordinary activities. And too often that causes the still-fragile bones to break yet again. If your housekeeper can keep young Chegwin here from making that mistake, it will be to his benefit in the long run."

De Grandison turned his attention to the young man lying in the bed. "Are you listening, Piran?"

"Aye, Father. I'll try to remember to behave myself."

"We'll leave you to it, then," said the infirmerer. "Ansfrid, can you bring the kitchen tray?"

As the monks took their leave, de Grandison sat down on the side of Piran's bed while Ned and Robin remained by the door, obviously uncomfortable. "So, Chegwin, how do you feel today?"

"I'm not really sure, Father. I haven't been awake for long, and it seems so strange to have slept through so many days."

"Are you still in pain?"

"Not when I stay still and remember not to take deep breaths. The brothers assure me things will get better every day, but in the meantime, I can't do anything without their assistance. I . . . I never imagined feeling so helpless." He paused, as if the effort of talking was taking a toll. "What did you and the infirmerer mean about Mistress Chert taking care of me?"

"As soon as they think you're ready, we'll be moving you to my lodgings so she can do just that."

"But shouldn't I just go back to St. Edmund Hall?"

"Not unless you want Mistress Chert moving into that small room with you and your mates. She's made it abundantly clear that no one else but her is going to look after you until you can once again look after yourself."

"There's nowhere for her there with four of us—" He stopped short, as if suddenly aware of the presence of his two friends. "Ned . . . Robin . . . where's James?"

The two exchanged a furtive glance before Robin diverted his gaze to the floor. "Well, Piran," Ned began, shuffling about, unable to look directly at his friend in the bed. "It's . . . well . . . it's like this . . ."

De Grandison understood that neither of these young men had ever had to break such news before. "I'm sorry to have to tell you this, Piran." He placed a comforting hand on Piran's right arm. "James did not survive the fight." The look on Piran's face changed from horror to fear to sorrow before tears began welling in his eyes. "I don't know exactly how it happened, lad – it was all over and the perpetrators had fled before I arrived on the scene – but Ned saw it all and can tell you when you're ready."

Grateful to be spared the task they'd been dreading, the other two came to Chegwin's bedside, Ned taking a seat on the stool and Robin standing behind.

"I want to know now," said Piran. "I don't want to be conjuring up thoughts in my mind that might not be true."

De Grandison maintained his steadying hand and a watchful eye on the young man who'd just emerged from healing sleep to haunting news. "He's right, Ned. Better he should know."

"He was trying to save your life, mate. We could all see de Villiers intended to stab you in the gut, but James was the closest. He lunged toward Martin – I think he was trying to grab the arm that was wielding the knife. Something happened I couldn't see, and then James and Martin fell to the ground in a heap, and Martin's knife plunged into James's back. Brother Infirmerer said the knife went between the ribs and straight into his heart, killing him instantly." Ned paused as a few tears escaped Piran's eyes and ran down onto his pillow. "He saved your life, Piran. Ours too, truth be told, because as soon as he understood what had happened, Martin scrambled out from under James, and he and his cronies couldn't run away fast enough."

By now, Robin had walked around and sat on the other side of Piran's bed. "I didn't see it all like he did, but Ned's right. James saved all our lives."

"What about de Villiers, Father?" Piran asked. "Does the sheriff have him?"

"Not yet, son. By the time the alarm could be raised, they'd all managed to go to ground somewhere. Both Master Bertran and I have urged the sheriff to keep up the search, but I don't know how much influence we wield, given the tensions between townies and university folk. That doesn't mean we won't keep pressing for them to be brought to justice." De Grandison squeezed Piran's arm. "But now I have to be on my way. I have a lecture to deliver. Will you be alright, Chegwin?"

"Don't worry, Father," said Ned. "We'll stay with him."

De Grandison rose. "Then I'll tell Brother Ansfrid to look in later, when it's time for you two to go back to your studies." He paused outside the door to listen and was heartened to hear Robin's voice trying to cheer his friend up.

"You're lucky this didn't happen in my village, mate. Any man got hurt that badly in a fight, they put him in a pile of fresh horse dung and made him drink some vile potion of cudweed and ale."

De Grandison smiled to himself and went in search of Brother Ansfrid.

XII

Piran was delivered into Mistress Chert's care on the following Saturday afternoon. Ned and Robin brought him on a litter made of canvas between two poles on which a prone man could be carried. Ned took one look at the steep stairs to the first floor and stopped in his tracks. "I don't know how we're going to get him up there, Mistress," he told the housekeeper.

"You're not, so don't even think about it. He's going to sleep in my room for now, so you just take him here, through the kitchen."

"But I can't take your bed, Mistress Chert," Piran protested.

"You can and you will, young man. Just like you'll do exactly what I tell you to heal those bones. There's three mattresses on that bed, and I've put one of them on the floor in the kitchen so I can sleep there and be close by if you need anything in the night. That leaves two on the bed, which is more than you had in that monk's cell you just left."

"But, Mistress, you can't sleep on the floor. It isn't right." Piran tried once again.

"It's right if I say it's right. Now you boys just bring him in here and let's get him settled."

That evening, de Grandison chose to take his meal in the kitchen with his housekeeper and her charge, who was now allowed to walk very short distances and sit at table or in a chair for brief periods. What struck him immediately was Chegwin's mood. He'd expected the lad to grieve the loss of his friend – even to fret over his own injuries – but there was something more profound in the young man's manner. His slumped posture, despite Mistress Chert's frequent admonishments to "Sit up straight so those bones heal right." A complete lack of light in his constantly downcast eyes. A reluctance to be drawn into conversation, his answers even to a direct question being monosyllabic at best, often little more than an incomprehensible mumble. Even the manner of his eating – as if it were a chore to be completed rather than something to savor.

When he downed the last of his ale and pushed himself up from the table using his good arm, de Grandison rose as well. "If you'll excuse me, Mistress Chert, I'll go help our young friend get settled back into his bed."

"You best take care, Father. Keep your arm under his shoulders and lower him gently. It's too soon for him to try doing it on his own."

He followed Piran into the housekeeper's room and knelt to take off the young man's slippers before carefully lowering him onto the pillows. Then he pulled the chair over to the bedside and settled into it. "Talk to me, Piran. I've never seen you so deeply troubled. Not even when it looked as if your dreams of becoming a priest were coming completely unraveled."

Chegwin turned his face toward the wall, apparently preferring his misery to the opportunity to unburden himself. Through the long moments of silence that ensued, de Grandison sat patiently, knowing that pent-up fears and longings and despair often came forth more as a trickle than as a gushing spring.

When, at long last, Piran turned back to face his mentor, his eyes glistened with moisture. "But it *is* completely unraveled now, isn't it, Father? De Villiers has won, and there's nothing I or you or anyone else can do about it."

"I'm not sure I agree, but tell me why you believe that."

"*Look* at me, Father."

Good, thought de Grandison. *Some emotion at last.*

"I can't even get out of this bed without help. How am I to finish my studies? And if I can't finish my degree, how can I take a place at Balliol? How can I even be a priest? All I've ever wanted . . . all my hopes for my life . . . gone. And the venerable Martinus roams free – gloating, no doubt, that he's finally made good on his intentions."

From the doorway came a female voice. "Oh, you'll finish your studies, young man." Mistress Chert had clearly been eavesdropping.

"*How?*" Piran's tone was a blend of frustration, anger, and despair. "How can I go to lectures when I can't walk farther than from here to the kitchen table? Tell me, Mistress. Tell me how."

"His holiness will see to it. He knows everything a man needs to know to be a priest and then some. He can teach you right here. And your friends can come and tell you what they've heard in their lectures. And as the weeks go by and you can move about more, you can write your treatises in Father's study, and I can deliver them to your master. You won't be giving up on your dream, young man. Not while *I* have anything to say about it." And with that, she turned on her heel and marched away.

Ah, Brother Infirmerer, thought the archdeacon as he watched a smile form on Piran's face. *If only you'd known just how quickly that sharp tongue would be needed. And for a soul as much as for the body.*

"She doesn't mince words, does she?" Piran almost chuckled.

"I thought you knew that."

"I guess I hadn't considered it lately." He paused and the smile disappeared. "But, Father, you have your own lectures to deliver. I can't take your time away from that."

"Do you imagine, Piran, that after all Bertran and I did to restore your good name, I wouldn't spare a bit of time to ensure you complete your last few weeks of study?"

"It's a lot to ask, Father. Most *especially* after what you've already done for me."

"It's not more than I choose to give." De Grandison paused then grinned. "And even if I didn't choose, do you really think I'd have much of a say in the matter?" They laughed together quietly, not eager to have to explain themselves should the subject of their amusement pop her head back in the door.

Life in the archdeacon's household quickly settled into a pattern. In the morning, Piran spent an hour or so at the kitchen table reading the passages de Grandison had selected for that day's lesson. Then he rested in his bed until the midday meal. In the early afternoon, when de Grandison returned from delivering his lectures, they sat together in Mistress Chert's little room – Piran propped up on the vast array of pillows the housekeeper had managed to procure – and discussed the lesson until Ned and Robin arrived. Mistress Chert always made sure there was enough food to invite them to stay for supper, which they were always happy to do since the fare was ever so much better that what was on offer in St. Edmund dining hall.

When he asked why she insisted on feeding all three students, de Grandison was once again reminded of the soft heart behind his housekeeper's brusque manner. "Our boy needs the comfort of feeling like his life is as it should be, even if he can't be living in the Hall right now," she'd said.

Every third or fourth day – at de Grandison's express request and to Mistress Chert's extreme consternation – Brother Infirmerer came to visit, bringing a supply of Saint Frideswide's healing waters and checking on Piran's progress. On his second visit, he took the stitches out of Piran's right arm and handed Mistress Chert a small pot of salve. "Apply this every day. It will keep the skin supple and prevent the scar from becoming too hard."

She gave the pot right back to the monk. "My mother used rendered pork fat for that, and I've made sure to have plenty on hand."

The infirmerer proffered the pot once again. "I've no doubt your remedy would have some effect, but I think you'll find the herbs in this smell much better."

Piran watched, his amusement suppressed with some difficulty, as they both stood their ground, the housekeeper with her arms folded across her chest, the monk holding out his pot of salve. When it seemed the impasse could go on forever, Piran knew it was up to him to help both of them preserve their dignity. "With all due respect for your mother, Mistress Chert, I think I'd rather have something that smells nice. Since I haven't had a bath in two weeks, I smell enough like a pig already without adding *actual* pig to the mix."

The housekeeper hesitated a moment longer then grudgingly took the pot. "Very well, if that's what the lad wants," she said. "But this better work as good as it smells."

After the monk's third visit, Mistress Chert could no longer contain herself and confronted de Grandison the moment he walked in the door from his lectures, following him into his study and complaining with every step. "That monk was here again today. And every time he comes, he checks on the lad. As if I don't know how to take care of him. Why do you let him do that, Father? Is it that *you* don't trust me to take care of the boy?"

De Grandison laid the heavy book he'd been carrying on the writing table and turned to face his angry housekeeper. "I asked the brother to come and bring the healing water. Surely you wouldn't deny Chegwin the help of a saint known by all hereabouts to be a healer."

"I'm perfectly capable of fetching that holy water myself. There's no need for him to be abandoning his monkly duties."

"I've no doubt you're capable, Mistress Chert. But think of this. What if something went wrong while you were gone and you weren't here to put things right? Something as simple as Chegwin needing to relieve himself and trying to get out of bed on his own? What if that set his healing back days or even weeks? I'd have trouble forgiving myself for allowing that to happen when I knew there was another way. Somehow, I think you would too."

"I could send someone to the priory to fetch the water instead of going myself." She wasn't willing to give in straightaway.

"Indeed you could. But think also of this. Each of you looks at our patient from a different perspective. You see the small steps, day-by-day. Brother Infirmerer sees what's changed over a longer span of time. And if you both see the same thing, then it must undoubtedly be true. I have no lack of trust in either of you. But knowing that you're in accord eases my mind considerably. So indulge me, if you will, and let the brother continue to give us his opinion."

"Well . . ." She paused for so long de Grandison was sure she was formulating yet another argument for denying the infirmerer's visits. Finally, her posture relaxed a bit and she added, "If it relieves your mind, then I'll try to put up with him."

Not quite acquiescence, de Grandison thought. *But probably as close as I'll get.*

As June gave way to July and Piran's stay in Mistress Chert's care entered its fourth week, the pattern began to change. First with Brother Infirmerer's visit on the Thursday – without the usual bottle of Saint Fridewside's water. "And what brings you here if you're not bringing the holy water?" Mistress Chert challenged as she followed him into the kitchen where Piran sat at the table reading.

"It's been nearly five weeks, Mistress – five weeks tomorrow since the actual fight. Time we start letting our patient ease back toward normal life, don't you think?"

"Five weeks isn't six, and bones take six weeks."

"Indeed they do, so I'm not suggesting we free him from all restrictions. Come in here and sit on the bed, lad." When Piran complied, he added, "Now let's remove your shirt." Then he carefully removed the bindings holding Piran's left arm in place and the wrapping from around his ribs. "Just let your arm hang naturally at your side."

Mistress Chert stood in the doorway, disapproval written all over her face. "You're not going to leave him like that, are you?"

"Not at all." Taking a fresh length of cloth from his satchel, the monk began rewrapping Piran's chest. "Much looser this time, young man. You need to breathe more freely so these ribs get used to doing their job once again." When he finished tying the cloth in place, he added, "Now take a deep breath, son," and watched as Piran complied. "How does that feel?"

"Strange." Piran breathed again. "I think I'm going to have to get used to it, Brother."

The monk grinned. "Slowly at first. Don't overdo it. And try not to cough or sneeze. If you feel something like that coming on, use your free hand to hold those ribs so they don't crack again. Now, for the cannel-bone." He ran his fingers along the bone then applied some pressure a short distance from where it joined the shoulder. When Piran didn't flinch, he pronounced, "Good. Healing very well. But I still don't want you using that arm for another week."

"And how am I supposed to keep him from doing that if he's got it all free?" the housekeeper interjected.

"It's not going to stay all free, Mistress. But first, I need to help him back into his shirt." That task complete, he took another piece of cloth from his satchel, this one a square that he folded so two opposite corners met. "Now, son, bend your arm at the elbow and hold the lower half across your chest." He finished by tying the cloth around Piran's neck, making a cradle to support his left arm. "There. You should be able to move around more freely now."

"And what if he gets in his head to take his arm out of that contraption?" Mistress Chert seemed determined to dispute the infirmerer's ministrations.

"I promise I won't, Mistress," Piran tried to placate her. "You said it's just for one more week, right?"

"A week and two days, if you count today."

"Then I'll count today, Mistress. I promise." Rising from the bed, he asked, "Does this also mean, Brother, that I can return to St. Edmund Hall and give Mistress Chert back her bed?"

"You'll be doing no such thing, young man," the housekeeper didn't give the monk a chance to reply. "Mayhap you can be moving upstairs, but you're not leaving this house until I decide you're fully fit to get on with your life."

"Just be careful going up and down the stairs, son," the infirmerer warned. "You don't want to fall now that you're so close to being what my colleague so aptly describes as fully fit."

"Colleague. Hmph," Mistress Chert grumbled as she stepped aside for Piran and the infirmerer to return to the kitchen.

"My esteemed colleague, in fact, Mistress. I commend you for the most excellent care you've given our patient. And when next I return, I believe we shall both be able to declare that he's ready to be out in the world once again. Now I'll just be on my way. I think you and young Piran have some reordering of sleeping arrangements to attend to."

The following morning, when Piran carefully negotiated the stairs after a restful night in what might have been the most comfortable bed he'd ever slept in, he found de Grandison waiting for him in the entrance hall. "No texts to read today, Chegwin. Instead, I want you to write a homily rooted in your current experience. You can use my study and any of the books you find there. We'll discuss it this afternoon." As he reached for the door latch to make his exit, he turned back. "And if a book's heavy, get Mistress Chert's help to move it from the shelf. It will keep us both in her good graces."

Piran laughed. "You can count on it, Father. I've sworn an oath to her to be on my best behavior for the next week."

But it didn't take long working on his assignment for Piran's mood to sour. In the preceding weeks, he hadn't had much time for contemplation. His time had been filled with study and meals and enjoying the company of his mates, and every evening he'd been so tired that the only thing he had any interest in was sleep. When he'd opined to the housekeeper that he'd never slept so much in his life, she'd said, "And that's as it should be, young man. Sleep is what helps a person recover from an illness."

"But I haven't been ill – just cracked some bones," he'd objected.

"One and the same thing," she declared. "Your body was broken. Sleep helps make it whole again."

Now, however, the archdeacon's assignment left him no choice but to ponder his circumstances. What *would* he say to a gathering of the faithful? Would he talk about evil in the world? How it's everywhere, all around us, every day. How it sneaks up on us when we least expect it. How we're often powerless in its grasp. How we have to be constantly on guard, always fearful lest we fall into its clutches. How it often wins in this world, leaving lives in tatters and dreams in shreds. How its practitioners can so easily draw others into their sphere and coerce others to do their bidding. And how they can get away with their evil deeds time and again with little or no earthly consequences. The more he went down that path, the darker his spirit grew.

At long last, after pacing around the study for what seemed like half the morning, he gradually came to a realization. *If these thoughts are distressing me so much, wouldn't speaking them aloud to my flock have the same effect on them? Shouldn't a good priest try to help his people find reason to hope even when things seem dark?*

So he pursued the opposite direction – one of hope and of cheer and the belief that the world is fundamentally good and that evil only rears its head now and again and that we needn't fear it lest we miss out on the joys of life. But in the end, that felt too naïve, too disconnected from his recent experience.

Unable to find something that satisfied him, he was grateful when Mistress Chert called him for the midday meal. But despite the fact that she was far more cheerful than usual – *probably because she got her first good night's rest since I got here, being back in her own bed at last*, he thought – and even commended him for following her instructions, he returned to the study with his thoughts still unsettled. And when de Grandison returned in the early afternoon, Piran's quill was still dry, the lid still on the inkpot, and the page he'd laid on the writing table still pristine.

As the archdeacon entered the study, he took in the situation but offered no comment, instead making his way to the chairs in front of the hearth and taking a seat. "Join me, Piran. Let's talk."

Looking utterly defeated, Piran complied. "I'm sorry, Father. I've failed. I tried, but I can't find the right words, the right tone, the right . . ." Unsure precisely what else wasn't right, he let the thought trail off into the air.

"Tell me what you've considered and why you've rejected it."

While Piran recited the litany of his morning's ruminations, de Grandison listened thoughtfully, now and again resting his chin on steepled fingers, occasionally raising his eyebrows, but never interrupting. "What I couldn't work out, Father," Piran concluded, "is how to help others make sense of what's happened when I still can't make sense of it myself." What he couldn't work out in the moment was the reason for the warm smile on his mentor's face.

"I'm actually quite proud of you, Chegwin. What I asked of you today is perhaps the greatest challenge any priest must face."

Piran looked puzzled. "I don't understand, Father."

"Ah, but you do. Your final remark. Helping others through a crisis when the crisis is ongoing, your understanding is limited, and the outcome is uncertain . . . it's inordinately difficult. But the ability to do that is what sets the good priests apart. Far too many fall back on the aphorism that we must simply accept God's will."

"Then I doubt I'll ever be a good priest." Piran sounded dejected.

"And I'm quite certain you will be. You got to the heart of the matter, which is the most important step, and you made thoughtful decisions about the paths you rejected. There's no question in my mind that if I gave you the same assignment tomorrow morning, I would return to find an acceptable homily lying on my writing table."

"I'm not so sure of that, Father."

"I said acceptable – not perfect. I'm not sure any of us ever gets it perfect. Take heart, Piran. You've done well with a difficult assignment."

And it wasn't just about what awaits me as a priest, Piran mused that night as sleep eluded him despite the comfort of his bed. *Father wanted me to find a way to make peace with what's happened . . . a way to put it behind me and look to the future.*

Do I still want to be a priest? Absolutely. And the fellowship at Balliol would make that path even easier. I still have most of the archdeacon's money since I've had no cause to spend it these past weeks. With that and what I could earn as a scribe, I could probably manage the first year. Was all of this God's way of making sure I could continue my studies? If it was, he certainly has a perverse way of going about things.

Don't go down that path, Piran. Remember what Father said about simply accepting God's will being the unthinking man's platitude.

Still, that doesn't negate the fact that I can now afford it . . . barely . . . but then again, that's a situation I know well.

And then his thoughts turned to James. To his friend who had his future all worked out. His friend who would never see that future unfold. He owed James his life. How, then, to use that life to honor James's sacrifice?

Sleep finally overtook him in that darkest hour of the night when the monks at the priory would be well into the liturgy of Matins. But when he awoke to the sounds of Mistress Chert busying herself in the kitchen below, he felt a new peace, despite having had such a short sleep. Descending the stairs, he was pleased to find the archdeacon in his study poring over a book at his writing table. Piran knocked softly on the doorframe, and de Grandison looked up. "God's good day to you, Chegwin. Is there something you wish to discuss?"

"Aye, Father. I've decided what I want to do with my life."

XIII

"Your sentiments are understandable, Chegwin – even admirable," said de Grandison in response to Piran's revelation that he wanted to petition Bishop Droxford to give him the post James would have had in Ashill. "But have you considered the risks?"

"You mean the risks of not extending my studies, Father? The only risk I see there is that I might spend the rest of my life in Ashill."

"No, Piran. I mean the risk to your very life. With de Villiers and the others still at large, that's a very real risk indeed. Your life is too precious to put in danger."

"And how would that risk be any different from James's?"

"In every way, Piran. James acted to help others. You would be acting out of a sense of guilt."

Piran's face fell. The peace he thought he'd found dissolved around him. Yet somewhere deep inside, he could feel the truth of the archdeacon's words. He'd felt the guilt from the moment he learned James's fate but had managed to repress it during the weeks when there'd been no time for contemplation. "Then I suppose," he began, his voice barely above a whisper, "I should accept Master de Seton's offer and continue my studies."

De Grandison didn't respond straightaway. When at long last he did, his tone was one of genuine concern. "In truth, Piran, I'm not sure anywhere in England is safe for you at this moment. Men like de Villiers can never accept defeat, and as long as he remains a free man, he remains a threat to your life."

"Isn't the sheriff still looking for them?"

"Another sad truth, I fear. Since they're no longer causing trouble here in Oxford, he's decided there's no reason to pursue them elsewhere."

"Wouldn't that mean I'd be safe at Balliol?"

"What do you think, Piran? You couldn't spend all your days and nights in your room. And de Villiers has already proven his skill at the unexpected attack."

"Then what am I to do, Father? I've never wanted the monastic life and yet, if you're right, a monastery is the only place I'd be out of his reach."

"Not the only place." From a drawer in his writing table, de Grandison retrieved what appeared to be a letter and rose from his chair. "Come sit with me in front of the hearth." Once they were settled, he continued. "I've taken the liberty of writing to a friend on your behalf. And yesterday, I received this." He held out the letter to Piran. "I think you should read it."

Piran unfolded the pages carefully then studied the words, his brow furrowing as he did so.

"Something wrong?" de Grandison asked.

"I . . . I can't make out the words, Father."

"Ah . . . I should have thought of that. You don't know French. Well, that's something else we'll need to attend to." He extended his hand. "Here . . . let me read it to you." Taking the pages, he added, "I'll just skip over the blessings and the personal greetings and get straight to the heart of the matter."

I'm not sure which intrigues me more, John – the possibility of adding a strong intellect to my staff or the possibility that I shall need a new category to put him in.

De Grandison looked up from the missive. "My friend finds it amusing to categorize the people who surround him and claims that, so far, they all fit neatly in one of three little boxes, none of which he regards very highly. I ventured to suggest you might not be such a neat fit."

"Me, Father?"

"Let me continue."

Your notion that he might begin in the Chancery is a good one as it will provide an opportunity to assess what he might be capable of. As much as I respect your judgment, John, I should like to observe this young priest myself to decide where he can be of the greatest service.

When you send him to me, ensure that he carries a letter of introduction from you, and I will ensure that he's not turned away when he requests an audience.

May God's blessings be with you always, my friend, and may we both be blessed to share a meal together soon.

Jacques

After a long pause, Piran asked, "Does this mean you've secured me a position, Father? With this Father Jacques, whoever he might be?"

"Indeed it does. And who he might be is the holiest of fathers. You might have heard of him. He frequently goes by the name John XXII."

Piran's jaw dropped. "The . . . the Pope, sir? You've secured me a position with the *Pope*?"

De Grandison grinned, enjoying his little surprise. "In the papal court, to be precise, but yes, there's no doubt you'll be in the presence of the Holy Father himself from time to time since one of the responsibilities of the Chancery is to record official proceedings."

XIV

Even as he stepped off the ship in Calais, Piran still couldn't quite believe what was happening. Surely it was some sort of dream and any moment he would wake and be back in . . . But every morning he woke to yet another sunrise on another once-inconceivable day in this new reality that was now his life.

It had been barely a month since that afternoon in the archdeacon's study when his path had veered sharply away from anything he'd ever envisioned. A month of sadness and joy, anticipation and anxiety, regret and renewal. Saying farewell to Ned and Robin was sad – he'd probably never see them again – but it had been expected. Even if he'd stayed in Oxford, they were moving on with their lives.

His parting from Brother Ansfrid was more poignant. Piran thought he'd be safe on the short walk to the priory in broad daylight, but Mistress Chert was having none of it. "His holiness would have my hide if anything happened to you, young man," she'd said on the morning he announced where he was going. "Now you just wait one moment while I take this pot off the fire and then we can be on our way." Thankfully, she chose to wait outside while he went into the church.

Saying a final prayer of thanks at St. Frideswide's shrine, he made his way to the south aisle to gaze at the stained glass window at the east end and recalled what Brother Ansfrid had said the first time he admired the window. "It tells of the union of England and France, you see. The lion of England and the fleur-de-lys of France at the top, the king and queen at the bottom depicting Edward and Isabella. And in the middle, St. Augustine, who founded our order, St. Thomas à Becket, and St. Martin de Tours, the patron of France. It was commissioned and installed before the current troubles between Edward and Isabella. But no matter their troubles, I still find it inspiring."

Did the window somehow also depict my future? Piran wondered. *Could that be why I've always been so drawn to it?*

"It's beautiful in the morning light, isn't it?" Brother Ansfrid's voice startled Piran from his musings.

"Aye, it is."

"And now you're going to France."

"It seems that's the path God has chosen for me."

They spent the next hour in quiet conversation until Piran could postpone his leaving no longer. "I shall pray for you, my son," said Ansfrid. "And know that you have a home here should God's path ever lead you back to us." They embraced and Piran left quickly lest he be overcome by the emotions that were roiling inside him.

When, later that same day, Master Bertran presented him the parchment attesting to his achievements at the university, the poignancy was swept away in a wave of joy and pride. Piran couldn't make out who was most pleased – himself, Master Bertran, or Father de Grandison. But that question was answered unequivocally when he returned home to discover Mistress Chert had prepared a feast befitting the crowning of a king, all in his honor. She absolutely glowed when de Grandison insisted she join them for the meal, and after they'd toasted Piran, she raised her glass again. "Don't you ever doubt what you're capable of, young man. You know *I* never will."

Though he regretted not being able to take up the fellowship at Balliol, he'd finally made peace with the truth of the threat to his life if he stayed in England. What he regretted far more deeply was that he'd been unable to go home to explain it all to his family. The archdeacon had been adamant that he mustn't travel alone. "Besides," he added, "there isn't time. You have to be here to receive your degree on St. Swithun's day, and if I'm to meet with the archbishop in York, attend to my duties in Nottingham, and be back in Oxford when I'm expected, then we must start our journey a day or two after that."

So he'd had no choice but to write a letter to his parents explaining how his life had changed. Not wanting them to worry, he described the position in the papal court as a rare opportunity rather than an escape from danger. But he knew they'd worry about his being so far from home, so he ended with a promise he didn't know if he'd ever be able to keep.

Maam . . . Tas . . . know that I love you and that my fondest desire, should the Holy Father offer me a respite from my duties, is to once again embrace you and enjoy the warmth of my family for whatever time is afforded me.

Mistress Chert had looked in the door once while he was writing and left without saying a word. Then, as if by divination, she returned just as he poured the wax to seal his missive. "Now, you be giving me that, young man, and I'll see to its delivery."

"I was thinking you might go with me to hire a messenger."

"Never you mind that. You give it to me, and I'll make sure it goes with the next coachman headed for Launceston. And I won't be scrimping pennies on what I pay him either, but don't you tell his holiness that. I wouldn't have him thinking I've turned into a waster." She crossed to the writing table and picked up the letter. "Don't you fret. This'll get to your parents as soon as may be."

De Grandison hired a carriage to take them to York and arranged to stop only in the finest inns, making the journey far more pleasant than Piran expected, his only previous experience with travelling long distances having been the crowded public coach he'd taken to Oxford. He hated to admit it, but he was really going to miss the comforts he enjoyed in the archdeacon's company. When he mentioned this to Father by way of thanking him for his generosity, de Grandison chuckled. "Ah, Piran, if you only knew what awaits you. You'll be surrounded by grandeur beyond anything you've ever seen before. It's a testament to the glory of God, of course, but also makes the lives of those who serve the Holy Father quite tolerable indeed. All your daily needs will be provided for, and you'll also receive a small stipend. It will be a very different life from that of the poor parish priest who more often gets paid with a chicken than a shilling."

They'd spent the long days in the carriage with de Grandison alternately preparing Piran for his ordination and teaching him some basic French. "Won't my Latin be enough?" The idea of trying to learn a new language in such a short time just added to the anxiety he already felt about this adventure. He had to get things right. He couldn't let down the man who'd already done so much for him.

"Once you're established in the papal court, yes," the archdeacon had replied. "But you have to get there first. And I rather suspect you'll want to eat and sleep along the way. Besides, if the Pope should decide he wants to speak with you privately, he'll be quite pleased if you can at least attempt his own language, even if all you can say is '*Je ne parle qu' un tout petit peu de français.*'"

"I suppose that means something like 'I can barely speak French.'" Piran chuckled then paused a moment before adding, "But won't I be able to find churches in the towns and villages along the way and won't they have priests who speak Latin?"

"In the larger towns, certainly. But in the poorer parishes or small villages, the priest may know no more Latin than the words of the mass. Not every priest has your education, Piran. Some are barely literate. Some chose that path because they had no other means to feed themselves. There are even a few reprobates who became priests to escape the clutches of the law. It's a failing of the Church that needs to be put right." De Grandison flexed his shoulders, as if shaking off something unpleasant, and sat up straighter. "Now, let's see if we can get you enough French that you don't turn up in Avignon looking like a starved orphan."

By the time they reached York, Piran could manage a few sentences on his own and could more or less understand de Grandison if the latter spoke slowly enough. Most importantly, he had what he expected to be his most useful phrase – *je ne comprends pas* – I don't understand – comfortably on his tongue.

De Grandison had assured him he was fully prepared for Archbishop Melton's examination of the candidate, but when they set foot inside York Minster, Piran's confidence flagged and he stopped just inside the entrance.

"I . . . What if I'm not found worthy, Father?"

The archdeacon smiled. "William Melton is not going to find you wanting, Chegwin. I have every reason to believe this will be no more than a formality." What he didn't add was that Melton already knew Piran was destined for the papal court.

Piran couldn't sleep that night. Tomorrow would be the most momentous day of his life. And when the time came and the prayers were said and he was clothed in his new vestments and his hands anointed, he knew beyond any doubt that he was ready. Feeling Bishop Melton's hands on his head, he also felt what he could only describe as a renewal of his soul as all that had gone before slipped away and he was imbued with an overwhelming joy for what lay ahead.

Two days later, the archdeacon accompanied the new priest, dressed in a fine new cassock, to Hull, paid for his passage to Calais, and admonished him, "Write to me, Piran. I shall be most eager to learn how you're getting on."

Now, as he set foot on French soil for the first time, what was foremost on his mind was food. He'd never quite gotten his sea legs. The salt pork and ship's biscuit he got with a mug of ale at mealtimes didn't help his slightly queasy stomach, but he discovered quickly it was best to forego the meat. He spent most of his time in his cot. The seamen assured him he'd feel better in the fresh air on deck, but he was too afraid of losing his footing and tumbling overboard. When they docked at Sluys to offload some bales of wool, the captain bartered some of the pork for a cask of pickled fish, which the crew ate with gusto. Just the smell of it was enough to send Piran rushing on deck to spew his guts out over the railing.

But with his feet finally on dry land, he slung his satchel over his shoulder, picked up his traveling bag, and set out in search of a meal. Remembering the archdeacon's warning about the taverns near the docks – *The men who frequent those places are a rough sort. They won't take kindly to a priest in their midst.* – he found his way into the town. After threading his way through a series of narrow alleys, he came out on a much wider street and found a tavern straightaway. Stepping inside with a certain amount of trepidation, he made his way slowly to the bar.

"*Bonjour, mon Père. Bienvenue.*" The landlord seemed friendly enough.

"*Je . . .*" Piran hesitated. "*Je . . . faim. J'ai faim.*" He hoped he'd managed to say he was hungry and not something rude.

"*Ah. Vous voulez manger, oui?*"

"*Oui. Manger.*" And then he remembered his manners. "*S'il vous plaît.*"

"*Alors, je vous en prie, asseyez-vous là.*"

Piran wasn't precisely sure what the man had said, but since he was gesturing toward an empty table, it seemed reasonable to assume this was an invitation to sit. He set his traveling bag under the table, placed his satchel beside the bag, and perched on a stool as the landlord disappeared through a curtained doorway behind the bar. He returned momentarily with a bowl of steaming potage, a large chunk of bread, and a glass of wine. "*Eh, bien . . . bon appétit!*"

Not wanting to appear impolite and knowing his stomach would fare better if not assaulted with the whole meal in a single gulp, Piran took his time over what turned out to be quite delicious fare. Finished, he beckoned the landlord to ask what he owed. "*Combien?*"

"*Le repas est gratuit pour un prêtre. Surtout un prêtre étranger.*" Seeing the puzzled look on his guest's face, he added, "*Rien pour vous.*"

The conversation was straining the limits of Piran's French, but he'd understood the word for "nothing" and tried to protest. "*Non, non . . . je . . . payer.*"

He started to reach for the pouch of French coins de Grandison had given him for the journey, but the landlord shook his head and held up his hands. "*Pas du tout, mon Père. C'est mon plaisir.*"

Having no idea how to respond, Piran said the only two words he could think of – "*Dieu . . . bénisse*" – and hoped the landlord would understand he was trying to invoke God's blessing. Then another thought occurred to him. "*Où est l'église?*" Surely in a city of this size the priests would be well-versed in Latin, and he could get some much needed help for continuing his journey. And surely this man could tell him where to find the nearest church . . . if he could just understand.

"*Suivez-moi.*" The landlord started for the door and beckoned for Piran to follow. Hoisting his satchel and traveling bag, Piran did as he was bid. Outside, the landlord pointed down the street that ran in front of the tavern. "*Tout droit. Et puis, tournez à droit à la troisième rue. Et voilà. L'église est juste en face de vous.*"

"*La troisième rue?*" The third street was all Piran had understood.

"*Marchez tout droit.*" The landlord pointed straight ahead with the forefinger of his left hand and mimed a walking movement with the first two fingers of his right. "*Alors. Un . . . deux . . . trois.*" He counted off with the fingers of his left hand while continuing the walking movement with the right. "*À la troisième rue, tournez à droit.*" Now, with his left hand, he pointed to the right.

Piran vigorously nodded his understanding. "*Merci. Merci beaucoup.*"

The landlord clapped him on the shoulder, smiled broadly, and said "*Allez-vous en*" before turning to go back into his establishment.

Exhausted from the effort of trying to converse in a language he really did not know, Piran made his way to the third cross street, turned right, and let out a huge sigh of relief. Straight ahead of him was a very large church with a beautiful rose window above the entrance. Yes, the priests here would speak Latin. And with a modicum of luck, they might also agree to give him lodging for the night. He had a long journey ahead of him – the longest of his life – and it seemed a good night's sleep, after the fitful rest he'd had on the sea voyage, would be the best way to begin. *Mistress Chert would be proud*, he told himself as he set off toward the church.

Marsh Baldon, England

"So the chick has flown the coop, Martin," said Bolam, the extra man who'd been recruited to assist with the attack on Chegwin.

De Villiers took a quick swallow of ale before asking, "Where to?"

They were sitting in the small, dark room that passed for a tavern in this tiny hamlet not far from Oxford. Not so dark during the long evenings of summer when light streamed in through the open door. And not really a tavern at all – certainly not a legal one. Just the front room of the somewhat dilapidated house next door to the smithy. The house belonged to the blacksmith – Bolam's cousin – who, being unmarried and needing only the back room for sleeping, had decided he could make a little extra money from his thirsty neighbors. A plank laid across two empty barrels served as a bar. A single table and a dozen or so stools were the only other furnishings. The ale came from Abingdon Abbey, where the blacksmith bartered his services whenever he needed a fresh barrel from their brewery.

De Villiers and the others had fled here after the wrong man died in the streets of Oxford that night, and they'd stayed out of sight for a week in the loft above the smithy. Unwilling to attract the attention of the Oxfordshire authorities to his little unlicensed enterprise, Bolam's cousin was only too happy not to mention to the sheriff's men that he was harboring the six fugitives.

Once the active search seemed to have been abandoned, they came out of hiding and made their way to Reading, convinced that no one in Berkshire would know they were fleeing a crime. Being the only one with any money, de Villiers rented a single room for them all to share in the cheapest inn he could find and sent the others out to find work so they could all eat. On the third evening, Snape didn't return.

"When I find that bastard," de Villiers had growled, "he'll wish he hadn't crossed me."

"Oh, just leave him be, Martin," said Wainwright. "What can he possibly do?"

"What can he do? Other than go to the authorities, you mean?"

"So what if he did?" asked Hawthorn. "As long as *we* all tell the same story, it's his word against ours and there's four of us, so who are they going to believe?"

"Is that what you think?" Martin sneered. "Well, think about this. First thing he'll do – no, second thing after he tells them what we did and where to find us – is to tell them about that archdeacon. *Then* who do you think they'll believe – us or the man in the cassock?"

While the others toiled at whatever work they could find, de Villiers had scoured all the back alleys of Reading in the hope of finding Snape cowering somewhere the little fool thought was safe. All to no avail, as it turned out. Snape had well and truly made his escape. And as the days wore on and the Reading sheriff took no notice of the rest of them, Martin finally acquiesced to Wainwright's nightly plea that he should leave well enough alone.

But when June gave way to July and St. Swithun's day was approaching, his compulsion to know where Chegwin would be once he received his degree and left the university overcame his concern about the risk of being in Oxfordshire. His vengeance on the Cornish pig wasn't complete, but once the pig was on his own, away from all his protectors, there would be opportunities. So they'd returned to Marsh Baldon, and he'd sent Bolam – whose face was unknown to anyone who mattered – to spy on what was happening.

For the first few nights, Bolam returned to report nothing of any real interest. At the end of the week, it wasn't Bolam but a filthy boy in a torn shirt who wandered into the makeshift tavern asking for Martinus. "I'm to tell you they're leaving and he's following," said the boy.

"Who gave you this message?"

"Don't know his name. Just that he paid me a farthing and said I was to tell someone called Martinus. And that's you, right?"

Martin didn't acknowledge who he was – just reached into his pocket and produced a penny, which he held up in front of the boy's face. "And I'm paying you a whole penny if you promise to keep your mouth shut. What do you say?"

The boy grabbed for the coin but Martin jerked it away. "You keep your mouth shut, right? You tell no one you came here. You tell no one you saw me – or any of us. You tell no one what you told me." He held the coin up again, this time just out of the boy's reach. "Right?"

Nodding, the boy said, "Right."

"You swear? Swear on your mother's soul."

"Don't got no ma. No pa neither."

"Then swear on your own soul. You keep your mouth shut, right? Because if I find out you've been talking, you'll be joining your ma and pa alongside the devil himself."

Fearless, the boy met Martin's gaze. "I swear. Now give me the penny."

Martin flipped the coin in the air, watched as the boy caught it deftly, then laughed as the lad ran away.

More than two weeks passed before Bolam returned, and now the idiot was more interested in emptying his mug than in answering Martin's question. "You can drink later, Bolam. Right now you need to tell me where the pig's gone. Or did you even think to ask where that ship was headed?"

His mug now empty, Bolam finally spoke. "Oh, I asked, Martin, but you won't like the answer. The harbor-master said that ship was bound for Sluys in the Low Countries, then Calais, then Hastings."

"And?" De Villiers lifted his mug, as if about to take a long, celebratory swallow.

"And he had absolutely no idea which of those places the priest was going to. Seems the man who arranged the passage did his business directly with the ship captain."

"*God's **bollocks**!*" Martin slammed the mug down on the table, sloshing ale all over himself, the table, and Wainwright, sitting next to him. Every man in the room turned to stare, and Martin glared at each in turn until they'd all diverted their eyes back to the studious examination of the contents of their own mugs. No one spoke. The silence went on and on and on.

At long last, Wainwright ventured, "What do we do now, Martin?"

XV

After two days of walking, Piran decided Father de Grandison had been right. It would be worth spending some of his money on a decent horse rather than arriving on the Pope's doorstep with holes in his boots. Worried that his limited French would make him an easy target for someone looking to get a high price for a broken-down nag, he enlisted the help of one of the priests at Thérouanne Cathedral to help with the transaction. Apparently, generosity to priests wasn't uncommon in this part of France as he ended up with quite a satisfactory mount for about half what he'd expected to pay. Even so – and even with the long summer days and the fact that he was a good horseman – it took him eleven days to reach Chalon-sur-Saône.

The priests at the cathedral there tried to convince him to overcome his anxiety about floating transport and find a boat to take him the rest of the way by river. "Find one that only puts in at Lyon and Valence, and you could arrive two or even three days sooner than going overland."

"I'll think about it," he told those who were so eager to help him, but in truth, his mind was already set. He'd become rather fond of his horse and its pleasantly smooth gaits and had no desire to experience water travel again so soon, even if it wasn't on the open seas.

Nonetheless, his route followed the river through miles and miles of vineyards that stretched from just south of Mâcon all the way to his destination. Spending his final night in France at the Abbaye Saint-André in Villeneuve-lès-Avignon, he decided this would be a suitable home for his horse and made a gift of it to the brothers. "All I ask," he told the abbot, "is that you take good care of her. She's sound and willing, and if she's well fed and not abused, she should have many good years left to give you."

The following morning, he stood for a long time outside the gatehouse at the Tour-Philippe-le-Bel. Once he crossed the Pont Saint-Bénézet, he would be in the Papal State and his new world. At long last, he hoisted his traveling bag and set out on this last, short portion of his journey.

At the papal palace, crossed halberds stopped his progress before he reached the entrance. Father de Grandison had warned him about the Swiss mercenaries who were employed to guard the Pope. "They're diligent in their duties, Piran," Father had said, "and they have absolutely no sense of humor. So don't do anything they might construe as reaching for a weapon." Remembering those words, Piran had already removed the letter of introduction from his satchel and offered it to the guards even before he was asked. The man who took it examined the seal then beckoned to a guard who stood beside the door. Piran couldn't understand their verbal exchange – he wasn't even sure if it was French – but when the first man turned back to him and barked "*Attendez ici*," Piran set his traveling bag down on the ground to show he intended to comply.

When the man who'd taken the letter inside returned, he was accompanied by a priest who was now in possession of the missive. "Father Chegwin?" the priest asked.

"I am."

"And I am Father Selvaggio. My instructions are to take you to Cardinal des Près." His next words were once again unintelligible, but the halberds immediately snapped to the vertical and the guards turned to face each other, inviting Piran to pass. *How many languages must one know to function here?* he wondered.

When he stepped through the entrance, it took all his concentration not to stop in his tracks and gape. De Grandison had said he'd be surrounded by grandeur, but Piran clearly hadn't understood his mentor. The word he'd taken in was "grandeur" – what he now realized was that the most important word was "surrounded." Wherever his gaze fell, it landed on opulence he could never have imagined. When he stumbled on an uneven bit of the stone floor and Selvaggio reached for his elbow to steady him, he apologized. "I'm sorry, Father. I should watch where I'm putting my feet."

Selvaggio chuckled. "It happens to every man who passes this way for the first time, Chegwin. And that's precisely what the Holy Father intended – to create something even finer than the Lateran. I'm afraid the rivalries within the papal court between Italy and France run deep indeed. But don't worry. You'll grow accustomed to your surroundings in due course."

They passed by two vast halls then wound their way through a labyrinth of corridors until Selvaggio finally stopped and knocked on a door. There was no response from the other side. "It's his habit," Selvaggio whispered, "to make people wait. Why is a bit of a mystery. But it's my observation that those who earn his respect are the ones who can avoid appearing flustered when they're finally admitted."

When the invitation to enter eventually came, Selvaggio stepped inside and waited for Piran to join him. "Father Chegwin, Eminence, as you requested." The man who rose from behind his writing table had a full, clean-shaven face, closely cropped hair, and was not exceedingly tall, but he wore the air of one who was accustomed to being respected. Making his way to where the two priests stood just inside the doorway, he extended his left hand toward Piran, who dutifully kissed the ring. "Chegwin," Selvaggio continued, "this is Cardinal des Près, Vice-Chancellor of the Holy Roman Church."

Piran bowed his head and said simply, "Your Eminence."

"Leave us for now," said the cardinal, "but wait in the corridor. If our interview goes well, I shall need you to show Father Chegwin to his post. If it does not . . ."

Another attempt to intimidate me? Piran wondered. He was, in fact, already quite intimidated by his surroundings and by being in the presence of such a high official of the Church, but he vowed to take Selvaggio's words to heart. *I won't give Father de Grandison any reason to regret sending me here.*

Des Près returned to the chair behind his writing table and gestured to the single chair opposite him. Leaving his traveling bag and satchel beside the door, Piran walked purposefully but not hurriedly across the room and took a seat. "I'm told," said the cardinal, "that you've been recommended directly to the Holy Father for a post here. That's highly irregular. Would you care to enlighten me?"

In that moment, it dawned on Piran that this was a test – the first step in proving himself worthy of the archdeacon's confidence. *Choose your words carefully, Piran.* "The Archdeacon of Nottingham took a favorable interest in my work at Oxford, Your Eminence. For which I'm grateful, as I would not, on my own, have thought of putting myself forward for such service."

"You're only recently ordained. Do you really think you're ready for such responsibility?"

Intimidation again. "I think perhaps I shouldn't be the one to judge my own readiness, sir. That said, what I *know* I'm ready for is to work diligently and learn quickly."

"Is it true there was some unfortunate incident you were involved in at the university? A fight of some sort? We have no need for men of violence here."

The cardinal's questions were a clear message that he was privy to whatever Father de Grandison had written to the Pope. Piran took a deep breath and refused to rise to the bait. "When I was ordained, I vowed to myself to put those events in the past and not speak of them further."

"In other words, you chose to renounce violence?"

"I never chose to embrace it, Eminence. My vow was to turn my back on those who wished me ill. I'm given to understand that the Holy Father is fully informed of what transpired."

"If you've been the victim, Chegwin, then would it not be in your interest to speak of it? To clear your name?"

Why is he pressing so hard? "I believe my name is clear, Eminence. And I have no wish to become the subject of gossip here."

Des Près bristled. "Are you comparing the papal court to a room full of women at their needlework?"

"Not at all, sir. I only know that it is in the nature of men that, if they know the hint of a story, their curiosity will compel them to pry for details or perhaps even to speculate on what those details might be. I have no desire to be an object of curiosity."

"You are indeed an interesting young man, Father Chegwin." The cardinal's demeanor finally relaxed. "One who appears to be well suited for the work we do. You see, it's my judgment that if a man can keep his own counsel about an unwarranted assault on his character and on his person, then he can be considered reliable to keep the secrets of others. And in the Chancery, we see the most important secrets of all and are sworn to keep them. Are you prepared to do that, Chegwin?"

Piran recognized that, now, a direct answer was the right course, so he answered with as much conviction as he could put into his voice. "I am, Your Eminence. And ready to swear an oath if that is what you require."

"No oath is necessary. Only your recognition that there is no tolerance for breaking the Holy Father's trust." He paused, but didn't seem to expect any further acknowledgment. "Now, you will begin as a *scritor*. Your stipend will be based on the number of documents you prepare. That is, the number you prepare correctly. You'll not be paid for work that must be redone. Excel in this role for a time and you'll be eligible for promotion to *abbreviator*. With sufficient experience and some training in canon law, you might even become an *auditor*."

"I won't disappoint you, Eminence."

"Selvaggio," the cardinal called out.

The door opened straightaway. "Yes, Eminence?"

"Father Chegwin will be joining the *scritores*. Assign him lodgings and then take him to his post."

"As you wish, Eminence." Selvaggio picked up Piran's traveling bag and satchel as Piran rose and bowed his head briefly to the cardinal. Once they were in the corridor with the door closed behind them, Selvaggio added, "Welcome to the Chancery, Chegwin. I think you'll soon discover how grateful your fellow *scritores* will be for the extra hand."

It took all of Piran's self-control to suppress the grin that threatened to spread across his face. He'd passed the test. His new life was about to begin.

XVI

Denying the prevalence of gossip in the papal court may have been the right answer for the cardinal. It would be surprising indeed if des Près himself actually believed such talk didn't exist. The whole point of his outrage at the mention of gossip had, after all, been to reinforce the importance of secrecy for those who worked in the Chancery. But it took no time at all for Piran to discover his instincts had been correct – not only about the existence of the gossip but that he was the current topic.

He took great pains with his first assignment, poring over the draft with its myriad crossed-out words and phrases and new text written in the margins, intent on making the final document perfect. As the other *scritores* began filing out at the end of the day, most didn't even cast a glance his way, though one paused beside his writing table and sneered "Hmph – one document" then moved on, elbowing the man beside him. "Won't succeed here at that rate, will he?"

"Pay Malatesta no mind," said the man still seated at the table to Piran's left. "First day is the same for everyone. Here, let me have a look." He stood and scrutinized Piran's finished document. "Nothing to find fault with there. Don't worry. After a few days, it gets easier and you get faster. Étienne Bonfils. And you are?"

"Piran Chegwin. Newly arrived from England."

"In that case, I suspect you're in need of a guide to find your way around."

"I'd be grateful. All I remember about how I got here was following in Father Selvaggio's footsteps."

Bonfils laughed aloud. "Also typical for everyone's first day. I think Selvaggio could navigate these corridors in the dark without a candle. Add to that the cardinal hammering home the fear of God – or rather the fear of des Près – and it's no wonder a man ends the day feeling like Theseus without a thread. Come along."

Back in the dormitory room where the junior priests slept, Piran was delighted to discover Bonfils had the bed just to his right. Étienne seemed like someone who could become a friend.

Over the next three days, Piran became discouraged when no one but Bonfils would even acknowledge his presence, much less chat with him during meals. So discouraged that he was compelled to ask why. "It happens with every new arrival," Étienne replied.

"Why?" Piran was thoroughly puzzled.

"You have to understand this world. Everyone is ambitious yet, to a man, they assert that they dislike ambition. But every new arrival is a threat to the ambition they pretend not to have."

"You mean they all aspire to one day be Pope?"

"Some, certainly. But more important in the short term is that each wants to achieve advancement or preferment before everyone else. Thus, every new arrival becomes the subject of gossip since he threatens to disrupt the established patterns. And you're particularly problematical because you're only recently ordained and haven't spent years toiling as a lowly priest in some cathedral as your path to the papal court."

Piran wasn't sure if he should ask the question that was forming in his mind. It might put him in a position he'd prefer to avoid. That said, he was already in an exceedingly uncomfortable position trying to find a place among men who seemed determined to shun him. *You'll never know if you don't ask*, he told himself. "Do you know what's being said, Étienne?"

"Some say the Holy Father himself appointed you to the position."

How could anyone have come so close to the truth? Piran's heart beat faster as he wondered what else might be known.

"Of course, that's said about anyone whose arrival is a surprise, no matter what their rank," Étienne went on, allowing Piran's heart to relax a bit. "Others think you have a champion somewhere in the court and are busy speculating on who that might be. Still others think you're running away from something." Piran's heart sped up again. "And there are a few who say that your name proves you're not English at all but maybe Irish or Scottish – or even Breton."

"And what do you think, Étienne?"

"I think it will all blow over in time and once the next thing captures their imagination, they'll accept you as if they'd never had any questions."

"I hope you're right. But as you're willing to be my friend, I'll tell you this. I did come with a letter of introduction from my master at Oxford." *That's not a lie – Father de Grandison **was** my master for a few months.* "But I had to pass Cardinal des Près's interview just like everyone else. And I'm English to the core. From Cornwall, to be precise, which is why my name is a little different from many Englishmen. But English nonetheless. And anyone who doubts that need only ask me to converse with them in the English language." He paused before adding, "There's no need to tell anyone any of this. It would only fuel more speculation. I just wanted you to know."

Bonfils clapped Piran on the shoulder. "You know, Chegwin, I think we're going to be very good friends. And I think it would be great fun to fuel the gossip by asking Cardinal Montfavez, who oversees my work, to take you on as well. If you agree, I'll ask him tomorrow."

"Let's give the gossip-mongers something new to talk about."

XVII

Oxford, England, January 1327

She'd been on alert for the sound of the front door ever since the priory bells had tolled midday, so Mistress Chert dashed from the kitchen the moment she heard the latch turn. She arrived in the entry hall as the archdeacon was closing the door, his back to her. Turning around to remove his cloak and gloves, de Grandison took a startled half-step backward. Even after a year, she could still surprise him by appearing when and where he least expected it. "Four more letters came today, Father," she announced. "I put them on your writing table."

"Thank you, Mistress Chert," he replied, hanging his cloak on the peg and laying his gloves on the little table alongside.

"There's one I think you're going to be right pleased to see," she added, following him into his study.

Has she been reading my correspondence? de Grandison wondered momentarily, then put the thought out of his mind. Never had a seal been broken on any of the letters he received. And there had been quite a number of them during the months since he'd returned from Nottingham.

It was while he was making his rounds of the most important parishes in the diocese that it occurred to him the secular authorities weren't the only ones capable of finding a person who'd gone missing. The church had eyes and ears all over the kingdom, in every parish, in every village church. So he'd asked the clergy in each parish he visited if they'd ever seen anyone matching de Villiers's description. None had, but he really hadn't expected Martin and his cronies would have come that far north. True, there had been enough time, but they had no connections to the area that de Grandison was aware of so it was probably an unlikely destination.

During the journey back to Oxford, he pondered the wisdom of what he was considering. If de Villiers could be located and brought to justice, it would be safe for Piran to return home and take up the vocation he'd had his heart set on. *But is it my role, as a man of God, to actively seek out miscreants? And what about the Church's tradition of offering sanctuary to those who seek it? It's often a delicate balance. If a person explicitly requests sanctuary and the prelate in charge grants it, then it's inviolate in the eyes of the Church and – usually – of the secular authorities. But if no such request is made, the Church certainly has no responsibility to protect a man from the consequences of his misdeeds.*

By the time he arrived home, he'd reached the conclusion that there was no moral argument against his making at least some effort to locate a man who'd violated both the law and one of God's sacred commandments. So he began writing letters, starting with the parishes not too far distant from Oxford.

Mistress Chert almost had an apoplexy when, at the end of his first week back, he presented her with a stack of a dozen letters to be delivered. "And just how am I supposed to do that, your holiness? There probably aren't that many messengers in all of Oxford. And do you have any idea how much paying all those messengers will cost?"

"Calm yourself, Mistress. Two messengers should suffice. One for the locations in Oxfordshire and another for Berkshire. They don't have to wait for replies."

"Be that as it may, that's still a lot of letters. No one will deliver a whole stack for the price of one."

"Don't fret about the money. Just tell me how much you need and I'll see that you have it."

Over the coming weeks, the housekeeper's objections had faded . . . along with de Grandison's hopes that his efforts might yield any fruit. The priests at both St. Giles and St. Laurence's in Reading reported some strangers around the town who might have been the group the archdeacon was looking for – but that was back during the height of summer and they hadn't been seen since. Beyond that, whatever replies arrived – and not all of his inquiries received a reply – had nothing helpful to report.

Leaning against the door frame, Mistress Chert waited patiently while the archdeacon read and discarded the first three letters in the stack and finally picked up the fourth one. "I take it then," he looked up as he addressed her, "this is the one you think I'll like?"

"Aye, Father."

He turned it over and looked at the seal. The unmistakable seal of the Apostolic Chancery. But his housekeeper wouldn't know that. "And what makes you so sure of that?"

"The messenger. Couldn't speak two words of English. Kept blabbering on in . . . French, I think it was. Sounded like what you speak sometimes . . . what you were teaching our boy."

"I hope you gave him half a pound for his troubles." De Grandison was taking a perverse pleasure from taunting his housekeeper. *It's really not fair,* he thought, *but I so rarely have a chance to get the upper hand.*

She pushed away from the door frame, her face and posture a portrait of indignation. "Two shillings was all he deserved and that's all he got. He'd already been paid for carrying the message, after all."

Best not to aggravate her further. De Grandison held the letter out toward her. "Shall I open it?"

"You do what you like." A reply that would normally have preceded a hasty retreat back to the kitchen, but this time Mistress Chert's feet remained firmly planted in the doorway.

The archdeacon broke the seal and unfolded the pages to reveal another missive tucked inside. "Shall I read it aloud?" he asked.

"You do what you like." This time her tone was subdued – almost plaintive – leaving him in no doubt of her wishes.

He laid the second letter aside and began to read.

Written at Avignon the third Sunday of Advent, 1326
In nomine Patris et Filii et Spiritus Sancti
To my dear master and friend, Archdeacon de Grandison
As we are well into the Advent season and I have been at my new post for a few months now, it seemed appropriate that I should take up my quill and heed your admonition to write to you. In truth, I'm most remiss for not having done

so sooner, but it has taken me this long to accumulate the funds necessary to pay the messenger. I hope you'll forgive what was a necessity rather than a lapse of manners or a lack of gratitude.

By the time you read this, the New Year will have begun, so I send you and Mistress Chert my fondest wishes for a year of good health and prosperity. I myself am quite well and hope the same is true for both of you. Please tell Mistress Chert that I remain deeply grateful for all she did for me and that she is always in my prayers.

De Grandison paused and looked up from the page just as Mistress Chert wiped at her eyes with the back of her hand. "That's really all I wanted to know. That our boy is safe and well," she said. "Now you get on with your reading, and I'll just see to the cook pot."

"I miss him too, Mistress."

Her hasty retreat told him she had no desire to reveal any more of her soft side, so he settled into a chair in front of the hearth to continue reading.

It may be well that I was unable to write to you sooner as I might have been inclined to complain, but I'm now well settled into this role and can assure you most fervently of my gratitude for making it possible. When I first arrived, however, I was met with a great deal of skepticism – and in many cases, I fear, resentment – for having been thrust into the midst of the established order. It was my great good fortune that Father Étienne Bonfils – who has now become a good friend – was not among the skeptics. Not only did he help me endure those early days when the other scritores shunned me but he also interceded with his own supervising notary, Cardinal Montfavez, to take me on. When the cardinal agreed, that seemed to make me legitimate in the eyes of the doubters.

Since that time, my mind has been in a complete whirl. For some reason, the cardinal offered to instruct me in canon law.

A smile came to de Grandison's face as he looked up at the fire. *Ah, Jacques,* he mused, *I see your fine hand in this. Is taking care of my protégé some small token of appreciation for my patient sojourn here in Oxford? Or might this be des Près's guidance to his notary? I'm quite keen to hear what you and*

Pierre both think once you've had more time to assess the young man. He cast his eyes back onto the page.

We've only just begun, but already I find it quite stimulating. The daily work of a scritor relies more on a steady hand than a curious mind, although I continue to be in awe of the scope of the matters that come before the Holy See. Far more than I could even conceive of as a naïve young man from the West Country or even as a somewhat more worldly student at Oxford. I can say no more than that as the work of the Chancery relies on the complete discretion of those of us so engaged, but I'm certain your more exalted position means you already know what I'm only just learning.

There is something peculiar that has struck me of late, Father. You'll remember how vehemently I protested that I had no interest in the monastic life. And yet that is precisely what I'm living at the moment. A gilded monastery, to be sure, but a monastery nonetheless. A community entirely of men, living apart from the real world and not ministering to the needs of the ordinary folk. Attending to the business of the Church in all its earthly glory rather than to the daily glorification of God. But a monastery nonetheless.

Once again, de Grandison paused to stare into the flames. *You're not precisely wrong, Piran, but you haven't been there long enough yet to have recognized that there's a reason it's called the papal "court" – that it far more resembles a royal court with all its intrigue and subterfuge and clamoring for position than any monastery you might ever encounter. But that's a realization for another day.* He set the pages aside, went to the sideboard and poured himself a goblet of wine, then returned to his reading.

What's even more peculiar, Father, is how easily I've slipped into being satisfied – quite content, even – with my current state. I've asked myself have I been lulled away from my earlier aspirations by the ease afforded me in these surroundings. And I'm not sure if I have no answer or if I simply prefer to avoid confronting the answer. Or if, perhaps, given the dangers I've managed to elude, the answer simply doesn't matter. Something to ponder, I suppose, though I increasingly have little time for rumination.

Each day, I find myself quite eager to complete my assigned documents so I can move on to my law lesson. Étienne told me the cardinal has a doctorate in law, but once again, I hadn't conceived of the depth of knowledge that implied. My hours with him and in the library studying the texts he recommends remind me of my time at Oxford and more than compensate for the disappointment of not being able to remain at Balliol.

And therein, Piran, de Grandison mused, *though you haven't realized it yet, lies the reason for your contentment. You're always happiest when your intellect is being challenged.* He took a sip of wine then returned to the letter.

You'll also be pleased to know that my French is improving, thanks to Étienne. Enough that, now and again, I can manage a brief conversation with the cardinal in his native tongue. For everything that matters, of course, we rely on Latin, but he's been kind enough to indulge my efforts without mocking my mistakes.

Finally, Father, I have a favor to ask. You've seen that I enclosed a letter to my kerens with this missive. As Mistress Chert was kind enough to arrange sending my last letter to them, I pray she'll find it in her heart to do so once again. I simply didn't have enough money to pay the messenger what he asked for going all the way to Cornwall. If this is too much of an imposition, please forgive my asking.

I did not realize until we parted company in Hull just how much I had enjoyed those last few weeks spent with you. Perhaps I was simply too self-absorbed with recovering from my injuries to acknowledge it at the time. Even though I now have new companions and a new teacher, it's my fondest hope that our paths will cross again. And that that should happen sooner than later.

May God keep you in his hands, Father, and bestow on you all the blessings you so richly deserve.

Piran

De Grandison sat quietly in front of the fire, contemplating just how much his protégé had matured from the earnest, eager, sometimes frightened, sometimes distraught young man he'd been during his final months as a theology student. With Montfavez to guide him and Jacques watching from behind the curtain, Chegwin would do well in the papal court. But then an unsettling thought struck him. *How many more years did Jacques have on this earth?*

Downing what was left in his goblet, he brushed that concern aside for the moment, retrieved Piran's other letter from his writing table, and went in search of Mistress Chert.

XVIII

Avignon, August 1327

"What in the name of the blessed Virgin is going on in Exeter?" No one in the audience chamber could doubt the Pope's displeasure, least of all the unfortunate Bishop of Chichester whose task it had been to deliver the news of the death of James Berkeley in late June and the rapid election of John Godeley to replace him. "Does no one even think to consult me anymore, Langton? Is it assumed I'm doted and have no opinion in the matter?"

"It's not for me to say, Holy Father, what any of my colleagues might assume—"

"Don't be spouting magged tales, Langton," the pontiff cut him off. "New bishops don't get elected without discussion among those participating. But don't bother trying to answer the question. It's not flattery I'm looking for. Respect would be nice though."

Chastised, Bishop Langton bowed his head. "Of course, Your Holiness."

"What *is* going on in Exeter?" the Pope repeated, his anger somewhat dissipated. "First Stapledon is murdered by a mob in London, then Berkeley's murdered as well. This can't continue. Besides, I have different plans for the diocese, and Godeley isn't part of them."

"And what should I tell my fellow bishops? And even Godeley, for that matter."

"That I've quashed the nomination. That I intend to put someone in charge who can bring order back to what is obviously a diocese in disarray. And that there will be a new bishop of *my* choosing in Exeter before the year is out."

"Yes, Holy Father."

"Have you brought any other news, Langton? Perhaps something I might find more palatable?"

"Only that the plotting to free the deposed king and restore him to the throne persists, that the queen has ordered Friar Thomas Dunheved's arrest, and that the Earl of Kent is still rumored to be in communication with the plotters. I suspect that isn't more palatable, Father, but at least it isn't specific to Exeter."

"Do you know if the rumors about Kent are true? I rather liked him when he came here as an emissary. Some seven years ago, as I recall."

"I'm skeptical, but many are convinced. As close as Kent was to his half-brother . . ." Langton let the thought hang in the air for the Pope to draw his own conclusions.

Duèze rose, signaling the end of the audience, and extended his hand for Langton to kiss the ring. As he exited through his private door, the ever-hovering Alphonse was waiting in the corridor. "Send Montfavez to me in my study, Alphonse," said Duèze. "And tell him to bring that new English priest with him. I have letters to be drafted."

"But, Holy Father, Chegwin is merely a *scritor*. Shouldn't the cardinal bring an *abbreviator*?"

"Just do as I say, Alphonse. And tell them to come straightaway."

Try as he might, Piran couldn't find a word to describe his reaction when Cardinal Montfavez told him they'd been summoned by the Pope. Trepidation? Excitement? Anxiety? Curiosity? Stark terror? There simply wasn't a word that encompassed all those emotions at once. "It's unconventional," Montfavez had said. "Ordinarily, I'd just find an *abbreviator* who wasn't otherwise occupied and take him along. But it seems

Duèze asked for you specifically." Words intended, no doubt, to reassure but that served only to augment the unnamable turmoil in Piran's gut.

He walked in silence beside the cardinal through corridors he'd never seen before, trying to identify landmarks should he be dismissed first and have to find his way back alone. *Don't bother,* he eventually chided himself. *You can always ask someone to show you the way. Keep your mind on how you want to present yourself to His Holiness. You have to make Father de Grandison proud.* That last thought calmed his nerves a bit . . . until it unsettled them once again as he recognized just how much was riding on his shoulders.

When they approached an elaborately carved and gilded double door with guards on each side, he knew they'd arrived at the Pope's private apartment. One guard moved so quickly to open the door that they didn't even have to break stride as they stepped inside. Piran was trying to take in the trappings of Jacques Duèze's living quarters by moving only his eyes, hoping this would maintain his dignity, when Montfavez came to his rescue. "It's your first time here, so have a look around. When des Près promotes you to *abbreviator,* you'll be here frequently. Some might say it's too grand for a man of God, but I'm more inclined to the view that the man who carries the weight of both Heaven and Earth on his shoulders is entitled to some comforts."

In the study, they found the Holy Father pacing back and forth in front of a large window. Piran held back while Montfavez strode in. "Good. You came quickly." Duèze stopped his pacing and gestured to the chairs in front of his writing table, where the cardinal immediately took a seat. "No need to loiter in the doorway, young man," the Pope admonished in Latin. Piran approached cautiously and, when Duèze extended his hand, dropped to one knee, kissed the ring, and said quietly, "*Sancte Pater.*" Rising to his feet, he stood in silence as the pontiff took the other chair in front of the table and addressed Montfavez. "*Comment vous trouvez ce jeune prêtre? Quel progrès fait-il dans ses études?*" French was the native tongue of both men.

"*Il a une compréhension rapide et s'applique avec diligence. Exactement comme des Près a entendu.*"

Piran understood the Pope was asking about his studies. But as the conversation between the two men progressed, it became more challenging for him to follow, though from the occasional word or phrase he *did* understand, it seemed as if the entire conversation was about him. The turmoil churned once again. *Was I brought here to be scrutinized? What if I don't measure up? Will I be dismissed?*

Switching to Latin, the Pope addressed Piran directly, startling him from his musings. "So, Father Chegwin, it seems you have a promising career in the Church."

Everything de Grandison had told him raced through his mind. *Greet him in French, even if it's only to say you don't speak French well. Don't flatter. Be honest and direct but not arrogant. Show your intelligence. Don't shy away from difficult subjects.* Girding all his courage, Piran hoped his fledgling French wouldn't fail him at this critical juncture. "*Ce serait mon espoir, Saint-Père.*"

Duèze's face lit up in a broad smile. "*Ah, vous parlez français!*"

"*Pas très bien en ce moment, mais j'apprends.*" At least Piran was confident in saying he didn't speak well but was learning.

"*Et qu'est-ce que vous pensez de ma maison ?*"

Another bit of de Grandison's advice flashed into Piran's mind. *He's exceedingly fond of his palace and will almost certainly ask you what you think of it.* And he'd just done precisely that. *Don't answer in generalities – he knows it's grand. Find something specific to mention.* Piran wracked his brain. What could he comment on? More to the point, what could he actually say in French? And then it struck him. "*Ma mère adore les belles tapisseries. J'amerais qu'elle . . .*" He stumbled, unsure of the right verb form. Nothing for it. He had to muddle through. "*. . . voir les vôtres.*"

Apparently sensing Piran's discomfort, the pontiff reverted to Latin. "It appears you're making as much progress in learning French as you are in learning the law. And I'm just as fond of beautiful tapestries as you say your mother is. But now we need to attend to the reason I summoned you both. Please, Father Chegwin . . ." He gestured to the chair behind the writing table – the place he would normally sit. ". . . take that chair. It's you who'll be doing the writing today.

"Now, Bertrand, you were in the room for Langton's audience, so you know what's on my mind. Is there anything in civil or canon law that prevents my simply declaring Godeley's election null and void?"

"Any authority local bishops or archbishops have to determine who fills a vacant episcopacy derives, according to the apostolic succession, directly from whoever consecrated them and thus, ultimately, from the Pope – not the man but the office. So you are the final arbiter."

"And there are no technicalities to attend to or circumvent?"

"None, in my opinion."

"Then here's what I want done. First, Chegwin, a letter to the Archbishop of Canterbury informing him of my decision. The cardinal here will give you the proper forms if you don't already know them. It's the archbishop's responsibility to inform Godeley and the others. Then a letter to Archdeacon de Grandison informing him that I've selected him to fill the vacancy at Exeter. Instruct him to make haste coming to Avignon as I want to consecrate him myself so there can be no doubt in anyone's mind of my intentions. Tell him also that I'll write to Bishop Lewis in the coming days with instructions to seek a new archdeacon." He paused and waited for Piran to finish writing. "You have all that, Chegwin?"

"Yes, Father."

"Then you two go get to work. I don't want any more time wasted in this matter."

As he and Montfavez made their way back through the labyrinth, Piran mulled over what had just happened. The Pope had given him a gift beyond measure. When Father de Grandison received the letter, he would recognize the handwriting and understand straightaway all that it implied. Piran's heart was full. The road to this moment may have been rocky and rutted, but the reward was a blessing he could never have imagined.

The cardinal broke into his thoughts. "We need to have those drafts done and ready for him by the end of the day. You can work in my study. It's little more than a closet, but you won't be distracted and I can look in from time to time in case there's anything you need."

"Of course, Eminence."

"And Piran . . . well done back there. I think the Holy Father is right. You almost certainly have a promising career ahead of you if you stick to your current path. But that isn't always the easiest thing for a man to do in this den of intrigue."

What did he mean by that? Piran wondered.

XIX

Avignon, October 1327

"Des Près wants to see you," the lad whispered in Piran's ear before scurrying away. He was one of several such, typically eleven or twelve years of age, employed in the papal court to run errands and carry messages. They were mostly second sons of less-well-off Avignon families who wouldn't have much of a future unless they found a place in the Church.

Piran carefully finished the document he was drafting then placed it in the drawer of his writing table for the ink to dry away from prying eyes. Not that the rules of the chancery didn't prohibit spying on another's work, but he knew that des Près's cardinal rule was "Make no assumptions and take no chances." Since he'd been promoted to *abbreviator* shortly after completing the letters for the Holy Father, he no longer feared such a summons, seeing it now as more likely a new opportunity than a looming chastisement. But he was totally unprepared for what awaited him in the cardinal's study.

When he reached the door, he found the lad who'd brought the message leaning against the corridor wall beside the doorframe. "He says you're to go straight inside."

That was unexpected. Ever since Selvaggio brought him here that first day, the ritual had always been the same. Knock. Wait. And eventually hear the invitation to enter.

He pushed the door barely open and stepped cautiously around it, hoping the boy had gotten things right and wasn't up to some sort of prank. "Come, come, Chegwin," des Près called out. "No need for timidity."

There was someone else in the room, sitting with his back to the door. Des Près had a broad smile on his face – yet another puzzling twist in what was turning out to be a most unusual summons. And then the other man rose from his chair and turned to face Piran . . . who froze in his tracks. "Father?"

De Grandison beamed and spread his arms. Piran snapped out of his momentary trance and rushed to embrace his dear friend. When they broke their embrace, des Près was still grinning from ear to ear. "Sit, Chegwin." He gestured to the empty chair beside de Grandison. "I wish you could have seen the look on your face. It's not often I get to surprise someone . . . at least, not in a good way." All three men chuckled. "But I do think I've managed it this time."

"You have indeed, Eminence," said Piran.

"Pierre was just singing your praises, Piran," said de Grandison.

"I fear that might have been a rather short song, Father."

"Quite the contrary. I hear you've recently been promoted and that Montfavez is quite pleased with your progress in studying canon law."

"You were right to send me here, Father. I'll admit the days as a simple *scritor* were rather boring, but the law and the new work are endlessly fascinating."

Des Près laughed aloud. "I've been wondering how long it would take you to complain about the tedium of mere scribing. You know, John, he never did. And that convinced me you were right about him."

Seeing the puzzled look on his protégé's face, de Grandison explained. "Pierre and I have been friends for years. I knew that if Jacques put you in the chancery, you'd be in good hands. And now, my friend . . ." He turned to the cardinal. ". . . I think Father Chegwin and I have some catching up to do. If you'll excuse us?"

"Of course. And Chegwin?"

"Yes, Eminence?"

"Whatever you were working on can wait until tomorrow."

"Thank you, Eminence."

As they made their way into the corridor, de Grandison told Piran, "I have a special message for you from Mistress Chert."

"And how does she fare?"

"As feisty and intransigent as ever. And just as soft-hearted inside. She tried not to let me see it, but there were tears welling in her eyes when I said my farewells. Anyway, she made me take an oath on the Bible that I'd tell you she was more proud of you than anyone who'd ever crossed her path and that if you ever come back to England she expects you to visit her."

They spent the rest of the afternoon and long into the night talking about all that had transpired in the past year. Eventually, Piran's curiosity won out over his resolve to keep the past in the past. "Was de Villiers ever found and brought to justice, Father?"

"Sadly, not yet. I actually tried to find him myself. But none of my letters yielded anything useful. I even wrote to the priest in his home parish, but no one there had seen him since he left for Oxford. After a few months, I had to admit it was a hopeless quest. Even if he'd been seen some place, what were the chances he'd still be there when the authorities went looking. I did my best, Piran, in the hope you could come home. But I fear finding him may be more a matter of chance than of intent."

"Oddly, I'm not heartbroken. Yes, it would be a weight off my mind to know for certain he's no longer a threat. But he can't threaten me here. And there's so much here to stimulate my mind, that I'm actually quite content."

"And now you know you have a friend in Cardinal des Près."

"Thank you for that, Father."

"Whatever the situation, Piran, if you need advice, you can turn to Pierre. He will never steer you wrong."

Wednesday, 28 October 1327
Piran stood among the prelates gathered in the Cathedral of Notre Dame des Doms for a special mass celebrated by the Pope himself for the consecration of John de Grandison as Bishop of Exeter. As he watched the

pontiff lay hands on de Grandison's head, bestowing the apostolic succession, Piran felt emotion that surpassed anything he'd ever experienced, even at his own ordination. Pride. Humility. Reverence. Another of those complex combinations that tended to defy naming. But in this case, Piran was sure there *was* a name – the Holy Spirit.

When Bishop de Grandison left Avignon two weeks later, their parting was poignant. As the bishop climbed into the carriage that would take him north to the next phase of his life, Piran watched from the steps of the papal palace. *How long will it be*, he wondered, *before I see him again?*

XX

Written from Exeter, September 1st, 1328
Salutations and most friendly greetings along with the blessings of God and ourselves.

To my dear friend, Piran

At long last, I am formally enthroned in my new cathedral and settling in to the enormous task before me. As Jacques so accurately described it, I have inherited a diocese in much disarray, a cathedral still under construction though it seems little work has been done in the time since Stapledon was murdered, substantial debt, and an empty purse.

Perhaps the lack of funds was the reason Berkeley suspended the work, but a house of God should not be left missing a full third of its structure with only scaffolding and boards to keep out the weather. What has been completed so far is quite magnificent and must be finished. I've already rehired the architect and a number of the craftsmen, and I have ideas of my own for some of the details. I wish you could see it, Piran, and perhaps one day you will.

As for the money, I must find it somehow, so that is my immediate task.

Written from Avignon, October 8th, 1328
To my dear friend, Bishop de Grandison
May the blessings of God be upon you always

I hope by the time this reaches you that you've had some success in raising money and that the work on the cathedral progresses. I was disappointed, during my journey to Oxford, that there wasn't time to see the cathedral as we passed through Exeter. Yet perhaps my reward for that omission will be the opportunity to see it in its full glory once it's been completed under your guidance.

Little has changed here, though we do have a new notary in the chancery. A Father Manuele Fieschi. Though not a cardinal, he was specifically appointed to the role by the Holy Father. He seems of a good disposition and quite knowledgeable, but my work with him has not been extensive.

On the subject of my work, it seems that I'm increasingly being entrusted with some of the more important matters coming to the Curia. And you will, I think, be as pleased as I was to hear that Cardinal des Près commended me on a document I prepared at his request.

Written at our manor of Chudleigh, March 11th, 1329

Fondest greetings and the blessings of God to you, my dear friend, Piran

With the Lenten season now underway, we eagerly await the first signs of spring here in the West Country. Most especially so that the temperatures are warm enough for the masons to work the mortar and continue their building.

Raising money has turned out to be far more daunting than I expected, not least because of the recalcitrant opposition of Sir Hugh de Courtenay. That gentleman actually had the audacity to suggest that I'm living a sumptuous lifestyle off the backs of my parishioners and that I would do well to curtail my excesses. I'm given to understand that his family has long believed they have complete primacy within Devon to do as they see fit and that prior kings have allowed their arrogance to go unchecked, apparently in the belief that if Devon remains subservient, the royal attention can be directed elsewhere. Sir Hugh appears to have no respect for my episcopal authority, and I fear our interactions will be contentious for some time to come.

You'll have noted that this letter comes to you from Chudleigh rather than Exeter. Though the bishop's palace at the cathedral is comfortable enough, the one at Chudleigh is rapidly becoming my favorite residence. It's peaceful here in the countryside, and I find that most conducive to reading and study and to the planning of all I wish to accomplish.

Written from Avignon, May 1st, 1329

My dear friend,

I was distressed to hear of your difficulties with Sir Hugh. Nonetheless, I know well your ability to find a path around obstacles so am hoping that your next letter reports just such a resolution.

Written at our manor of Chudleigh, December 15th 1330

Fondest greetings to you my dear friend

I have recently returned from my first meeting of Parliament. There have been previous summonses, which I should perhaps have heeded but, being consumed with the urgent needs of the diocese, I sent my regrets. This time, Parliament assembled in Salisbury, making the journey much shorter. And I now recognize that my presence in Parliament serves to balance de Courtenay's pretensions to authority over both temporal and spiritual matters in Devon.

Sitting among the lords proved quite poignant for me as I had never – even in my most fanciful musings – imagined that I would be sitting there alongside my father. And what gladdened my heart even more is that my well beloved sister, Katherine, accompanied her husband so that I was reunited with two of the people I love most in this world.

*Many of my fellow bishops – and even the Archbishop of Canterbury himself – urged me to pursue an office in the royal court. Being a man of good manners, I agreed to consider the idea. But in truth, there is nothing **to** consider. I've already done such service in the papal court so am not inclined to repeat the experience in a secular one. My interests now lie in the liturgy, in defining and refining the order of service, in recording the lives of the saints, and in creating a collection of important books as a library for the cathedral.*

Written from Avignon, May27th, 1331

To my dear friend

It has been a most interesting time here these past weeks. The Holy Father has had a visitor who remained with us for fifteen days. The only opportunity I had to be in a gathering where he was present was when the Pope celebrated mass in the cathedral during the visit. But I was at some distance from the altar and unable to really get a glimpse of the man's face. The rumors flying through the palace said that he was the deposed king of England.

That scarcely seems credible, given what we heard about his burial and elaborate tomb in Gloucester. Father Fieschi had been in the first audience with the visitor, so I asked him discreetly if there was any substance to the rumors. He was extremely circumspect, saying only that the Holy Father was pleased to offer his hospitality and to reminisce about the guest's brother's last visit here. So it remains a mystery, but it certainly caused a stir within the court.

Written at our manor of Chudleigh, October 16th, 1331

God's blessings upon you my dear Piran along with my prayer that you'll forgive my delay in replying to your last missive

The visit you report is curious indeed. Most especially in light of the fact that rumors still persist here – even after all this time – that the man laid to rest in Gloucester is not our late king Edward II.

Written from Avignon, December 5th, 1334

It is with a heavy heart that I take up my quill this day, my dear friend. Yesterday, God called his servant, our Holy Father, to his heavenly home. I know you will mourn him more than most, and I pray most fervently that God comforts you in your grief.

Written from Avignon, December 20th, 1334

To my dear friend

It is late in the evening as I sit down to write to you. We have just learned that the Conclave has concluded and that we have a new pontiff. Thankfully, the deliberations were not protracted, though many here feared a repeat of the rifts that crippled the previous Conclave. Despite the fact that what transpires in those deliberations is sacrosanct, it was well understood here that the central issue was whether the Holy See would return to Rome or remain in Avignon.

In the end, they chose Cardinal Fournier, and we are told that he has decided to be known as Benedict XII.

Written from Exeter, January 16th, 1335

Salutations, and may God bless you in this new year

Though I was informed through the official channels of the events of December, your letter brought me more comfort than anyone else could offer. I am, in fact, quite pleased with the outcome of the Conclave. Jacques Fournier was one of my teachers at the University of Paris, and I both like and respect him. The Church is in good hands.

Written from Avignon, September 11th, 1338

My dear friend

Much has changed here since our new pontiff was enthroned, the greatest of which is the place in which we live and work. As the Holy Father had no liking for his predecessor's palace, he has set out to replace it, dismantling the old as the new one is constructed. The tower that houses his apartment and the Treasury is complete. But to my eyes, the new edifice looks more like a fortress than a comfortable palace.

Written at our manor of Chudleigh, January 4th, 1339

Ah, Piran, how I wish it was safe for you to come here. I should so like you to be part of the collegiate foundation I have established at Ottery St. Mary. You would also be a great help in the work I've undertaken to document and elucidate the lives of the Cornish saints.

Written from Avignon, July 27th, 1340

As you predicted, my dear friend, my career is progressing. Some two weeks ago, Archbishop de Valle, the Pope's camerlengo, tapped me to take over the management of the accounts for the construction of the new palace, which proceeds apace. You will no doubt laugh when I tell you how astonished I was to learn all that must be paid for on such a project, even down to oats for the animals that transport new materials from the sources where we acquire them. The roll for this year alone is already three parchments stitched together and the year is barely half over.

Written from Avignon, May 8th, 1342

Once again, my dear friend, I write with both sad news and glad tidings. The Holy Father went to be with God on April 24th. Even as we prayed for his soul, a Conclave assembled on May 5th and in just two days, elected a new pontiff. Cardinal Roger has chosen to be known as Clement VI.

The camerlengo assures me that my position remains unaltered. So I shall continue the job of disbursing and recording payments for pounds of oats, mountains of hay, tons of stone, piles of sand and lime, salaries for masons and stone carvers and fresco artists, decorative tiles for floors and ceilings, timber and nails and pigments and tools and items I'm not even sure what they are. Oh, and eggs. Dozens of eggs. It seems the artists use the yolks to mix their paints. I cannot help but wonder what happens to all the whites.

XXI

Avignon, mid-July 1346

Making their way back to their work after the midday meal, Piran and Étienne were discussing the recent rise in price for the slaked lime needed for making mortar. "That's not the only thing that's costing us more," said Étienne. "Just yesterday I was questioning what we now pay for oats and looked back at last year's account roll. Those prices have gone up as well."

They'd been working together in the *camerlengo*'s chambers for the past three years. Mere weeks after his enthronement, Pope Clement had announced his plans for a substantial extension to the papal palace. Piran couldn't decide if this was to satisfy the Pope's personal vanity or to declare to the world that the Holy See would henceforth remain in Avignon. In truth, he didn't care. What he *did* care about was that the pontiff's insistence on accelerating the pace of construction had made his workload untenable, so he'd petitioned Archbishop de Valle for help and specifically asked for Étienne – and the *camerlengo* was all too happy to oblige.

Now, as they turned into the corridor that led past the main audience and reception rooms, Piran's heart skipped a beat. Three or four beats, if he was honest with himself. Two men were headed toward them. A cardinal and a priest. Piran fought to maintain his composure, to keep his expression neutral and his eyes straight ahead, to keep putting one foot in front of the other. When the two pairs of men passed, the other priest said "Pig" in a hushed voice, not intended for his companion the cardinal to hear.

Piran kept putting one foot in front of the other, trying to still his now-racing heartbeat and calm his breathing. "Did he just call you a pig?" Étienne asked.

"Not here, Étienne." At the next corridor, Piran turned left toward the entrance rather than continuing ahead to the *camerlengo*'s chambers. Étienne followed . . . out of the palace, across the square, into the cathedral. Piran didn't stop, didn't utter another word, until he entered the Chapel of the Virgin, dropped to his knees, and began the prayer to the Blessed Mother.

Ave Maria, gratia plena, Dominus tecum.
Benedicta tu in mulieribus, et benedictus fructus ventris tui, Jesus.
Sancta Maria, Mater Dei, ora pro nobis peccatoribus, nunc, et in hora
mortis nostrae.
Amen

Étienne watched as Piran crossed himself then went to sit on the narrow stone bench at the side of the chapel and buried his face in his hands. Joining his friend on the bench, Étienne said quietly, "Talk to me, Piran. What just happened?"

When he finally spoke, Piran's voice cracked with emotion. "The one thing that was never supposed to be possible here in this place." For the next half hour, he poured out the whole story to Étienne, ending with, "There was supposed to be no way de Villiers could threaten me here. How could he even have ended up here . . . and in the company of a cardinal, no less?"

"You've just had a terrible surprise," Étienne put an arm around Piran's shoulders, trying to offer some comfort. "I can scarcely imagine your distress. But once you can think clearly, you'll realize you're not without advantage."

"What advantage could I possibly have?"

"You know he killed a man. I would wager my last *denier* he has somehow buried that so far in his past that no one – especially not that cardinal he was with – has any idea. But he knows you know. So the scales are balanced."

"I wish I could believe that."

"Take heart, my friend. Let me find out who the new cardinal is. And you know as well as I do there'll soon be plenty of gossip about the priest he has in tow. Now..." Étienne clapped Piran on the shoulder and stood. "Let's go back to work. Finding the three new masons we need should take your mind off this de Villiers character."

As Étienne made his way out of the chapel, Piran said one last quick prayer to the Virgin. *Holy Mary, grant that this cardinal is just here for a visit and that he leaves soon and takes his acolyte with him. In nomine Patris et Filii et Spiritus Sancti. Amen.*

For seven long days, Piran lived in dread of encountering de Villiers again. He'd prayed to Saint Piran for protection, and every night, as he climbed into bed with no further sighting of his nemesis, he sent a little prayer of gratitude to his namesake. Now, as the bells tolled midday, he put down his quill and rose to walk with Étienne to the dining hall. "If it's all the same to you," said Étienne, "I'd rather have fresh air than food at the moment." Piran gave him a puzzled look. "A little fasting now and then can be good for the soul, don't you agree?"

Outside in the square, Étienne picked up the pace, striding vigorously up the path to the top of the hill beyond the cathedral where there was a magnificent vista of the Rhône, the Pont St. Bénézet, and Villeneuve-lès-Avignon on the far bank. "Impressive, isn't it?" said Étienne. "Somehow, from this high up, it all looks so peaceful."

"Come on, Étienne. Don't keep me on tenterhooks. You didn't bring me here to admire the view."

"No, I didn't. Let's sit over there on those rocks." When they'd found two that weren't terribly uncomfortable, Étienne continued. "The new cardinal is Adhémar Robert . . . holds the title of Cardinal-Priest of Sant'Anastasia, so he has Italian connections. Also, he's a relative of the Pope ... nephew or maybe cousin. And he's been made a notary, so he's not going anywhere."

"Any insight on how de Villiers came to be with him?"

"It happened when Cardinal Robert visited his titular church in Rome. From what I've been able to work out, it seems de Villiers wormed his way into the cardinal's confidence with a bit of flattery and what appear to be impeccable credentials. A doctorate in theology from the University of Bologna."

Piran couldn't contain himself. "A *what*?" he blurted out.

"Doctorate in—"

"I heard what you said, but that's impossible. Martin had no interest in studying and couldn't put two coherent sentences together for his assignments at Oxford."

"Perhaps he changed after his narrow escape from the authorities."

"More likely he paid someone to do the work and took all the credit, including the degree."

"Be that as it may, he convinced the cardinal to take him on as some sort of personal *scritor*. It's already been noticed that he considers himself superior to everyone in the chancery."

"The great Martinus considers himself superior to everyone on God's earth." There was no mistaking the disgust in Piran's tone. "I've no doubt he's hoping to ride the tails of the cardinal's cassock to his own advancement."

"Gather yourself, Piran," said Étienne. "You've seen enough of how the factions here compete against each other to recognize that *that* grand game, though on a very personal scale, is what you now have to play. You're not powerless, Piran. Don't ever forget that."

That night, Piran lay awake long after the sound of snoring permeated the dormitory. Normally a strange sort of lullaby, tonight the rhythmic snuffles and snorts seemed more a drumbeat of the lurking threat de Villiers's presence signified. When at long last he was about to drift off to sleep, his eyes suddenly popped wide open as realization dawned. *You know how the game is played, Étienne had said. Yes, Martin has a powerful cardinal on his side – a close relative of the Pope. But so do I.*

⟠ ⟠ ⟠ ⟠ ⟠

Three days later, he had the pretext he needed – a long letter from Bishop de Grandison devoted mostly to the progress on rebuilding the parish church at Ottery St. Mary. *I have imitated many of the details from the cathedral at Exeter,* he wrote, *though on not so grand a scale.* But it was the final paragraph that caused Piran to send a heartfelt prayer of thanks to the Blessed Virgin.

To my great delight, the artisans have just completed installation of the astronomical clock in the south transept. Not only does it have a functional purpose, but it is also most beautiful with a brilliant azure face, gilded decoration, a golden ball to represent the sun, and a half-black, half-white ball for the moon. And my own coat of arms represented in each of the top corners. I have long desired that one of my churches should have such a fine mechanism for tracking the passage of the hours and the days. It's a wish I've had in common with Pierre des Près, and so perhaps you would be kind enough to find an opportunity to tell him of my pleasure in finally accomplishing something we've often talked about.

At the appointed time, he stood before the door to the Vice-Chancellor's office and took a deep breath to quiet his nerves before knocking. Predictably, there was silence from within, but Piran somehow found reassurance in the predictability. Life was normal. Finally, the invitation came. "Enter."

Knowing what was expected, Piran quickly stepped inside, shut the door behind him, and knelt to kiss the offered ring. "Eminence."

"Father Chegwin. You have news from our mutual friend, I'm told."

"I do indeed. News he urged me to share with you." He handed de Grandison's letter to the cardinal, who read it quickly.

"Well, well. So he finally got his clock. I must write to him and express both my admiration and my envy. Maybe I should build my own collegiate church and get an even finer clock." Des Près laughed. "He was first, but I could be best." He refolded the letter and handed it back to Piran. "But tell me, Chegwin," he continued, his tone more serious. "How do you fare these days?"

"Awash in bills for oats and special pigments and blacksmiths's services, sir."

"De Valle tells me he couldn't manage the accounts for all this construction without you."

"That's kind of him to say."

"Is there anything else on your mind, Father Chegwin?"

The opening he needed. In other places, he would just enumerate the issues and ask for help. But that's not how the game was played here. The question meant des Près knew there was a problem and most likely knew precisely what it was. And Piran knew what he had to do was acknowledge that truth and put his faith in the cardinal's support. "In truth, Eminence, I'm rather glad not to be in the midst of the turmoil that happens when a new notary joins the chancery." He hesitated briefly. "Much as I enjoyed my time serving you there."

Was that the hint of a smile he saw in the cardinal's eyes? *Or am I just imagining what I want to see?*

"When you reply to the bishop, please convey my wishes for his continued favor in God's eyes."

An oblique indication that I have his support? A suggestion, perhaps, that I should tell Father of my plight? Piran knew he would get no more in the moment, so he smiled and said, "Of course, Eminence."

The cardinal rose from his seat. The audience was concluded. Piran followed suit, bowing slightly with a final "Thank you, Your Eminence," and left the room.

He'd done what he could.

XXII

July gave way to August with no further encounters with de Villiers. Étienne was optimistic. "It seems to me he's intentionally avoiding you, Piran. What you know would be poison to his career, and he knows that. He's unlikely to do anything to draw attention to himself." They were once again in the Chapel of the Virgin in the cathedral. Piran had made a habit of going there once each week to appeal to the Blessed Mother for her protection. Despite Piran's protests that he didn't require company, Étienne had made it his mission to keep his friend's spirits up until it was clear there was no cause for concern.

"I wish that were true," said Piran. "But unless he's changed, de Villiers likes nothing more than drawing attention to himself. He's just biding his time. I can feel it in my bones."

"It's been . . . how many years now? Twenty? That's long enough for anyone to learn from his experiences and become a better man for it."

"But not long enough for him to forget his favorite epithet for me."

By the time they celebrated the feast day of Saint Dominic, Piran knew his bones had been right. At first, it was nothing more than someone looking at him slightly askance as they passed in the corridor. Within a week, few of his former colleagues from the chancery would join him and Étienne in the dining hall. And as the feast day of Saint Bernard de Clairvaux approached, de Villiers began frequenting the common dining hall, always in the company of half a dozen priests from the chancery. When, near the end of August, the *camerlengo* began asking to see Piran's accounts at the end of each day, there could be no doubt what was afoot.

One evening, Étienne waited while the accounts were being scrutinized. "Come with me," he told his friend when the review was complete. Leaving the palace, he turned left instead of right and left again on the narrow alley just south of the current construction. Neither said a word until they came to a small church Piran had never seen before. "It's the Église des Cordéliers," Étienne explained. "No one will look for us here. You need privacy to hear what I have to tell you."

Exeter, September 1346

Returning from the king's latest Parliament, Bishop de Grandison made the decision to spend a few days in Exeter before going on to Chudleigh. It had been almost a month since he'd checked on the work at the cathedral, and this was the perfect opportunity before the approaching cold weather began to affect what could be done. As he descended from his carriage, he was surprised to see the Dean of the Cathedral rushing out to meet him. "Thanks be to God you're back," de Braylegh seemed almost breathless.

"Is there some crisis?"

"It would seem so, Bishop, but of what nature I can't say. I only know that four letters have arrived for you from Avignon this week, and one of the messengers has stayed for the last three days. It seems his instructions were to wait for a reply."

De Grandison furrowed his brow as he fell into step beside de Braylegh, headed for his study. "Somewhat out of the ordinary, I agree, but what has you so concerned, Richard?"

"One bears the seal of the Vice-Chancellor, one of the Pope's *camerlengo*, and two of the chambers of the *camerlengo*. Not only that, but the messenger who's waiting said his instructions came directly from Cardinal des Près." Now concerned, de Grandison quickened his pace. "The letters are in your study," de Braylegh added. "I removed them from my strongbox as soon as they told me your carriage was approaching."

"Thank you, Richard. I trust you'll have someone see to my traveling trunk. I'll be staying here for a few days."

"Already being attended to, Bishop."

De Grandison gazed at the four letters arranged neatly in the center of his writing table, the seals intact. The handwriting on one was quite familiar and he was tempted to read it first, but something drew his attention to the other missive bearing the seal of the *camerlengo*'s chambers. Who else there would have business with him?

In nomine Patris et Filii et Spiritus Sancti

I write to you, Lord Bishop, because I am bereft of other ideas for how to help our mutual friend, Father Piran Chegwin. Events from long ago have recently manifested themselves here in the papal court, much to his detriment and undeservedly so in my opinion. I have for these past weeks been urging him to write to you and know that he has now done so. What I don't know is if he has fully expressed to you either the increasingly dire nature of his circumstances or the despair that he tries most diligently to mask from all but myself.

As I have now exhausted all means at my disposal to help him, I turn to you, Lord Bishop, and most urgently beseech you to intervene in whatever manner you can on behalf of our dear friend.

Yours in Christ and may the blessings of our Lord Jesus be upon you, sir
Father Étienne Bonfils
Written at Avignon, September 7th, 1346

Dark clouds began to gather in de Grandison's mind as he opened Piran's letter.

I hope, my dear friend, that this letter finds you in good health and that God has blessed you that all your good works are progressing successfully. I fear that my own news is not of such a fortuitous nature.

You may not have been able to find Martin de Villiers when you searched for him all those years ago, Father, but he has now found me. Quite by chance,

I believe, as he arrived here in the company of Cardinal Adhémar Robert, who is newly appointed as protonotary apostolic. It was clear from our first brief encounter that nothing in his attitude toward me has changed.

And so I write to you today to ask if there might be a role in which I could serve you within your diocese. You once mentioned that I might be of assistance in your documentation of the lives of the Cornish saints, a task I would happily undertake. Nor would I be unhappy to serve in one of your parishes, should there be a need that is now unfulfilled. I hope you agree it would be safe for me to return to England now that we are certain of where de Villiers is and that he is likely to remain here for some time to come.

I would also like very much to see my kerens once again before they depart this earth.

Piran

Written at Avignon, September 6th, 1346

The bishop sighed deeply as he laid the page on the table. Bonfils was right. Piran hadn't dwelt on his problems – merely advocated a solution. But de Grandison was in no doubt about the peril his protégé now found himself in. Perhaps one of the other letters would provide some detail. He picked up the one bearing the *camerlengo*'s seal next.

In nomine Patris et Filii et Spiritus Sancti

To John de Grandison, Bishop of Exeter

I write to you in hopes of some elucidation on a matter that is most troubling to me. I am given to understand that Father Piran Chegwin was commended to the papal court by yourself during the reign of our late, much-beloved John XXII. Said Father Chegwin was then commended to me by Cardinal Montfavez and even by our late Benedict XII as a diligent and reliable man to assist with the disbursement and recording of payments associated with the construction of the new palace.

In all the years he has performed this role, I have found him to be everything that he was represented to be. Such that, some two years past, I gave him responsibility for overseeing all the financial dealings associated with the said construction. And I have never had any reason to question his honesty or his devotion to God and to his duty.

In recent weeks, however, this has all been called into question. A new arrival here, a protégé of Cardinal Robert, has brought to our attention that Father Chegwin has a most unseemly past. To wit that he was found to be cheating in his final year of study at Oxford, that he passed the work of others off as his own, that he caused a fight in which a man was killed, that he might even have been the one who wielded the fatal knife, and that he was never called upon to answer for any of his misdeeds. The priest who alleges all these things and says he observed them personally during his own studies at Oxford is a man of impeccable credentials, having received a doctorate in theology from the University of Bologna and enjoying the unassailable support of Cardinal Robert.

As this information came to light, I resumed direct supervision of Father Chegwin's work and have found no discrepancy and no deviation from his prior diligence. At the same time, he has not stepped forward to refute any of what is being said.

I am therefore most puzzled, Bishop de Grandison, by the discord between what I hear with my ears and what I see with my eyes. I would be most grateful for any insight you can offer so that I might know how to act.

Yours in Christ

Gasbert de Valle, Archbishop of Narbonne, Camerlengo of the Holy Roman Church

Written at Avignon, September 8th, 1346

"That bastard son of the devil's own whore!" De Grandison slammed a palm on the table as he permitted himself a rare expletive. If ever there was a time and a cause for a colorful curse, this was it. He rose and began pacing around the room in an attempt to temper his fury, but it didn't seem to help. Returning to sit at his writing table, he picked up the final letter. *Please, Pierre, tell me you're doing something about this.*

May the blessings of God be upon you, my dear friend

This is a most difficult letter to write as I have yet to get to the heart of the matter. When Cardinal Robert arrived some weeks ago, he was accompanied by a priest whose surname was familiar to me from our conversations years ago about Chegwin's difficulties at Oxford and your search for the perpetrator. At first, I paid little attention as the name is not uncommon in France.

But then I thought perhaps I shouldn't be so quick to assume. Chegwin's guarded response when I questioned him on the day he brought me news of your clock further aroused my curiosity. So when the initial whisperings began, I wrote to Bologna to inquire about this de Villiers's claimed credentials. The University asserts that they did award the degree he claims, but I still question its validity though Robert clearly will not. Nor will he permit this de Villiers to do the usual work of the chancery but retains him in some sort of ill-defined role that is highly unusual for a papal notary.

I can't help but wonder if there is some personal connection, though I won't speculate as to what, or if de Villiers possesses knowledge that Robert wants to remain concealed. Whatever the reason, Robert will hear nothing ill said about his protégé nor will he even entertain casual questions about what the man does or how he came to be in the personal service of a cardinal.

What de Villiers asserts to anyone who will listen is exactly what happened in Oxford all those years ago but with the roles of perpetrator and victim reversed. As you know, what starts as a whisper increases in volume with each repetition, and the doubt growing around Chegwin is now difficult to contain.

Absent proof of a false representation of de Villiers's credentials, I have little hope of refuting Robert's adamant support of his minion. Documentation of the dismissal from Oxford would only go so far, as Robert's rebuttal would almost certainly cite the Bologna doctorate as proof of a change of heart.

*Beyond that, John, I have a greater good to consider. The rift within the College of Cardinals between the French and Italian factions persists despite the façade of cordiality that marks their day-to-day interactions. As dean, my task must be to strive for consensus and, failing that – which I must admit is more or less a foregone conclusion – to narrow the gap to the greatest extent possible. To introduce yet another point of contention by pitting them against one another over the veracity and merit of two ordinary priests would **not** be in the best interests of the Church. Having them both remain within the papal court would, I fear, serve only to ensure that the conflict is visible every day to everyone here. I cannot order Robert to dismiss his protégé. Nor would it be wise to draw the Holy Father into this matter. But I can appeal to you to once again extricate Chegwin from being unjustly discredited.*

I hope he has written to you, but in the event he has not, I urge you to find a place for him under your care. He deserves to leave here of his own volition rather than in disgrace.

Pierre

Two hours later, de Grandison found the dean consulting with the head of the craftsmen working on the carvings for the singing gallery. Despite being impatient to get the letters he'd just finished on their way, he took a moment to admire the work. "And the angels are all to be beautifully painted?" he asked.

"The artists are ready to begin as soon as the carvers finish, my lord Bishop," the craftsman said.

"And how soon can we begin using the gallery?"

"The gallery itself can be used now. It's only the decorations that still have to be finished," said the craftsman.

"Good news indeed. I'm quite eager, Father de Braylegh ..." de Grandison addressed his next remark to the dean. ". . . to hear what the choir sounds like when we elevate some of the voices."

"As am I, Father. Is there something you wanted?"

"The messenger you mentioned. Could you have him found and sent to my study?"

"Of course, Father."

A quarter hour later, a surprisingly prosperous looking man with a satchel slung across his body – *Papal messengers must get paid well*, thought de Grandison – knelt to kiss the bishop's ring – a carved image of the Madonna and Child enameled in pale blue. "Bless you, my son. I'm told you were sent by Cardinal des Près himself."

"That's right, Father. The cardinal was most insistent that I make haste getting here and the same getting your message back to him."

"In fact, I have three letters to be delivered. Would you be willing to accept an additional fee to carry them all?"

"As you wish, Father."

De Grandison handed him a small pouch containing four gold florins. The messenger had the good manners not to open it then and there, but de Grandison knew the amount, while somewhat excessive, would ensure his instructions were followed without question. As he handed over the letters, he said, "These are all to be given to Cardinal des Près and no one else. Into the cardinal's hands only. Is that understood?"

"Aye, Father. Only the cardinal."

"It's urgent, my good man. I trust you'll be as speedy going home as you were in coming here."

"Those were the cardinal's orders. You can count on me, sir. Is there anything else?"

"Only God's blessings upon you, my son, and may He grant you a safe and swift journey."

When the messenger had gone, de Grandison walked over to the window and looked out onto the small courtyard below. However swift the man might be, it would be weeks before any further news. *Blessed Mary, grant that no harm come to Piran in that time.*

XXIII

Avignon, October 18th, 1346

The past three months had been difficult for Piran. He'd learned in Oxford that he couldn't leap to his own defense – that he had to put his trust in others. But he could see no sign of anyone defending him. *Patience*, he kept reminding himself. *It takes time. It has to be done quietly and carefully.* And so he had plodded along. Doing his work exactly as he'd done for the past twenty years. Taking care that his demeanor didn't betray his inner thoughts.

But those inner thoughts were as despondent as his darkest days in Oxford. He slept poorly, if at all, his dreams filled with demons, and spent more time at prayer than at meals, so he was starting to lose weight. Étienne was a gift from God. Never wavering in his friendship. Accepting of Piran's refusal to mount his own defense. Providing a welcome distraction, yet knowing when distraction was unwelcome.

So when Archbishop de Valle approached his writing table in midafternoon, Piran was certain his worst fears were about to be realized. "Cardinal des Près would like to see you, Chegwin," de Valle said quietly, as if he didn't want to be overheard.

Try as he might to maintain his composure, Piran's hand shook as he laid down his quill. And as he rose to his feet, it seemed as if his whole body was quivering.

"Calm yourself, my son." The archbishop placed a comforting hand on Piran's shoulder. "There's no need for alarm."

Piran glanced toward Étienne. *Is this the last time I'll see him?* His friend simply nodded, as if to reassure.

As he made his way to des Près's study, his thoughts, like a weathercock in a violent storm, swung wildly back and forth between trust and trepidation. When, for the second time ever, the cardinal bid him enter the moment he knocked on the door, he knew his gut was right – this was to be a life-altering meeting.

The smile on des Près's face gave Piran reason to hope even as his gut refused to calm itself. "Father Chegwin, do sit, please." The cardinal didn't bother with the formalities. "I have something for you." Opening a drawer in his writing table, he retrieved a letter that he passed to Piran – a letter in a hand and with a seal that Piran recognized immediately. "It was delivered just this morning by my personal messenger, and I wanted you to be able read it in privacy, without others knowing anything about it. Shall I step into the corridor while you read?"

"That won't be necessary, Eminence." Somehow Piran managed a smile. "Besides, it would look quite peculiar, should anyone pass by, for you to be loitering in the corridor outside your own study."

As the cardinal leaned back in his chair and folded his hands over his belly, Piran broke the seal and unfolded the page.

To my dear friend, Piran, with the blessings of God and of ourselves

My dismay at learning what has transpired is matched only by my delight in knowing that you will soon be back in England and that, even more happily, you will become part of all the good work we are doing here in Exeter. And to that end, I encourage you to make haste in coming to us. There is much to be done, which will benefit greatly from a man of your intellect and temperament.

I must, however, most strongly insist that you should not travel alone. The risks are likely small, but there is no sound reason not to avoid them. To that end, you must find someone you trust completely to accompany you and hire a carriage for the land portion of the journey. Even if the carriage and the sea passage require all your money, spend it and I will refill your purse as soon as you arrive.

Know that my dear friend Pierre is privy to what I ask of you in that I have written separately to him so that he may sanction your departure and see you safely on your way. None, including Cardinal Robert, will challenge the decision of the Dean of the College of Cardinals, so everything about your departure will be above suspicion.

And now, my dear friend, I can do no more than wait in eager anticipation for your arrival. Come straight to Chudleigh where I will be preparing my thoughts and orders of service for the Advent season.

John de Grandison
Written at Exeter the 27th September 1346

Piran's eyes glistened as he folded the page and struggled to compose himself. At long last, he looked back up to meet the cardinal's gaze. "Thank you, Eminence." He could only hope des Près recognized that the gratitude was for more than just giving him the letter.

"Somehow, Chegwin, in this place where the stakes are always so high, it is often those who least merit it that suffer from the ambitions of others. What disturbs me most, is that the animosity in this instance derives from prejudice and not from just cause. How one can call himself a theologian and not understand that we are all God's creatures, all made in his image, and that Christ called on us to love our fellow man without exception is something I will never understand." He shook his head sadly. "Be that as it may. In his letter to me, John said that he told you I know of his instructions as they pertain to your travel."

"He did, indeed, sir."

"Then I hope you'll have no objection to the fact that I've already undertaken certain things on your behalf. I've spoken to Father Bonfils. I wanted him to be prepared when you broke the news to him. He was determined to be the one who accompanies you to England, and I've agreed. Further, I've hired a carriage to take you to Bordeaux, where you can get passage to Plymouth or Weymouth and have but a short land journey to Chudleigh." He paused and reached into his drawer again, producing a leather pouch. "This purse contains twenty-five florins. It should be ample to cover ship's passage for you and Bonfils and your expenses during the journey." He pushed the pouch across the table.

"I can't take your money, Eminence. That's far too much."

"It's no more than the Holy See owes you, Chegwin. I'll make it known that you leave with my approval to take up a new post. That said, de Valle and Montfavez are already in my confidence, and Dupuis will be before the end of the day. Those of us who matter most will know the truth and will always be grateful for the work you've done here." Des Près rose and Piran followed suit, leaving the pouch on the table. The cardinal picked it up and pressed it into Piran's hands. "You must take this. And there's one more thing you should know, Chegwin. As long as I am Dean of the College of Cardinals, there is no hope that Adhémar Robert will ever be considered as even a potential candidate for the papacy."

There was yet one more thing, which des Près chose not to reveal – the last paragraph of his letter from de Grandison.

You may be inclined, Pierre, to take steps to expose de Villiers for what he is. It would absolutely be his just deserts to be called to account by none other than the man who ranks second only to the Holy Father. But after much thought on the matter, I'm asking you to refrain. After two decades of uncertainty, we finally know where the villain is. And that knowledge is Piran's protection. I therefore beseech you in the name of our long friendship to let it be. Once Piran leaves, the matter will soon be forgotten and the court will move on to some new gossip or intrigue. As long as de Villiers is in Avignon, I can rest easy. And if something should sever his ties to Robert and he seeks to leave, I know I can count on you to tell me what's afoot.

Feast Day of St. Martin de Tours
Not normally inclined to concern himself with household matters, de Grandison had been fussing for the past three days over the arrangements for the expected arrivals. The housekeeper was at her wits' end. Yes, the best

guest rooms had been cleaned and dusted. Yes, the finest sheets were on the beds. Yes, the windows had been opened, despite the chill, to air out the rooms. Yes, the wood was laid and ready to light the fires at a moment's notice, and yes, there were extra logs in the wood boxes to keep the fires going. No, Cook had no further questions about the meal to be served on the first evening. Yes, the jeweled goblets were polished, and, of course, there was a plentiful supply of the bishop's favorite wine in the cellar. So when the carriage pulled into the forecourt in midafternoon, the entire household heaved a collective sigh of relief.

Any thought of a bishop's dignity left for another time and place, de Grandison rushed out the front door just as Piran and Étienne descended from the carriage. Stepping aside, Étienne watched, a warm smile on his face, as the two friends embraced. When, at long last, they stood apart, de Grandison clapped Étienne on the shoulder. "Welcome, Bonfils. I'm so glad it was you he chose to accompany him."

"Oh, he had no say in the matter, Father. Cardinal des Près and I would have it no other way."

De Grandison laughed, put an arm around each of the younger men, and started toward the steps that led to the entrance. "Let's get inside where it's warmer. Everything is ready, the fires are being lit in your rooms even as we speak, and we'll have a celebratory meal this evening." Once inside, when Piran and Étienne removed their cloaks and gave them to the servants, he added, "A meal that it looks like you might be in need of, Piran. Your cassock is hanging on your frame."

"The anxiety of these past months stole my appetite, Father."

"Plus, he didn't eat more than a couple of ship's biscuits on the entire voyage," said Étienne.

"Sea travel doesn't agree with me," said Piran.

"He's right, Father. I've never seen anyone so green."

"Then let's hope it's the last sea voyage you need to make in this life," said the bishop. "Now, my housekeeper will show you to your rooms. Once you get settled, come join me in my sitting room. Any of the household staff can show you the way. I want to hear all about what happened in Avignon."

As they talked through every detail of those long weeks, Piran felt the weight slowly slide from his shoulders. So much that, when the housekeeper announced the evening meal, he bounded up from his chair before either of his companions. "Hungry, Piran?" asked de Grandisson.

"Ravenous, actually. I hadn't realized just how much I'd needed to talk with you about things. Talking to God is all well and good, but . . ."

De Grandison and Étienne both chuckled. "Sounds as if I'm a poor substitute for *you*, Father," said Étienne.

Clearly discomfited, Piran tried to make amends. "Oh, I never meant you weren't helpful, Étienne, it's just that . . ."

Bonfils clapped him on the shoulder as they left the sitting room. "Never you mind, Piran. God and I together can't hold a candle to the exalted bishop. At least I'm in good company."

Finally able to laugh for the first time since hearing the hated epithet from so long ago, Piran joined in the merriment as they walked into the dining room and took their places at table. He couldn't remember when he'd seen such a feast as what was arrayed on that table. But before he could take a bite, de Grandison raised his goblet. "To homecomings." Then, turning to Bonfils, he added. "And to those who see us safely home."

As they ate, conversation naturally turned to what the future might have in store. "You should stay here, as my guests," said de Grandison, "through Advent and the Christmas season. I'm just putting the finishing touches on a new order of service for Christmas Eve, and I'd like you both to be there. Then, after Twelfth Night, I thought you might want to visit your parents, Piran."

"I'd like that very much, Father."

"You should stay as long as you want. In truth, if it hadn't been for the risk, des Près and de Valle would both have given you time for visits long since. Take Bonfils with you if you'd like. Unless, that is . . ." he turned to Étienne, ". . . you must return to Avignon straightaway."

"Cardinal des Près left the choice up to me, Father. He said I would be welcome back any time if I chose to return but that I was under no instructions to do so." He paused for a sip of wine. "I think . . . if you'll permit . . . I should like to stay for a while."

"You're welcome for as long as you like, my son."

Warmed by the food and the wine and the companionship, Piran raised his goblet. "To the best friends a man could have."

"And a future of contentment and peace," Étienne added.

Fairfield, Derbyshire, December 23rd, 1346

His nose wrinkled in distaste, his gut churning with unease, Father Wainwright laid the letter he'd just read on the eating table in his small cottage near the chapel. How, after all this time, had Martin discovered where he was? It had been almost fifteen years since they'd parted company in Bologna.

After they'd lost track of Chegwin, Martin had convinced Wainwright to go to Italy, certain they could complete their studies there. As things turned out, they'd had to start from the beginning to avoid having to reveal their dismissal from Oxford. Martin had wormed his way into the good graces of a minor nobleman in the city who agreed to pay their way. Wainwright found their benefactor somewhat unsavory but preferred not to know how Martin courted the man's favor.

They'd quarreled over what to do once they were ordained. Martin was determined to obtain a doctorate and then go to Rome, convinced that was the right place to begin what he saw as his inevitable rise through the Church hierarchy.

"That's only because the last two Popes have been Frenchmen," Martin had scoffed when Wainwright pointed out that the Holy See was in Avignon. "But mark my words. They'll elect an Italian when this one dies and everyone will come back to Rome. Just wait and see."

But Wainwright had no interest in waiting. He'd grown tired of Italy, tired of universities, and tired of Martin's grandiose ambitions and wanted nothing more than to return to England and get on with his life. Martin called him pathetic, tossed him three florins, and said, "Good luck getting home on *that*. But it's probably the most money you'll see the rest of your life."

It had taken him over a month to get back to England, relying on the hospitality of churches along the way for a bit of food and a place to sleep and ordinary people's generosity to a priest whenever a church wasn't conveniently at hand – guarding those precious florins to pay for the passage from Calais to Dover. When he finally set foot on English soil, he had three pennies to his name and no prospects of obtaining a parish of his own, so he'd gone home to Derbyshire and lived with his brother's family for most of a year until the opening in the chapelry at Fairfield, within the Royal Forest of High Peak, came available. What might otherwise have been a poor living benefited from the generosity of the king and his nobles whenever they came to one of their favorite hunting grounds. Wainwright was content.

Or at least he had been until that letter arrived just after the midday meal. He picked it up and read it again.

God's blessings to you, Wainwright, even though you be but a poor priest and I now roam the corridors of the Holy See itself. You will scarcely credit what transpired during the past summer and autumn. Barely two weeks after I arrived here in the company of Cardinal Robert, I chanced to encounter none other than the Cornish pig Chegwin and learned that he had somehow managed to achieve a position of some importance, though why a Cornishman would be allowed inside these hallowed walls much less given advancement is beyond my ken.

Once I knew he was here, I could take no chances that he might reveal my past. I have learned, Wainwright, that a rumor is a powerful thing. Turn one loose and it spreads and gets embellished along the way and its subject is powerless against the tide. Within weeks, the pig was thoroughly discredited, and all the working priests in the Chancery were hanging on my every word.

He was gone by St. Frideswide's feast day, but no one will say where. Only that he left to take up a new assignment. But I'd wager my last meal I know where he's gone. That archdeacon who came to his rescue in Oxford is now Bishop of Exeter. No doubt that's where the pig has found a new sty.

I need you to go to Exeter and find out exactly where Chegwin is. Once you've found him, write to me and I'll give you instructions on what you're to do. We have to finish this once and for all.
Martinus

What was distaste on first reading became disgust on the second. Having freed himself from Martin's clutches, Wainwright had no wish to be drawn back in. The self-important bastard could solve his own problems. He tossed the letter onto the fire. As he watched it flare and then crumble to ash, a momentary thought crossed his mind. *Should I write to the bishop and tell him about this?*

But that would have to wait. Tomorrow was Christmas Eve, and he had to prepare for important services over the next few days.

XXIV

England, 1348

It was the second time the king had summoned Parliament this year. The first meeting was in January and February, and de Grandison had declined to go. He'd never liked winter travel, and as he'd gotten older, he found it quite intolerable. But this summons was for the 31st of March, so the temperatures should be warmer and the roads less likely to be snowbound. There were other reasons to go. It would be an opportunity to see his brother, who now held the family title and estates, and his nephew, who was now the Earl of Salisbury. And on his return, he could spend some time with Katherine. Since her husband had died four years earlier after being wounded in a tournament, his sister rarely left her manor house at Bisham Abbey, and she would certainly not be inclined to make the journey to Chudleigh.

Piran had returned shortly before Advent of the previous year, having stayed in Launceston during his mother's final illness. He and Bonfils were now engaged in working on the lives of the saints. De Braylegh had the remaining work on the cathedral well in hand. There was really no reason not to go.

Much of the business of the Parliament was predictable. Edward needed money to continue prosecuting his war against France, which he was granted, but with stipulations. The recently formed Commons were flexing their muscles and insisted on a provision that the funds could not be used to pay off previously incurred debts and that the tax would be cancelled in the event of peace – or even a truce.

When the session finally came to a close on April 13th and the lords were slowly dispersing from the meeting hall, de Grandison was surprised to be approached by a yeoman wearing the king's livery. "Begging your pardon, My Lord Bishop, His Grace requests a word, if you please."

What could this be about? de Grandison wondered. "Is there an appointed time?"

"If you'll just come with me, my lord."

The yeoman led the way up stairways and through corridors that de Grandison had never traversed and finally stopped before a single, elaborately decorated door. He rapped twice on the door then opened it and stepped inside, leaving de Grandison standing in the doorway. It was a small but richly furnished room with a writing table, two large windows, and, on the opposite wall, a carved stone hearth with two chairs set before it. The king had his back to the room, his attention on something outside. "Bishop de Grandison, Your Grace," the yeoman announced before stepping aside to allow the bishop to enter and then departing straightaway, closing the door behind him.

Edward turned, a smile on his face. "I find it amusing to watch the little groups that invariably seem to form as men are leaving one of these meetings. Some, no doubt, congratulating or commiserating with one another. Alliances forming, shifting, changing. Or maybe just friends arranging the next gathering at someone's hunting lodge. Please, Bishop . . ." He gestured toward the hearth as he began to make his way across the room. "Do be seated."

Two glasses of wine stood in readiness on the low table between the chairs. Edward took a sip from his, the signal that his guest should follow suit. "From Gascony," said the king. "Quite to my liking, so I'm in hopes we have a plentiful supply as there may not be much of a harvest there this year. The plague is raging across southern France and making its way north quite rapidly, I'm told."

"I've heard similar reports. A most virulent disease, by all accounts."

"Which is why I wanted to speak with you. There are some who avow we'll be safe since we're surrounded by water on all sides. But I think they're fools. I think it's the water that brings it. Well, not the water precisely, but the ships that ply the waters. Why else does it always break out first in a port city? Sicily, then Genoa, then Marseilles. It's only a matter of time, de Grandison, before it arrives on these shores. And we won't know when or where until it's already among us."

He paused for another sip of wine and gazed for quite some moments at the glowing embers in the hearth. "I find it disconcerting, Bishop, to feel so powerless to protect those who matter to me. But Philippa reminds me that those are the times when one must put their faith in God."

"It seems to me the queen is wise." De Grandison had no idea where this conversation was going – only that he had to let Edward come to the point in his own time and his own way.

"I learned long ago her advice is worth heeding. So I have determined to do all I can to invoke God's protection for my son and heir, and to that end, I wish to commission mass and prayers to be said for him daily in all the places and for all the titles that he holds. As Duke of Cornwall, he holds a castle at Tintagel where, if my memory is correct, there is an ancient and holy chapel on the headland. And that is where I would like to petition God's intercession. Find a good priest, de Grandison – a man who is devoted to Christ – and give him this assignment. I'll provide fifty shillings every year. And you should know this commission is likely to last well beyond the plague. My son has proven himself an able commander, so when our campaigns in France resume, he will take my place in the field and will need God's protection from weapons as well as from disease."

"As you wish."

Edward downed what was left in his glass. "That is a great weight off my mind."

"When would you like this commission to begin?"

"As soon as may be. But I suspect you may be planning to visit your sister before returning home."

"Indeed I was, but if this is more pressing."

"Visit her. William's loss was as great a blow to me as it was to her, but the pressing needs of the kingdom make it difficult for us to visit her even briefly. Give her my assurances that her son is doing well as the new earl."

"I'm sure she'll take comfort from that. Is there anything else?"

"Only my thanks. The yeoman will be waiting in the corridor to show you the way out. This is a rather out-of-the-way corner of the palace, but I like it because it's a quiet place to think."

"God be with you, my son" said de Grandison as he rose to leave.

He stayed longer at Bisham Abbey than he'd originally planned so it was Midsummer's Eve before de Grandison was back in Chudleigh. And the news he brought was dire. "We heard as we passed through Yeovil that there's plague in Weymouth," he told Piran and Étienne over supper.

Piran shook his head sadly. "I suppose it was too much to hope that we'd escaped the danger when we left France before it arrived there. Seems it just followed us here."

"There may be more truth in what you say than you realize," said de Grandison. "The word in Yeovil is that it came on a ship from Bordeaux – that there were two seamen on board who were ill and within a week every man on the ship was dead and people in the town were starting to get sick."

They finished their meal in grim silence before moving to the bishop's sitting room to share a final pitcher of wine before retiring for the night. "What are we going to do?" Piran finally asked.

"Is there anything anyone *can* do?" said Étienne. "I don't think anyone knows."

"I've been thinking about that," said de Grandison. "It seems almost everyone who comes into contact with a sick person also gets sick, especially if they're shut up together in one place, like those men on the ship. And yet there are some who don't. No one knows why. Which leads me to think perhaps being here in the countryside and not in the towns and cities may be safer. Maybe the answer is to be in as remote a place as possible."

Piran sensed that the bishop was being reticent – as if there was something he either wasn't prepared to say or didn't know how to broach the subject. "Is there something on your mind, Father?"

De Grandison didn't answer straightaway. Instead, he rose and went to gaze out the window that looked across the meadow to the little pond where deer liked to come for a drink in the long summer twilight. At long last, he turned back to face the two younger men. "Yes, Piran, there is. I hope and pray that we can stay safe here in the manor. But there *is* one thing I can do. The king gave me a commission for a priest to say mass and prayers for the Duke of Cornwall in a very remote part of that county. Tintagel Castle, to be precise. I would send both of you if I could, but the stipend is barely enough for one man, let alone two. Which means I have to choose. A choice I do not wish to make, but that I must, nonetheless." He turned back to gaze at the deepening twilight.

At long last, Étienne broke the silence. "It seems to me, Father, that there's only one choice. It has to be Piran. If God's grace is to be sought for Cornwall, then it should be done by a Cornishman."

De Grandison took his time before turning slowly back around. "Are you sure about that, Bonfils?"

"Quite sure, Father. You've already been kinder to me than I could have asked by letting me stay here rather than return to France. So I'll take my chances alongside you here in Chudleigh . . . if you'll allow me to."

"I'd be grateful for the company, my son. If what's happened in France is any indication, we may be in for some long, dark days."

"Then I'll go find my bed and leave you two to talk," said Étienne.

When he had left, de Grandison came to sit beside Piran. "I don't like the thought of sending you so far away, Piran. But I can think of no safer place for you to be in the face of what's about to happen. While you pray for the duke there, I shall be praying for you here."

"My prayers won't just be for the duke, Father. They'll be for you and Étienne and everyone here as well."

The following morning, the servants began loading a wagon with supplies. Barrels of flour and oats, barley for brewing ale, sacks of dried beans and lentils, dried beef and venison, crates containing bottles of wine, seeds for planting next year, winter clothing and blankets – anything that might be needed if the priest and the caretaker had to remain isolated in the castle for months on end. Piran had tried to object. "I can't take all this, Father. What will you do for supplies here?"

"We can get more before the plague makes it here. That will be much harder for you at the end of the world."

Everything was loaded and the horses hitched and ready by the time the village church bells tolled midday. Piran embraced Bonfils first. "Take care of him, Étienne. I owe him my life many times over."

"You can count on me, my friend. And you keep yourself safe."

Then it was time. This parting was more heart-wrenching than when he and de Grandison had said farewell in Hull so many years ago. Then, they knew they'd see each other again. Today, it was hard even to imagine what might lie ahead. They held their embrace for longer than ever before. Finally, de Grandison stepped back and handed Piran two small pouches. "In the black one is your stipend for the year. The red one contains a rosary that belonged to my mother. I want you to have it."

Piran kissed the red velvet pouch. "I'll cherish it always, Father."

"Now, you'd best be on your way. I'll write to you whenever it's safe to send a messenger. Godspeed, my son."

Piran climbed into the wagon, took the reins in hand, and clucked to the horse. He looked over his shoulder and waved a long farewell, then turned his eyes to the road as the tears began to flow. It was Midsummer's Day – the longest day of the year – and it felt like it would be the longest day of his life.

XXV

He chose the route over the north side of the moor as the ascents weren't as high and it would be easier on the horses. Besides, that route would take him directly into Launceston, where he planned to give the horses a rest while he spent a couple of days with his family.

Throughout that first afternoon, he wrestled with his conscience over whether he should tell people about the coming plague. Was it right to withhold the knowledge that it was already in the kingdom? Did they not deserve to know what they might soon be facing? On the other hand, there really was nothing they could do to prepare. This wasn't like foreknowledge of warring armies approaching, where the ordinary folk could flee to some place safe, out of the path of destruction. Could they flee the plague – go to some place more remote as he was doing? In the end, though, that would only change where people were crowded together – possibly even create the kind of conditions that existed in a city, where the disease could run rampant. No, they would be safer in smaller villages. And what would telling them now accomplish besides sowing fear? Fear that might even trigger behavior that would make them less safe in the long run. Might it not be better for them to enjoy their ordinary lives until they were disrupted? Some places might escape entirely, so was it right to frighten them about something that would never happen? And what about his own safety? He had a commission from the king to fulfill – a commission for which he'd already been paid. If he told people the plague was here, would they turn against him – maybe even do him harm – fearing that he, a stranger, was bringing it into their midst?

He wished he'd talked this over with Father de Grandison before he'd left Chudleigh. And then he remembered what Father had said all those years ago in Oxford when he'd struggled with the homily he'd been assigned to write. *What I asked of you today is perhaps the greatest challenge any priest must face. Helping others through a crisis when the crisis is ongoing, your understanding is limited, and the outcome is uncertain . . . it's inordinately difficult. But the ability to do that is what sets the good priests apart.* He had wondered then if he would ever be a good priest. He wondered the same thing now.

He stopped for the night in Moretonhampstead. The horses deserved a rest after pulling the heavy wagon up onto the moor. Over a hearty supper and some excellent ale at the small tavern on the ground floor of the inn where he'd found a room, he observed the people around him. All going about their usual business, friendly enough to a traveler in their midst. *Is that just because of my cassock?* Piran wondered. He remembered the kindness of the first tavern keeper he'd encountered in France. This one wasn't so generous, demanding payment for the room and the meal in advance. But he was friendly enough to a stranger and quite jovial with his local patrons.

By the time he fell asleep, Piran had made up his mind. If people he encountered asked him about the plague, he would be forthright and try to help them with their fears. If they didn't ask, he would leave them in peace. As for his own family, all he could do was trust God to guide him once he was with them.

He let the horses set their own pace over the climbs and descents as they traversed the moor, stopping the next night at Bridestowe. Tomorrow would be an easier day, and he would be in Launceston by early afternoon. But tonight, St. Bridget's Church beckoned him. The old Norman arch at the entrance to the churchyard spoke of how long this had been a sacred place. It seemed a fitting place to say the first prayers of his commission, so he stepped inside and knelt before the altar, asking God's protection for the

Duke of Cornwall. His obligation accomplished, he stayed for another half hour, absorbing the serenity and spirituality of the place, hoping it would prepare him for the morrow.

In the end, he told his family only about the plague in France. But he was quite stern when he said, "If it comes here, the only way to protect yourselves is to keep to yourselves. Don't be tempted to help your neighbors if they become ill, no matter how un-Christian that may seem. And don't let anyone who might have been near a sick person inside your door. Don't even open the door to their knocking. We know from France that anyone who's been around a sick person will almost certainly get sick themselves. And anyone who gets this disease will almost certainly die. Take my words to heart. For the sake of your children, my nieces and nephews." He'd done what he could, but still, he left with a heavy heart, not knowing if he would ever again see these people he loved so much.

He arrived at Tintagel Castle on the eve of the feast day of Saints Peter and Paul to the complete surprise of the caretaker who met him outside the gate. "Nobody say anybody be coming. And what's in the wagon?" The man exuded distrust.

As well he should, Piran thought. *After all, it's his job to protect the king's property. Though, from the looks of things, it's more in need of repair than protection.* And in that moment, he decided cheerfulness was most likely the best way to allay suspicion. "No need to fret, my good man. I'm here at the king's behest. To say mass and pray for his son, the Duke of Cornwall."

"Anybody could put on cassock. How I know it's truth?"

Recognizing the man's discomfort with English, Piran switched to Cornish, hoping to garner some goodwill. "Well, I suppose you don't. But here's what I was told. There's a little chapel on the headland, outside the curtain wall, that's dedicated to St. Julitta. And the king wants mass said there every day on his son's behalf. I'm Father Chegwin … and my Christian name is Piran. No one said this to my face, but I think maybe the king believes that having a man named for one Cornish saint praying in the chapel of another Cornish saint might be the best way to invoke God's protection for the duke."

The caretaker's aggressive posture had relaxed ever so slightly as Piran spoke. "And why might the duke need God's protection?"

"Because it won't be long before the king resumes his war with France, and the duke will be leading the English armies."

"And I'm supposed to house you and feed you here?"

"I don't come empty-handed, my good man. And the king will pay me every year, just like he does you."

The caretaker walked around the wagon, inspecting the load, the wagon itself, and the horses. "Fine animals. And a good, sturdy wagon too. How'd you come by them, you being just a poor priest?"

"The Bishop of Exeter gave them to me when he gave me the king's commission. They're ours to use as we might need." Piran paused, but the caretaker said nothing further. Clearly, he was mulling over in his mind what to do about this stranger who'd just showed up at his gate. "I've told you my name," Piran continued. "Perhaps you can tell me yours, since it appears we're going to be spending quite a bit of time together."

The man hesitated then seemed to reach a decision. "Tregurtha. Jori Tregurtha. Mayhap you can come inside. But I warn you, you'd best not try to do me harm or steal anything. I trained with the king's army – fought for him in Scotland – so I know a thing or two about taking care of myself and what's mine to protect."

Piran laughed. "You've nothing to fear from me, Jori. The only time I was ever in a fight was when I was a student at Oxford. My mates and I were set upon late one night in a dark lane, and I ended up with a broken cannel-bone and three broken ribs. Trust me, I never want to have that experience again." *Was that almost a smile on Jori's face?*

"Then I guess there's nothing for it but for you to come inside." He opened the gate wide enough for the wagon to pass then bolted it once it stopped a few feet beyond.

"Ride with me," Piran called. "Show me where to go."

"Across the bridge to the other courtyard."

It took them the rest of the afternoon to get the supplies stored, the horses groomed and fed and turned out into a paddock with Jori's horse, and the wagon secured. "Guess it's best you share my lodgings," Jori told Piran. "You can have the upper floor. It has two rooms and there's a fireplace in one of them, like on the ground floor. You'll take your meals in the kitchen like I do. Saves having to carry things across the path and then back again. The staircase to your rooms is outside, so you can come and go without bothering me. But mind, I'll be keeping an eye on you for now."

Piran understood these first few days were about building trust. Of course, that went both ways. When it was time for supper, he was surprised to find two bottles of wine on the table. Bottles he recognized straightaway. "Where did this wine come from, Jori?"

"Those crates we unloaded earlier. I snatched us a couple so's we could drink to your arrival. See, I know a man'll tell you things about himself when he's cup-shotten that he wouldn't say otherwise, so I figure that's the fastest way to get to know what he might be hiding."

"Well, if you want to get me drunk, you'll have to find another way. That's sacramental wine – blessed by the bishop himself for the Eucharist for all those masses I have to celebrate for the duke. So, unless what you want tonight is just a tiny sip with a morsel of bread while I pray for your soul, you'd best put these back where you found them." Jori looked at Piran askance. "Better still, I'll put them back and then fetch the bottle that's in my traveling bag so you can ply me with wine and ask anything you want. I promise to answer truthfully. But you have to promise *me* something, Jori."

"Depends what it is."

"You have to promise to keep your hands off the sacred wine." He paused, but Jori said nothing. "Jori, I'll know if any of it goes missing." The caretaker still held his tongue. "Come now, Jori, it should be an easy promise to make. You don't strike me as the type of man who'd want pilfering God's wine on your conscience."

"Alright, you have your promise. Now fetch something we can drink right now."

Piran quickly gathered up the two bottles, planning to store them in his room. "I'll be right back." At the door, he turned before stepping outside. "And if you're really determined to get me drunk, I'd wager you have a bottle of your own that we could open once we've drained mine."

At long last, Jori broke into a smile. "I think maybe I'm going to like you, Priest."

XXVI

Piran woke the next morning suffering no ill effects from the previous night's indulgence. Not that he himself had indulged all that much. It was Jori who downed most of the wine – and Jori who started the day complaining of a pounding head and a fuzzy tongue.

"How do I find the chapel?" Piran asked, taking care to keep his voice low.

"There's a little back gate."

"Where?"

"God's teeth, my head hurts!" Jori rubbed his forehead. "Sorry, Father. Can you fetch me a cup of small ale?"

"Where would I find that?"

"In the buttery . . . where we stowed your wine yesterday."

"Alright. I'll be back in a minute."

Piran found what looked like clean cups on the big kitchen table and two small casks on a shelf in the buttery with no indication of what was in either. He opened the tap on one and dribbled a bit of liquid into the cup to taste. Full-bodied ale. But surprisingly good. The other cask had what he was looking for. Cup filled, he returned to Jori's rooms.

"Took you long enough."

"Had to figure out which cask was which."

"Never been any need to mark them with just me here." He took a long swallow from the cup. "God's **bollocks** but my throat is dry! Sorry, Father." He took another swallow – a smaller one this time. "How is it you're so full of life this morning?"

"Just lucky, I guess." *No need to tell him I let him do most of the drinking last night.* "And a good thing, because I have an obligation to celebrate mass. It's Sunday, it's a feast day for two very important saints, and I have prayers to say for the duke. So three obligations, really. And I haven't even seen the chapel yet. Speaking of which . . ."

"Out the back gate."

"Which is where?"

"Just go along the curtain wall. You'll find it." He reached under his pillow and pulled out a ring holding a dozen keys. "Here, take my keys."

Apparently his trust is metered out based on the size of his headache. Piran smiled inwardly but gave no hint of his amusement to the suffering caretaker. "Which one?"

"You'll figure it out. Now just go on and let me be for a while."

Piran picked up the bag that held his vestments and the other accoutrements he would need for the mass and headed back to the kitchen to collect a bottle of the sacramental wine and the chunk of bread that he'd taken care to save from last night's supper. It would suffice for today.

It was easy enough to find the little gate, and the third key he tried unlocked it with no effort. Just a short walk up the hill, the chapel was small but looked to be in good repair. On the south side were two windows with Norman arches, one of which looked like it might once have been the entrance. Above the opening from the little narthex to the nave was a carving unlike anything Piran had ever seen before. A stone shaped into a triangle, each apex ever so slightly rounded. A perfect circle had been carved to touch each of the three sides, and in the center of the circle was a six-petaled flower. Three different symbols he didn't recognize filled the spaces outside the circle. The nave was simple, devoid of decoration, though it might once have been brightly painted. Twenty people – perhaps thirty if they were crowded together – could gather there for a service. The wooden screen separating the nave from the chancel was equally simple, but served its purpose. The altar cloth looked as if it had once been quite fine, but now it was faded and frayed. Piran was glad he had thought to bring a new one. Two bronze candlesticks sat on each end of the altar, devoid of any candles. That was something he would have to remedy before winter set in. Even now, at midday in the peak of summer, the small windows didn't admit much light. A small crucifix hung on the wall behind the altar.

In some ways, the little chapel felt cozy and comfortable. In others, it seemed forlorn and forgotten. Only time would tell how much one could feel God's presence in this humble setting. He donned his vestments and prepared his mind for the ceremony he was about to conduct.

Once again, Piran's life settled into a new pattern. Having celebrated his first mass at midday, he decided that would become his ritual. Something about sending his prayers aloft when the sun was at its zenith gave him a sense of closeness to God that he couldn't explain rationally. It was as if the sun was somehow adding its own blessing to his supplication.

In the mornings, he read from the Bible or from one of the books that Father de Grandison had insisted he bring with him. Afternoons were devoted to helping in the kitchen. Jori, it turned out, was a pretty fair cook. "Learned in the army," he told Piran. "Never enough camp followers in Scotland to feed everyone. Who wanted to go to Scotland, after all? Not me. But a soldier goes where he's told. Brutal, the Scots could be. Anyway, without enough camp followers, if a man wanted to eat, he had to learn to make his own potage. Some of the archers decided mine was better than what they were getting, so they started foraging for wild onions and herbs and mushrooms for me. As for the bread, a widow in the village used to bring me some now and then, but I got tired of waiting until she took it into her head to bring me a loaf, so I made her teach me. Haven't had flour as good as what you brought in a long time though."

Whether it was the flour or that first night's drinking together or just a relief from loneliness in this remote place, Jori's initial suspicions had vanished almost overnight. Over their suppers, he regaled Piran with stories from his days in the king's army. And he seemed to have an endless supply of them.

Yet for Piran, this new life brought a loneliness he'd never experienced before. Even in those dreadful days in Avignon when he was shunned by everyone except Étienne, he was still surrounded by people. Here, he was surrounded only by stone walls and neglected buildings – a place that was once grand but now seemed forgotten by its owner. But he vowed not to let himself become despondent. Isolation, he knew, was the sacrifice he'd accepted to protect himself from the plague.

Jori had been paying a man in the village to bring in supplies once a month, so Piran insisted they keep to that habit, replacing whatever they used so they always had a surplus. But he also insisted the man leave the supplies outside the gate for them to collect later. Jori thought Piran was being peculiar and said as much. Piran laughed it off, not wanting to mention plague unless it really became necessary.

But as the seasons passed and spring turned to summer and June gave way to July, necessity loomed. No one came to bring Piran's stipend for the coming year. Jori made light of it. "The duke's never sent me money on time since I first got here. Goes off to war, see, and forgets to tell someone he's got a castle out here what needs taking care of."

But Piran knew better. As the July days marched on and still no messenger arrived from the bishop, he understood how dire the situation must be. "I don't think they'll be coming this year," he told Jori over supper one evening when the caretaker had been grumping about his dwindling funds.

"What makes you say that?"

"Because there's something I didn't see any need to mention before now."

"You been holding something back on me?" Jori's tone carried the same suspicion it had on the day of Piran's arrival.

"Only because there was no need to frighten you."

"So out with it now."

"The plague had been in France for a year, claiming lives everywhere, and it arrived in England just before I came here. Since no one's come with my stipend, the only conclusion I can draw is that it's spread as it did in France and is now ravaging the kingdom. The only way to avoid contracting it is to avoid people who might be sick. I don't think it's in Cornwall yet – we haven't heard about people getting sick and dying – but we can't take any chances. That's why I won't let the man who brings our supplies come inside."

"And here I thought you were just being peculiar." Jori chuckled, trying to make light of things.

"It's no laughing matter, Jori. Part of my prayers for the duke are supposed to ask God to protect him from the plague. People who get this disease die. And it's a horrible death. As long as we keep to ourselves here in the castle and don't come into contact with anyone else, we'll be safe, even when the plague comes to Cornwall."

"You said it's not here."

"We don't have any signs it's here now, but think about it, Jori. It wasn't in England . . . and then suddenly, it was. So we can't assume it won't come here."

Jori's brow furrowed. "That's why you keep insisting we can't use up our supplies, isn't it? On account of we might run out of food out here all by ourselves if this plague gets loose. So how long does it last? I mean, how long does it stay around?"

"I don't know. I don't think anyone does."

"In that case, maybe we best stop eating so much."

"We'll be alright, Jori. Remember those seeds I brought? We'll plant them in the spring and grow our own food. We'll make it through, Jori."

A week later, there was panic in the village. People were dying in Bodmin, more and more every day. Piran and Jori barred the gate to the castle. "Maybe we should raise the drawbridge as well," Piran suggested. "Men with ladders could scale the curtain wall."

"Bridge hasn't been raised in decades," Jori replied. "Not even sure if it works anymore. Probably couldn't get it up, just the two of us. And even if we did, we might never get it back down again."

"Alright, then we'll just bar the gates at both ends and keep to ourselves on this side of the ravine."

In the months that followed, Piran's sense of isolation deepened. He no longer prayed just for the Duke of Cornwall but for Étienne and Father de Grandison and Cardinal des Près and Archbishop de Valle and Ned and Robin and Mistress Chert, pray God she still lives, and Brother Ansfrid and Brother Infirmerer and his own family in Launceston and the people of the village and Jori and even for himself. And he prayed to St. Piran and to St. Frideswide, and every night he prayed the rosary with de Grandison's mother's beads. And as the dark days of winter came and the wind howled on the headland and the sea crashed into the cliffs, he pondered the question Jori continued to ask every couple of weeks. How *will* we know when it's over?

XXVII

Avignon, April 1352

Anyone who had eyes could see that it wouldn't be long now before Cardinal Robert went to be with God. Well, anyone who had eyes and permission to enter his chamber, and Martin de Villiers had both. The old man was growing more doted by the day. Sometimes he knew who was with him, but more often, he asked over and over, "Now, who are you?" Once rather corpulent, he now refused food as often as he took it, leaving him gaunt and frail.

Martin knew it was time to hitch his wagon to another pony. Robert had gotten him into the Church's corridors of power but had done little else to advance his career. Of course, the plague had arrived in Avignon little more than a year after they had, and very little happened until the Black Death had run its course. Which it now had. He had a future, even if Robert did not, and it was time he did something about it. So he began whispering in the ears of anyone who would listen than he was available for service once the cardinal had no more need of him.

The summons to the Vice-Chancellor's study took Martin by surprise. Was he about to be assigned as a common scribbler? Or had the whispers made their way to someone with *real* power? He knocked on the door, but there was no response from within. Impatient, he knocked again, with the same result. *Who does he think he is to make me wait like a servant?* Then it dawned on him. *He's Dean of the College of Cardinals – the most influential man here save only the Pope. This calls for charm not contempt.* He took a deep breath, squared his shoulders, and imagined every benefice that was in this man's power to grant. When the summons to enter finally came, he strode confidently across the room to kneel and kiss the ring on des Près's outstretched hand.

"Please take a seat, Father de Villiers," said the cardinal.

"Thank you, Eminence."

"I think we both know why you're here. With Cardinal Robert failing, you find yourself in need of a new role."

"That will be the case eventually, Eminence, but I pray every day that the cardinal might be restored to his former robust health."

Save me from the glavering platitudes. Does he think I'm an idiot? I'll tell you who the idiot is. Des Près kept his irritation to himself and his tone even. "As I'm sure we all do, but equally, we all know how unlikely that is. Which means you are in need of a new role." Des Près paused, expecting another obsequiousness, but this time, De Villiers held his tongue. "I'm given to understand," the cardinal continued, "that you believe your experience in Robert's service has prepared you to be a bishop. That's quite an elevation from an ordinary priest. Perhaps a more suitable next step would be dean of a cathedral chapter or archdeacon."

"As you say, Eminence, I've spent much time under Cardinal Robert's tutelage. And unlike an ordinary parish priest, I have experience of the workings of the Church at the most exalted levels, having been here for six years now. I do believe I'm ready for the bishop's throne." He noticed des Près's steepled fingers and slightly furrowed brow. *Time for some charm.* "But if, in your wisdom, sir, you consider that one should first serve as an archdeacon, I would step into that role. Especially if I had some indication of when I might expect to be advanced to the episcopacy."

"You do know, de Villiers, that neither of these positions just come available whenever someone wants to step into them. Someone must be promoted first . . . or someone must die."

"As many dioceses as there are, surely that happens all the time."

What a self-centered arse-monger! "There are openings from time to time. But if I understand you, it's not your wish to be relegated to some remote diocese in Hungary. It will take me some time to find you a suitable position. In the meantime, you must be patient and accept whatever assignments are given to you here. Is that a path you're prepared to follow?"

"It is, Eminence. Consider me to be in your service."

No, just under my supervision. "Very well, de Villiers. For now, continue to attend Robert and provide him whatever comfort you can in his final days. I'll have an assignment for you when the time comes." Des Près stood, signaling the end of the meeting. "Do not mess this up, de Villiers, or that purple sash you so covet will become forever out of your reach."

Martin gave a little bow of his head. "Yes, Eminence."

Once out in the corridor, he broke into a big grin. He'd done it. He was now the protégé of the most powerful cardinal in the Holy See.

Now he could think about that other business with the Cornish pig. He hadn't heard back from Wainwright. But the plague had interfered with that as well. Had Wainwright succumbed? Or was he just being stubborn? Time for another letter.

You're mine now, de Villiers, thought des Près. *You're so self-centered you think I've promised to make you a bishop. Think what you like. But you've no notion of the infinite number of ways I can keep you in line. You have a lot to learn about how things work in this place and in the Church.*

The blank page, ink pot, and quill were already in position on his writing table – something he'd seen to while he made de Villiers wait in the corridor. Sitting back down, he picked up the quill and dipped it in the ink.

May the blessings of God be upon you, my dear friend, as they most surely have been upon us both to have come through the years of plague unscathed. The disease ravaged this city, killing half of its inhabitants, and the Holy Father had to consecrate the river as a sacred burial place since there was no land left for interments. I know not if it was God or the walls of this fortress in which we live and work that protected us, but I'm grateful for both. Sadly, the Church lost six of her cardinals, as I'm sure you know by now.

However, it's not to speak of past sickness that I take up my quill but to tell you that both Adhémar Robert and Pierre Roger are in ill health. I fear I shall have to preside over a Conclave before the year is out.

Nor is it of that particular task that I write to you but of the decidedly distasteful one I've just completed. I learned long ago that it's best, on such occasions, to simply squeeze one's nose and get on with it, which is precisely what I've done. This morning, I summoned Martin de Villiers to my study. Even in this brief encounter, his manner was undisguised.

As I write this, John, I'm reminded of Duèze's categories. I can just imagine him, Solomon-like, splitting the man in half and dropping one half into the ambitious and the other into the sycophants.

But I digress. What matters is that, in anticipation of Robert departing this earth, I've taken de Villiers under my personal control. In his pompousness, he's construed my words to convince himself I've promised to make him a bishop, but of course, I've done no such thing. If I'm any judge of men, though, I think believing himself to be attached to my high office will be sufficient to keep him here, poised to be the first to present himself when a diocese that he considers worthy should come open. To that end, John, we must both pray for the good health and long life of every bishop this side of Constantinople.

Pierre

Written at Avignon on the XXVII day of April in the year of our Lord MCCCLII

Fairfield, Derbyshire, May 25th, 1352

Father Wainwright handed the messenger a farthing for his trouble. Clearly disgruntled, the man looked from his still outstretched hand to Wainwright and back again. "I'm sorry, it's all I have. The coffers are empty." The man growled something in a language Wainwright didn't understand, leapt onto his horse, and galloped away.

Opening the letter, Wainwright glanced at the signature and let out a deep sigh. The first thought that crossed his mind was decidedly uncharitable. *Too bad the plague didn't put you out of your misery, Martin. Or more to the point, out of **my** misery.*

Without even reading the missive, he walked inside and tossed it onto the cooking fire. *Nothing wrong with letting him think the plague found its way here.* But then another thought struck him. *If he's still obsessed with his crusade against Chegwin, maybe I really **should** write to that bishop this time.*

But it would have to wait. The king's hunting party was due to arrive on the morrow. They would expect him to bless the hunt and might even want a mass of thanksgiving for their continued good health. Then, two days later was Whitsunday. And he didn't know how long the king expected to remain in these parts. At least when they left, his coffers would be full once again.

XXVIII

Tintagel, June 1358

They'd known it was over when Étienne arrived at the gate driving a pony cart laden with crates of sacramental wine and dried meat. No one had ventured close to the gates much less banged on them so relentlessly since they'd barred them against the plague, so it took some time to remove the heavy bars and haul open the gates on either side of the drawbridge before they could make their way to where Étienne waited, alternately pounding on the gate and calling out, "Piran, it's me . . . Bonfils. If you're not all dead in there, let me in."

When they finally got the outer gate opened, Étienne drove the cart inside then jumped down and the two friends embraced as Jori looked on. When they broke the embrace, Piran assailed Étienne with questions. "Give us the news. We haven't had any since the plague came to Bodmin and we locked ourselves in here. Did it come to Chudleigh? Is Father well? What about those in Exeter? And Launceston. Did you see my family on the way here?"

"Slow down, Piran," said Étienne. "One question at a time."

As he closed the gate, Jori muttered, "Wonderful. I survive a plague of sickness and now I'm visited by a plague of priests." Piran roared with laughter as he translated Jori's words for Étienne.

"You can leave the gate unbarred, Piran," said Étienne. "It's over at last."

Since Étienne showed no sign of returning to the cart, Jori jumped in, grabbed the reins, and clucked to the pony. The two priests followed on foot.

"Is it really over, Étienne?" asked Piran.

"It seems to be. King Edward has resumed the fighting in France. The French broke the truce at the beginning of this year and tried to retake Calais, but the English quickly quashed the attempt. And it's generally expected that Edward will summon Parliament to meet early next year.

"So for the rest of your questions. We, all of us, in Chudleigh survived. We got in extra supplies after you left, and then Father insisted that no one leave the manor. Anything that was delivered to us had to be left outside and brought in later. It never came to the village either."

"And Father?"

"Is well. Now. Two of his sisters died. Agnes two years ago, Katherine late last year. Katherine's death hit him really hard and he grieved deeply throughout the winter. I have a letter from him in my satchel. I don't know how much he'll say about how deeply saddened he was, but since the spring flowers arrived, his spirit appears renewed.

"And yes, I did check on your family on my way here. All is well. You father is showing his age a bit more than when I first met him, but that's most likely from worry over the past couple of years."

That had been eight years ago. Étienne came back just before Christmas that same year. Together, he and Piran had celebrated Christmas Eve mass using de Grandison's new order of service. The only music they had was what they could make with their own voices – which both agreed was a far cry from what would be heard in the cathedral that night – but the very act of trying made them both feel closer to the days before the specter of disease and death changed everything. Étienne had stayed through Twelfth Night. That year, even in the tiny village of Tintagel, which had mostly escaped the ravages of the plague, the revels of Twelfth Night were more about celebrating their freedom to get on with life than anything else. Someone had brought a fresh barrel of ale from Bodmin, and it was empty by the time the cock crowed on the morning of January 7th.

Since that time, every June brought a visit from either Étienne or the archdeacon, and every visit brought Piran's salary and a letter from Father de Grandison – from Étienne as well, if it was the archdeacon who came. Piran answered every letter with joy, feeling the bonds of friendship as strongly as ever despite his remoteness from those friends. And every year, Jori complained that the wine they brought was "that holy stuff and not something a man can get drunk on."

Four years ago, Piran had questioned Étienne about the bishop's plans and when someone else might be assigned to take over the king's commission. "After all, he gave me the commission to be safe from the plague, which is well and truly over now. Surely some parish has become available where I could be of more use than staying here."

"I've asked him that myself," Étienne had replied, "and don't have a really satisfactory answer for you. I know he's still worried about the specter of de Villiers. When Cardinal Robert died, de Villiers lost what he saw as his path to advancement. Cardinal des Près has kept him in Avignon for now, but Father's worried de Villiers might grow restive in the confines of the papal court and that he might decide to go elsewhere to find a new champion to press his cause. If we lost track of him . . ." Étienne let the thought hang in the air for a moment. "The only thing I can say, Piran, is that Father's first concern is for your safety. Perhaps, in a while, if de Villiers shows no inclination to leave Avignon . . ."

It wasn't the answer Piran was hoping for, but at least it was an explanation.

This year, Étienne's visit was to be longer than ever. "Any objection if I stay through St. Morwenna's day?" he asked when he arrived on Midsummer's Eve.

Piran could barely contain his delight. Jori was rather more sanguine about the idea until he discovered that two of the crates contained wine from the bishop's cellar that had absolutely no connection to the Eucharist. "Just don't drink it all at once, Jori," Piran admonished. "I'd really like to have some for myself."

Jori grinned. "Well, now, mayhap you can have a glass or two."

"Mayhap we should put some of it back so we can both have a glass or two now and again even after Étienne leaves."

"You see what I have to put up with, Father Bonfils? This one has no notion of a good time."

Piran and Étienne celebrated the daily masses together, often incorporating some of Father de Grandison's new orders of service. "All England's still talking about the prince's great victory at Poitiers last autumn and how he captured the French king," Étienne said as they left the little chapel on the first day. "Seems your prayers are powerful indeed, my friend."

"I can't take all the credit," said Piran. "The prince has other titles, so I've no doubt there are priests in Wales and Woodstock adding to my own poor entreaties. And probably Westminster and Canterbury too, just for good measure."

They spent the afternoons walking about the headland, often going right to the edge of the cliffs to watch the waves crashing below. Or they'd make their way down to the haven with its natural stone quay where a single ship could shelter from the wind and surf to load or unload men or supplies. On the south side of the haven was a little beach where they could watch the waves crashing into the cave and, if the day was particularly warm, remove their shoes and wade in the water's edge. But it was a long climb back up to the chapel. In the evenings, they'd find themselves in the kitchen, enjoying Jori's tasty meals. The little garden Piran and Jori had planted during the plague years still flourished, and Jori worked magic with its produce.

On the evening before Étienne was to depart, Piran was in a particularly pensive mood. "Chin up, old friend," Étienne said. "Yes, I have to go home, but it's not like I won't be back. And who knows . . . your duty here may soon be finished. If the French king can raise the ransom Edward has demanded, the war may come to a close. And if it does, the prince will no longer be in danger."

"Oh, it's not your departure that's on my mind, though I'll miss you – there's no question of that. No, it's something else. Of late, I feel a presence on the headland. Yes, I feel the presence of God in the chapel and all about – like I always have – but this is something different – something I can't put a name to. I feel it most strongly in the meadow around the chapel but also along the southern cliffs. Do you sense it too, Étienne?"

"I hadn't noticed anything unusual, but maybe I just don't know what to look for or listen for or . . ."

"Nor would I even know how to tell you. I can't help but wonder, Étienne . . . have I been here so long that the remoteness is starting to play tricks on my mind?"

"Your mind seems as sound to me as it always has, Piran."

"But you're not inside my head. You don't feel what I feel in my . . . I don't know . . . Is it in my bones? In my soul?"

Despite the fact that Jori hadn't said a word, Piran realized the caretaker had been staring at him intently, his brow furrowed. *Is that because he's struggling to understand what I'm saying?* Piran wondered. *I **was** speaking English, wasn't I?* Though Piran and Étienne usually lapsed into French – the language in which they'd become friends – when they were alone, they always reverted to English in Jori's presence. The caretaker was still more comfortable with Cornish, but he usually managed to keep up well enough. "What's troubling you, Jori?" Piran asked. "Are we speaking too fast?"

"Oh, no, Father. It just be . . . well, mayhap you be right."

"Right that my mind is playing tricks on me?"

"Nay. Right in what you be feeling. The villagers, they tell stories."

"What kind of stories, Jori?"

"About what happened here . . . back in the dark times."

"Tell us," said Étienne.

"'Twere back when Gorlois ruled in these parts. Weren't called England then. Not Kernow either. The stories say Gorlois had a great fortress here . . . out on the headland. And that was where Ygraine betrayed Gorlois with Uther. Or Uther betrayed Gorlois with Ygraine. Depends who tells the story. There's an old man in the village – he says it's the spirit of those times."

"You mean like ghosts?" Étienne asked.

"Not so much ghosts . . . not people in Purgatory. More like . . . Don't know how to say in English."

"Then tell me," said Piran, "and I'll explain it to Étienne."

"The old man says it's everything about that time and place and what happened trying to come back. Trying to prove they're not just legends but something that really happened. Like they don't want to be forgotten. The old folks say that's why, when the feeling is strongest, there'll be stormy weather . . . like the past is trying to break through."

"Do you feel it too, Jori?"

"Aye. But it's been a long time."

"Why haven't you said anything?"

"People who don't sense it think you're crazy . . . think you've been at the drink too much or are possessed by the devil. And you being a priest and all . . ."

Piran took a moment to tell Étienne what the caretaker was saying and then reverted back to Cornish. "When did you last feel it, Jori?"

"The year before you came. And oh, we had some bad storms that summer. Some nights, the lightning lit up the sky like it was broad daylight. And the thunder was fierce."

"That's been a long time."

"The old folks say it's impossible to know when it will happen. And I just thought maybe all your Godliness was keeping the ancient spirits at bay."

"So why do you think they've come back?"

"Maybe they were just biding their time . . . waiting until they could reach through to you. But now they have, there'll be storms this summer. You mark my words."

XXIX

The two weeks following Étienne's departure brought some of the most glorious summer weather Piran could remember at Tintagel. Sunny skies. Now and then a puffy white cloud in the brilliant blue sky. Sunsets so magnificent that they warranted walking out to sit at the cliff edge and watch the great orange orb slip below the edge of the sea in the far distance while the waves crashed against the rocks below.

Still, he couldn't shake the feeling that there was another presence on the headland. He told himself he'd allowed Jori's stories about the dark times to infect his mind – to overcome rational thinking. Surely there was nothing more to it than folklore and ancient superstitions. But folklore had deep traditions, almost always rooted in some ancient truth and passed from generation to generation during the time when common folk could neither read nor write. If souls lost in Purgatory could manifest as ghosts, could it be that these really were lost souls? But didn't ghosts take on their likeness from life so their descendants would recognize them? He'd seen no wraiths – no ethereal forms. Only felt a power that he couldn't name.

On the feast day of St. Etheidwitha, they woke to a gentle rain – exactly what their little garden needed to be sure the plants didn't wither before they could produce their bounty. When it was time to celebrate the daily mass, Piran threw his oiled wool cloak over his cassock and pulled up the hood. Even though the rain wasn't coming down in torrents, he preferred not to put his vestments on over wet clothing. If the vestments got wet, they wouldn't dry easily inside the cool, dark chapel, even in summer.

In addition to his prayers for the duke this morning, he invoked God's blessing on his eldest sister's family. Étienne had stopped in Launceston on the way, as he always did, and reported that there was a new life expected to arrive sometime in July. Piran was to be a great-uncle. So he prayed that his niece would be safely delivered and that the child would thrive.

And wondered how long it might be before he was able to see the wee one for himself. Now that the plague was long gone, Piran was beginning to feel the constraints of his commitment to daily masses so far from those he loved. Perhaps he should write to Father and ask if the king would begrudge him a brief leave to visit his family. He chastised himself for not thinking of that before Étienne left. *Nothing for it now, Piran. You'll either have to go into Bodmin to find a messenger or wait until next year.*

When he emerged from the chapel, the rain had stopped and the clouds had vanished. The wet grass gleamed in the brilliant sunshine, and the droplets of rain still clinging to the shrubs and garden plants sparkled like gemstones.

As he made his way across the meadow, he was drawn toward a sound that seemed to come from somewhere near the south cliffs. Music? It reminded him of songs he'd heard played on the harp when the lord of the manor where his father worked would hold a banquet in summer. They'd leave all the windows open so the music wafted outside, and Piran's father would let his children sit on the lawn to listen.

But there were no musicians here on the headland. No harp. Yet Piran felt himself inexorably drawn to the sound and his feet propelled him toward the cliffs. *Perhaps it's water dripping on the rocks below. That happens sometimes after a rain.* But he'd never heard real melodies before – just a ping, ping, ping. And when he looked over the cliff edge, the little pools left in the depressions in the rock were all smooth as glass and the sun caught no glimmer of falling droplets.

Turning to retrace his steps, he tried to shake off the experience. Surely this was nothing more than his memories of those childhood days on the baron's lawn coming back to him strongly as he'd thought of his sister and her children and the grandchild soon to be born.

Later, over supper, he asked Jori, "Have you ever heard the sound of music out in the meadow?"

"Sometimes, when the wind blows from just the right direction, it reverberates in the cave and sounds almost like someone playing a flute."

"Whatever this was, it seemed to be coming from the south cliffs. And it didn't sound at all like a flute. More like a harp or maybe a gittern."

Jori looked up from his potage long enough to give Piran a quizzical look, then resumed eating. They finished the meal in silence, but as Jori gathered up the empty bowls and spoons, he said, "You know, the old folks say Ygraine played the harp."

They passed the rest of the evening as they did most nights – Piran reading for the fourth or fifth time one of the books in the small library he'd assembled from what he'd brought with him and Étienne's occasional additions and Jori mending a harness or polishing a saddle or honing a knife or tool. Nothing more was said about music on the headland.

But as Piran climbed into his bed, Jori's words echoed in his mind. "They say Ygraine played the harp."

XXX

For the next week, Piran walked the headland every day, hoping to discover what phenomenon had caused the musical sounds he'd heard. Perhaps if he could hear it again – not being so surprised as the first time – he could act more quickly to find the source. *After all,* he reasoned, *it's not out of the question that my original notion of water dropping on the rocks was right and, by the time I got to the cliffs, there were no more droplets left to fall.* But no matter how many times he crisscrossed the meadows or walked the full circuit around the outer edge, the only sounds he heard were the wind and the waves and the calls of the sea birds soaring overhead.

Yet that feeling of another presence persisted. And sometimes, if he woke in the middle of the night, that melody echoed in his mind. *Am I going mad?* he would wonder at such times. *I've heard it said that people who spend too much time alone – men locked up in a dungeon for months or years – even hermits, at times – actually lose their minds and see and hear things that aren't there.* But the morning light would always bring reassurance. He wasn't completely alone. Jori would notice if something was that wrong. And he wasn't having visions. Mad people, it was said, often had visions.

Perhaps, though, there was a way to begin to make sense of whatever this was. Over supper one evening, he asked Jori, "The old man in the village . . .

the one who knows about the dark times . . . do you think he'd speak with me?"

"He might. I'll ask his daughter."

The daughter, it turned out, was a grandmother – or more likely, a great-grandmother. When she met them at the door of one of the larger cottages in the village, her welcome was effusive. "I'm *so* glad you're here. My father's been beside himself all morning, knowing you were coming. I haven't seen him so excited in . . . well, I can't remember when."

From inside came a voice. "Don't you be talking about me like I can't hear you, Morgana. And don't leave them on the doorstep. Bring them in, girl. Bring them in."

In the small but well-lit sitting room, an ancient man sat beside the window, a blanket across his legs for warmth. "Come in, come in." He waved a hand energetically to beckon them in. "Best ye sit right here beside me, young man." He pointed to Piran then patted the seat of the chair next to his. Piran turned the chair slightly before sitting down so they'd be face to face.

"I knew you would come," the old man continued. "The feelings were so strong this summer, it had to be more than just the past times wanting to be heard."

"Jori's told me you know a lot about the past times, sir," said Piran.

"Aye. And I know about the spirit of those times. It doesn't come to me so strong now that I can't walk the headland, but it comes nonetheless. And you feel it too, don't you? That's why you're here, isn't it?"

"I feel something, yes. I just don't know what it is."

The old man reached out and patted Piran's arm. "'Tis the past, my boy. 'Tis what happened on that headland so long ago. And folks today – they think it's just made-up stories – just legends from some long-ago ballad singer made up to pass the long winter nights. But I know better."

"Will you tell me?"

The old man studied Piran for a long moment then nodded his head. "'Twas all about Ygraine, you see. Everything that happened. She was the most beautiful woman anyone had ever seen in these parts, and Gorlois had won her hand. But he knew men would lust after her, so he installed her in his fortress here on the headland where he knew no one could steal her away.

"But he hadn't counted on Merlin."

Piran held up his hand to interrupt. "Who's Merlin?"

"No one's really sure. It's said he was a wizard. Could transform himself into an owl when it suited his needs. Could transform a man into someone else. Had potions to make a man fall in love or fall asleep or forget things or grow old or stay youthful or be strong in battle. That cave you can see from the haven? 'Twas his. He could disappear into the cave and come out at any place on earth he wanted to be. And he used all his powers, all his magic, in the service of Uther Pendragon. And that's how it all went wrong."

The old man paused and gazed wistfully out the window. When it seemed as if he'd forgotten he wasn't alone, his daughter prompted from across the room where she and Jori sat watching. "Go on, *Tasik*."

He turned his gaze back to Piran, scrutinizing him again just as he had before. "It was Merlin who made it possible for Uther to bed Ygraine. And that's what led to the great battle. And everything that followed . . . well, men today think it's just a story . . . just a romantic notion of a golden age that never really was. But I know better . . . and my grandfather knew better . . . and his grandfather before him . . . all the way back to those times. And that's why sometimes the spirits of those times speak to us . . . to remind us never to let it be forgotten. *That's* what you're sensing, my boy.

"My grandson never felt the call, and now he's been gone these last fifteen years. But I told Morgana there would be another. I was sure of it. And now you've come. But there's something else you should know."

"What's that, sir?" Piran asked.

"You'll never see ghosts. But there'll be signs. Something you hear. A scent on the wind. A fleeting glance of something that's not there when you look back. And whenever the feeling's the strongest, you can be certain there'll be a storm and that storm will rage as the battle when Gorlois discovered Uther's treachery."

"You mean like the music I thought I heard near the south cliffs one day?"

The old man's eyes lit up. "You see, Morgana?" He shook a bony finger at his daughter. "I told you there'd be another." Then he turned his attention back to Piran. "Aye, son. Just so." Then he began humming a melody – the same melody Piran had heard – the same melody that had played in his dreams from time to time since that day by the cliff.

"And you experienced all these things yourself?" Piran asked.

"Aye. Especially when I could walk the headland. But I'm old now and too feeble to go there anymore."

"How old are you, sir?"

"I've lost track. But I know I was fourteen when I marched with Longshanks the first time he went to conquer the Welsh. An army as big as anyone had ever seen. They said there were fifteen thousand of us. And I marched proudly with Earl Richard's men. It was the year after Earl Richard finished his castle – the same one they're letting crumble to ruin now."

Piran quickly did the arithmetic in his head. That would make the old man ninety-five or thereabouts if he really was fourteen at the time. Boys younger than that had been known to go to war, but even so . . . "That must have been quite a sight, sir," Piran said.

The old man reached out and patted Piran's arm once again. "That it was. You come visit me again sometime and I'll tell you all about it. And call me Arthur. 'Twas my grandfather's name and his grandfather before him. 'Tis what we should have called my grandson, but Morgana wouldn't have it. Insisted on calling him Jago, after his father."

Piran rose from his chair. "Best we go now, Arthur. I don't want to tire you too much. But thank you for seeing me."

"You come back any time, boy. You come back and, if you like, I'll tell you all about the dark times."

"I'd like that very much."

As they stepped outside, Morgana stood in the open doorway. "Please come back, Father. It may not mean that much to you, but it would mean the world to him. Ever since my son died . . . nay, even before that . . . ever since my *tas* knew that Jago didn't feel the spirits, he's fretted that their stories would be lost. When I've tried to reassure him that others know the legends, he dismisses me, insisting no one knows all that he does. So if you could humor him a bit in his old age, I'd be truly grateful."

"Put your mind at rest, mistress," said Piran. "I'll be back from time to time."

XXXI

As July rolled into August with only the occasional light rain shower, Piran chided Jori. "I thought you promised dreadful storms this summer."

"Summer isn't over yet. Neither are my feelings about another presence with us here on the headland."

Piran hadn't paid much attention to presences of late. Much more on his mind was a growing desire to see his family. His little great-niece or nephew would have come into the world by now, and he was surprised at how much he longed to see the child. He hadn't felt this way when any of his sisters' children were born. What was different this time? Had the plague made so great an impression on him of his own mortality? Or was it merely the fact that Launceston was both so close and so out of reach?

He'd decided not to write directly to de Grandison about his desire to visit his family but to first seek Étienne's opinion. He'd been mulling that letter in his head for the past few weeks, but the knowledge that the following day would be Jori's monthly trip to Bodmin for supplies finally spurred him to action

My dear Étienne,

Time moves on apace here on the headland. July brought several gentle rains with the result that our little garden is on the brink of providing our best

harvest ever. I've no doubt that we will have enough to share with the villagers, which makes my heart filled with the joy of God's grace.

There's a matter that I was remiss in not discussing with you during your stay here and that now weighs on my mind from time to time. I know that my commission from the king is for mass to be celebrated every day for his son. Yet I'm beset by a longing to see my family and see for myself how they fare. It has, after all, been ten years since last I was in Launceston.

My question to you is whether it would even be fitting for me to ask Father if I might be permitted a visit. Perhaps he might allow you to say mass there for the duke while I'm away. It would not be here in this chapel, as the king prescribed, but it would ensure that the daily masses continue uninterrupted.

I have no wish to place the burden on you to make the request on my behalf – only that you tell me whether you think it wise for me to write to Father myself.

May God's blessings be upon you, Étienne, and upon Father de Grandison
Piran
Written at Tintagel, the 7th day of August 1358

He would have to trust Jori to find a reliable messenger. It took half a day to get to Bodmin, so Jori usually made the journey south one day, bought his supplies, then made the return journey the next day. Even if he managed to buy his supplies straightaway and return before nightfall, the trip took a full day. That meant Piran couldn't go along since he needed to celebrate mass every day. So he gave Jori some extra money to pay the messenger and said a little prayer that the letter would eventually find its way to Étienne.

Jori returned with flour, wine, barley for brewing ale, even a bit of fresh meat – and a decidedly unfavorable opinion of the cost of a messenger. "Wanted a whole shilling to go to Chudleigh and wait for a reply. A shilling for four, maybe five days' work when good messengers for the army get maybe eight, nine shillings for a whole year? Not worth more than three pennies, by my reckoning. But the butcher said the man was reliable, and I know how much store you set by having that letter get where it's going, so I bargained him down to nine pennies and he didn't have to travel on days it was raining. Course, that means you owe me another three pennies on top of the extra you already gave me."

Piran was highly amused by Jori's pique, but merely smiled. "It's alright, Jori. Think about it. The man probably doesn't get many jobs during the year, but he's still got to feed his family."

"Buy himself extra drink, more like." Jori was in no mood to be appeased.

"Just let me run up to my room and fetch your pennies, then I'll help you unload the wagon."

When he finished celebrating mass on the feast day of St. Just – with an extra prayer that Étienne might be, even in that moment, writing a reply to his letter – Piran decided it was time he paid another visit to old Arthur. In other circumstances, he might have first inquired of Morgana when would be an opportune time for a visit, but her plea at the door for him to return seemed a sufficient invitation to come at any time. Arthur certainly had little to occupy his days, and spending some time with the old man might just take the edge off Piran's impatience to learn when he might visit his family.

Morgana's cheery welcome proved his assumption correct. "*Tasik*, look who's come back," she announced as she showed Piran into the sitting room where Arthur sat in exactly the same place Piran had first met him. It was as if he hadn't moved at all in the intervening two weeks.

And just as he had before, Arthur beckoned to Piran and patted the seat of the nearest chair. "I told you he'd be back, Morgana. Now you fetch us some small ale, girl. Wouldn't help if my tongue should go dry while we talk." As Morgana left to do Arthur's bidding, Piran made himself comfortable across from the old man, who added, "You're back to hear about the dark times, aren't you, lad?"

"Aye, Arthur. If you're willing to talk about them."

Arthur's eyes sparkled and he sat up a bit straighter. "It was all about Ygraine, you see. Such a beauty she was. Hair like spun gold. Eyes the color of the sky on a cloudless summer day. The skin of her face and hands a soft ivory. And she played the harp more beautifully than any angel ever did. Gorlois could scarcely believe his luck in winning her hand.

"He was content, hoping to soon welcome his heir into the world, when things took an unexpected turn. The Deheubarth began raiding the northern coast along the Mor Havren. So he had to muster his forces to repel the invaders, lest they gain a foothold from which they could march on his lands. And that's where he encountered Uther Pendragon."

He paused when Morgana returned with two mugs of small ale. "You just let me know, Father, if you need more," she said, handing Piran one of the mugs as she set the other on the small table beside her father's chair. "You're welcome to stay as long as you want."

Arthur waved her away. "Shoo, girl. I was just about to tell him how Gorlois met Uther." Morgana smiled broadly and hurried away as Arthur took a long swallow from his mug before continuing. "Now where was I? Oh, yes. Uther's stronghold was near Ynys Witrin, but he had the same concerns about the Deheubarth and had marched his own army. When they met in the field, they decided to join forces, and together, they sent the Deheubarth scurrying back across the water to their own lands."

"Were those lands what we now call Wales?" Piran asked.

"Aye. Some of the same places we went when I marched with Longshanks all those years ago. I was too young then to care about such things, but when Longshanks had to put down the Welsh yet again – seven years later it was – it came to me that those Welsh rebels had to be descendants of the Deheubarth – still trying to encroach into another kingdom."

"Did you fight with the English that second time?"

"Nay, I had a wife by then and they weren't mustering nearly as many men, so there was no reason for me to go."

"That must have been a relief."

"Aye. Who knows what might have happened if I'd been in battle again? I might not have survived. Might not be here to tell you the tale and be sure what happened isn't forgotten."

"So what did happen?"

"When they repelled the Deheubarth together, Gorlois declared Uther his best friend, and they swore to remain allies to keep the peace and keep the invaders out. To celebrate the victory and their alliance, Gorlois brought Uther to the fortress on the headland for a great feast, and that's when Uther first laid eyes on Ygraine. He was smitten with her straightaway. But he managed to conceal his fascination from Gorlois, and they returned to the north coast as great friends.

"Despite his outward demeanor of loyalty to his friend and ally, Uther was consumed with a desire for Ygraine that he couldn't suppress, which led him to enlist Merlin's help so that he might bed her. And that's where things began to go wrong."

"You said Merlin was thought to be some kind of sorcerer. Some kind of specter, perhaps?" said Piran.

"Oh, he was flesh and blood, but he had skills no ordinary man possessed and could see things and do things no ordinary man could accomplish. But that's a story for another day. For the next time you come."

Piran wasn't certain if Arthur was tiring or if he was just wanted to ensure there'd be another visit. Either way, Piran was happy to go along. "I'll visit again, Arthur. You can be sure of that."

"Best you do, boy. I have to be sure you know everything so what really happened isn't lost in the mists."

As he made his way back home, it occurred to Piran that he could give Arthur a gift beyond just the time to listen to the stories. *If I write them down, I can show him they won't be forgotten. Even if he can't read, Morgana can see to it that the pages are passed down through the generations of her family. And surely there are some among the younger ones now who **can** read.*

XXXII

As the days of August marched on, the weather remained fair. But on the eve of the feast day of St. Hugh the Little, the late afternoon brought a strong breeze from the northwest and a build-up of clouds over the sea. Even before sundown, the clouds approaching the land were dark and threatening. By the time Piran found his bed for the night, the storm was raging in the distance.

Were these the storms Jori had predicted? The storms the old villagers claimed were the past trying to break through? A shiver suddenly ran down Piran's spine. He hadn't been aware of that mysterious presence on the headland recently, but now . . .

Get a grip on yourself, Piran. Jori can no more predict the future than the past can reassert itself into the present. He said a quick prayer that the storm would remain north of them and not beat down their flourishing garden then climbed into bed.

Sometime in the middle of the night, a loud clap of thunder brought him instantly awake. Was the storm closer? He rose from his bed to look out the window, but could see little besides the buildings across the way and the flashes of light to the north. Anxious about what might be happening outside, he opened the door and stepped onto landing at the top of the stairs leading from his rooms to the ground. Here, he had a better view of the lightning streaking across the sky. It appeared Trevethy and Trevelgi were taking the brunt of the storm; here there was nothing more than a bit of wind and the sound of the distant thunder. *So why had the thunder-clap that woke him seemed so near?*

And then he heard something different. The call of an owl. It seemed to come from the general direction of the stable. He didn't remember having seen an owl on the headland before but they were, after all, nocturnal, so that shouldn't necessarily surprise him. *But why haven't I ever heard one before in all these years?* He stepped back inside and made sure the door was securely latched against the wind then climbed back into bed.

He woke the next morning in a state of bewilderment. After he'd returned to bed, his sleep was troubled by an odd series of dreams. In one, he watched a man in a woodland clearing mixing paint and then applying it to pieces of cloth. One seemed to be a tunic with a coat of arms on it, to which the man added a yellow crown. The rest were just strips of linen that he smeared with an odd shade of red that looked a bit like dried blood.

That dream disappeared to be replaced by one with a man standing on a drawbridge by the gatehouse of a fortress. Was it the same man he'd seen in the forest clearing? The face seemed vaguely similar, but this man looked like a wounded soldier. Whoever he was, he was talking with someone unseen, apparently inside the barely open entrance door to the fortress.

"Everything alright out there?" came from inside.

"Quiet as can be. Heard an owl earlier, but that's all."

The door opened a little more, but no one came out. "Where's your partner?" asked the voice.

"Taking a piss."

"Don't see him. No need to go anywhere to do that. Just piss off the side of the bridge."

"Well . . . Don't tell anyone, alright? He's having a swive with the village trollop at the edge of the ravine on the other end of the bridge."

Silence from inside. At long last, there was a quiet laugh. "He's not the first, is he?"

"Won't be the last either, by my reckoning."

"Alright, then, I'll just get back to my rounds."

And at that moment, the rooster crowed, jarring Piran to wakefulness. Splashing some cold water on his face seemed to dispel some of the cobwebs, and when he stepped out onto the landing, the air was crisp and clear, as so often happened after a storm. He found Jori just finishing his inspections. "Not sure we even got much rain, Father," the caretaker said. "Water barrels look about the same level as yesterday."

"Did you hear that loud crack of thunder sometime in the middle of the night?"

"Slept like a log. Didn't hear a thing – not even the wind – after I climbed into bed."

*How could something have seemed that loud to me and **he** never even noticed it?* Piran wondered. Aloud, he said, "Then I suppose you didn't hear the owl either."

"Owl? Haven't heard one in an age. Not sure they much like the wind that swirls around the headland. As long as there's good hunting inland, where it's calmer, there's no need for them to venture out here."

When Piran still felt disoriented by his dreams after he finished celebrating mass, he decided a visit to Arthur was in order. Collecting the pages he'd written after their last conversation, he made his way to the old man's cottage.

"I thought you might come today" were the first words out of Arthur's mouth.

"I had a restless night, Arthur, and thought you might help me make sense of it."

Arthur smiled. "The presence was strong. I could sense it even here. And you have questions, don't you?"

Piran found the old man's apparent ability to see inside his head unnerving, but in truth, that's why he had come here, after all. "Did you hear that great clap of thunder in the middle of the night, Arthur? It was so loud, I thought the storm was right on top of us."

"Morgana told me this morning no such thing happened."

"Jori said the same, but that's what woke me up. When I stepped outside, all signs of the storm were away to the north. That's when I heard the owl, but Jori says owls don't frequent the headland."

Arthur's entire face lit up, his eyes ablaze with excitement. "That was Merlin making his presence known. Remember when you first came here and I told you there'd be signs? What else did you hear last night?"

"Nothing, but I had two very strange dreams." Piran proceeded to describe his dreams, surprised at how much detail he remembered.

"Ah, my boy ..." Arthur reached out and patted Piran's arm. "You truly are the one the spirits are speaking to. So best I get on with their story."

"Please. I need to find some way to make sense of the strange things happening in my mind."

"Gorlois and Uther were back in the north, their armies spread out all along the coast. The Deheubarth were making new forays across the Mor Havren, just one or two boats at a time, testing the defenses, looking for a weak point where they could bring a large army ashore, while Gorlois and Uther tried to decide where to eventually amass their forces to prevent an invasion.

"But Uther was still obsessed with Ygraine, and Merlin knew Uther wouldn't rest until he got his wish – until he bedded Ygraine. Merlin also knew it was up to him to satisfy his master's desires in complete secrecy. So he devised a reason for the two of them to ride south – scouting for Deheubarth activity along the west coast. When they reached Tintagel, Merlin transformed Uther to look like Gorlois, put the sentries into a deep sleep, and stood guard while Uther had his way with Ygraine. Then they rode back north, scouting enough possible landing sites along the way to give a factual report on their return. Of course, Merlin had removed their disguises and restored the sentries to wakefulness shortly after they left Tintagel.

"Uther basked in contentment, assuring Merlin it was the sweetest experience ever a man could have and that it had all been worth it. The stories say Merlin was less sanguine about the adventure having been a good idea.

"So the owl you heard last night, my boy, was Merlin announcing his presence. And your dreams? Bits and pieces of what happened coming through. Just not enough for you to see the whole picture."

Piran wasn't sure if this was comforting or not. One thing he was certain of. "I . . . I've never experienced anything like this, Arthur. I don't quite know what to make of it."

"The headland is a mystical place, lad. And I think mayhap it's because you already deal in the spiritual – albeit with God and Heaven and all – that you have a natural connection to other spirits."

"But pagan spirits?"

"Were they pagan or Christian? I don't know. Does it matter?"

"I don't know. I suppose they could have been either. Certainly St. Piran came to Cornwall not too long after the Romans left, so maybe . . ."

"Either way, they've sought you out, lad, and this won't be the last you'll hear from them."

As he was preparing to leave, Piran remembered the pages he'd brought with him and produced them from inside the sleeve of his cassock. "I know you're worried, Arthur, that the stories will be lost, so I've taken the liberty of writing down everything you've told me. If you'll allow me, I'll keep doing it and then you can pass everything on to your great-grandchildren and they to theirs, to keep the stories alive."

Arthur's eyes glistened with moisture as he reached for the pages. "You'd do this for me?"

"Of course."

"Then you truly are a gift from God."

Piran didn't go straight back to his rooms. He needed time to think – to try to make sense of what was happening to him. Arthur had said it was mystical. Mysticism was certainly a well-known phenomenon among saints and hermits and holy men. But he was no saint, despite his name, so why would he have a mystical experience?

Surely it was nothing more than his mind playing tricks on him in his dreams. Like the time he was so badly injured in the fight and slept for three days, dreaming all the time that he was at home in the care of his loved ones. That was undoubtedly his mind seeking some form of comfort after the assault his body had endured. But what was his mind seeking here? Relief from the years of isolation in this remote place? That made sense.

It also made sense that he might dream about the stories Arthur told. But how could it be that he dreamed about something before Arthur actually related it?

Maybe it's better not to dwell on it, Piran, he told himself. *That way lies madness. Just think about the joy you're bringing into an old man's life. Would it really be all that different if you were a priest in a tiny village somewhere?*

He walked past the little garden, its plants standing proud in the afternoon sunshine. They'd already enjoyed beans, carrots, and parsnips, and it looked as if more onions would be ready in the next day or so. The small pear tree they'd planted five years ago was covered in fruit, and a few birds were helping themselves to a midday meal. Piran was happy to share the bounty with God's furry and feathered creatures, but it was time to claim some for himself and Jori.

He fetched a basket from the buttery and began collecting fruit from the lower branches. Any that had already been sampled he left for the next creature's meal. But there were many unmolested ones that went straight into the basket. When a pear he reached for came straight off in his hand without requiring a twist to separate it from the branch, he checked its ripeness by pressing gently on the neck. It gave to his touch, but wasn't mushy. Just right. He sank his teeth into the bulbous portion of the fruit, tearing away a generous bite, and began to chew. The sweetest pear he'd ever tasted.

XXXIII

Tintagel, June 1359

It was the archdeacon who brought Piran's purse and letters this year. Unlike in the past, he was accompanied by a man who drove the cart. "My messenger, driver . . . whatever I need him to be," said the archdeacon, omitting to mention the man's name. Too eager to read de Grandison's letter, Piran didn't pause to ask. Since he'd finally received Étienne's reply last autumn, he'd been on tenterhooks to learn if he would be permitted to visit his family.

When the messenger hired to take Piran's request to Chudleigh had seemingly disappeared, Piran had to reluctantly admit that Jori might have been right. For two months, Piran had wrestled with whether or not Étienne had even received his missive. Had the so-called messenger simply taken his nine pennies and gone his merry way? Piran had contemplated writing another letter but remained indecisive – what good would *that* do if there was no reliable messenger?

Then, near the end of October, Étienne's reply had arrived.

My dear Piran,

I can but imagine how impatient you've been with the delay in my reply and beg your forgiveness. I mulled your question for several days before deciding there was no harm in asking Father directly. He was sympathetic but unwilling to grant you permission without consulting the king. In fact, his exact words were, "I have no inclination to run afoul of the king's famous temper, so it's best we ask rather than assume."

But he has promised to put your request forward at the next meeting of Parliament and to give it his full endorsement if the king seems receptive to an ecclesiastical opinion. So now, all that remains is for the king to summon Parliament, which seems long overdue. Know that I'll be praying your request is granted . . . and soon.

Étienne

Now, thankful that the archdeacon was eager to be on his way, Piran helped Jori unload the cart and watched the visitors drive away before racing up to his room to open Father's letter.

Salutations with the blessings of God and ourselves
My dear Piran
As I am in no doubt what is foremost on your mind, I'll answer that question before proceeding to the news from here. Sadly, I have no answer at all. The king has not summoned Parliament so far this year. I can only surmise that it is because of the lull in the war and his expectation of receiving a sizable ransom from the French for the return of their king. Thus, he has no need of money at the moment and therefore no need of Parliament. I'm sure Étienne explained my reluctance to incite the king's ire. While it's known that he's far more temperate than his grandfather, Longshanks, it's equally known that, once angered, his rage can be just as fierce.

I have not forgotten you, Piran. And if I were certain it was within my power to grant, you would have been with your family long since. I beg you not to be disheartened. I will advocate for you at the very first opportunity.

Disappointment flooded through him. He set the letter aside. Perhaps he'd read the rest of it later. What he needed now was to find a way to make peace with another year of isolation here. *It may not be a year,* he told himself as he left his room and headed toward the gate that led out onto the headland. Jori had abandoned the idea of keeping the gate locked years ago when it had become too much trouble to produce the key day after day after day for Piran to go to the chapel.

Which was where he headed now. When he stepped inside, he was overcome by a sense of futility. *Does any of this really matter? If I didn't celebrate mass today – didn't pray for blessings on the duke – who would know? Would it make any difference at all to his fate? Surely God already knows what's to become of him. Does my meager intercession count for anything at all?*

Nevertheless, he donned his vestments and began the familiar ritual. And by the time he reached the final Amen, he'd found a sense of calm. Not real peace. Certainly not joy. But the earlier despair and disillusionment had faded enough that he felt ready to return to Father's letter and prepare his reply. Which, he now realized, would have to be sent by messenger since he'd been so self-absorbed he forgot to remind the archdeacon to wait for his missives. *Well, no messenger is getting nine pennies from me this time.* The thought brought a half-smile to his face.

Closing the chapel door behind him, he decided to walk about the headland for some fresh air and exercise, as there was no pressing need to return to his correspondence. One of his favorite walks was a complete circuit of the cliff tops, starting where they overlooked the haven then heading north – a walk that eventually brought him back to the gate through the curtain wall. It was from the tops of the western cliffs, looking out over the great expanse of the sea, hearing the waves crashing below that he felt such a confluence of emotions. The wonder of God's creation. The isolation and loneliness of life in this place at the very end of the world, so far from what he'd thought his life would be. And that sense of another, unseen presence in this place that had never completely left him since he'd first become aware of it a year ago.

As he approached the south cliffs, he heard a sharp cry and looked skyward for the gulls he was certain must be the source. They often called to one another as they soared above the cliffs, but none were in sight. And then he heard it again. Thinking they might be perched on the rocks below, squabbling over a fish, he walked to the very edge and peered over. Still nothing. Shaking his head, he turned to continue his walk. Just as he reached the gate, he heard another cry. *Maybe they're on the beach in the haven. It's a favorite resting spot. Maybe it's just the wind playing tricks on me, making me think the sound is coming from the other side.*

But there were no sea birds there either. No razorbills on the little beach. No gulls or terns in the air. *Why am I hearing things again when there's nothing to hear? Arthur would say the spirits are telling you something – like perhaps it's time you pay him another visit.*

That thought brought a smile to Piran's face. Quite a few weeks had passed since he'd spent time with the old man. It had been a particularly cold winter, and Morganna had sent word that her father was spending most of his time in bed just to keep warm. But once the spring flowers began to appear, Piran paid him a visit and found him just as ever – happy to hold court from his chair beside the window. What he wanted to talk about then was his experience in Longshanks's army – even down to the food they ate in camp. This, too, Piran wrote down, knowing how happy it made Arthur to have these stories preserved for his family.

So with nothing better to do, he made his way to the village and knocked on the cottage door. Morganna opened the door shaking her head. "Blessed Mary, if I live as long as Methuselah, I'll *never* understand how he does it."

"How he does what?" Piran asked.

"He announced this morning you'd be coming today. I tried to talk him out of it – not wanting him to be disappointed – but he'd have none of it. Insisted you'd be visiting. And now, here you stand." She stepped back to let him in. "Go on through, Father. You know where to find him. I'll just go fetch the small ale."

He found Arthur in his usual spot grinning from ear to ear. "One of these days, my boy, that girl is going to start believing me when I tell her something."

"So how *did* you know I'd be here, Arthur?" Piran asked as he arranged his chair and sat down.

"The presence was strong when I woke up this morning, so I knew it would be for you too. Simple as that."

"Well, maybe it's not so simple for your daughter."

"Most times she's just too practical. I ask her all the time, 'If you can believe in God and angels, why can't you believe in other spirits?' She just dismisses it as nonsense and gets on with her business. Just as well, I suppose. If she doesn't have time for the past, then they don't have time for her."

"If I weren't so busy keeping this household going, I might have time for such foolishness," said Morgana, who had come in with the mugs of small ale while her father was talking.

"You see, boy?" said Arthur.

Piran smiled. "What I see is a woman who loves her father and wants to be sure he has a comfortable life."

Morgana beamed and turned to leave, calling "You two have a nice chat" over her shoulder.

"I was right, wasn't I, son? You saw or heard something this morning, didn't you?"

"Yes, you were right. And it's what I heard. Sounded like gulls calling. But there wasn't a bird in the sky – or anywhere around that I could find."

Arthur chuckled. "Tell me, son. Have you ever heard a woman cry out when she's birthing a child?" Piran shook his head. "I didn't think so. 'Cause if you had, you'd have recognized the sound for what it was. Not birds at all, but a mother's travail."

"Ygraine?"

Arthur beamed. "You're beginning to understand. Yes, Ygraine gave birth to a baby boy while Gorlois and Uther were still in the north, playing cat and mouse with the Deheubarth. She sent word to her husband straightaway that he had a son. Gorlois was so overjoyed that he ordered an enormous celebration for the whole camp – Uther's camp too.

"If the Deheubarth had been smart, that's when they would have attacked. There was so much ale consumed – so much revelry – that no soldier would have been able to figure out which end of his sword to grasp. But they stayed on their side of the water for the moment.

"At one point, Gorlois's squire dared ask his master if the timing of the birth was suspect, given how long they had been there in the north. Gorlois just roared with laughter and chided the man. 'Don't you know no one could get to her in that fortress? She just waited a couple of months to be sure the child would thrive before telling me. Sending a man at war news he has a son and then just weeks later sending word the son has died wouldn't be very smart, would it? Now, fetch me some more ale.'"

"But the child wasn't Gorlois's, was it?" said Piran.

"Indeed it wasn't. But it would be some time before anyone understood that. Even Ygraine herself still believed it was Gorlois who had come to her that time in the middle of the night."

"So what happened next?"

"Thankfully, the Deheubarth stayed on their side of the water for a bit longer, so the men had time to recover their senses before it mattered. And Gorlois and Uther had time to devise their trap.

"When the enemy came again, they came with a massive fleet. More ships and small boats than had ever been seen along that coast. Gorlois and Uther waited . . . let them come ashore. Then, as they began to march inland, the trap was sprung. The lead elements of the Deheubarth were annihilated, and then Uther and Gorlois began a merciless drive to push the remainder of the invaders back into the sea. By the time they watched the last of the Deheubarth ships sail northward, there were scores upon scores of enemy bodies littering the ground.

"'They won't be back,' Gorlois told Uther as they surveyed the carnage. Nonetheless, they stayed in the north for a while, just to be sure. But when spring returned and the Deheubarth didn't, they each took their armies home."

"And you think that's what the descendants of the Deheubarth were trying to avenge when the Welsh rose up against Longshanks?"

"Most likely no one remembered what had happened in the dark times. But the spirits of the Deheubarth flowed down from one generation to the next to the next. Spirits are strong, my boy. So even if the Welsh didn't know it was revenge they were seeking, the spirits knew and propelled the rebels."

Piran wasn't so sure that was even possible, but he had no wish to spoil an old man's cherished beliefs. "It's a remarkable tale, Arthur."

"You'll write it down for me? Like all the others?"

"Of course. And I'll bring you the pages as soon as I've finished."

XXXIV

Tintagel, 1360

Midsummer's Day had come and gone with no sign of either Étienne or the archdeacon. Piran didn't initially fret, but when the second week of July passed with no sign of anyone from Exeter, he became concerned the plague might have returned. There'd been no mention of another outbreak when Jori had made the trip to Bodmin for supplies. But then again, its arrival in Bodmin the last time had been sudden and with no warning.

Piran had carefully guarded the meager funds left over from what Cardinal des Près had given him for the trip from Avignon to Exeter, but he'd had to dip into them to pay for his share of the latest supplies. If there was plague . . . if he and Jori had to go two years without salary as they had before . . . The first time, they'd been able to rely on what he'd brought with him. Now they had no reserves. *Should we curtail our eating and build up our stores?* he wondered. *Eat only what our little garden produces? Even so, how could we ever accumulate enough, given what little money we have? What a cruel fate it would be to die of starvation while staying safe from illness!* It didn't bear contemplating.

So it was a double blessing when St. Swithun's day dawned fair and the little pony cart pulled up to the gate in early afternoon. Curiously, the only occupant was the man who'd been the archdeacon's driver the previous year. "Archdeacon's ailing," the driver explained. "Couldn't make the trip, but said you had to have your money and that." He inclined his head toward the back of the wagon then drove the wagon through the gate and jumped down to the ground. "Get this stuff unloaded so I can be on my way."

"Not here." Jori wasn't about to be tricked into carrying everything from the gate across the bridge to the buttery. "Drive across the bridge. We unload there." When the driver didn't budge, Jori jumped up onto the wagon, took the reins, and clucked to the pony. "Alright, you can walk then." He urged the pony to a trot to make his point.

As they walked behind the cart, the driver tossed Piran a purse. "Here. Archdeacon said give you this."

Somehow, the purse felt light. *Because it's cloth and not leather?* Piran wondered. But something didn't seem right. Why was this driver so eager to get away? He opened the purse and quickly counted the coins. "Where's the rest?"

"That's what I was given."

"Don't you have something else for me?"

"Like I said, that's what I was given." The driver's tone was surly.

By now, they had crossed the bridge and caught up to Jori and the cart. "I'm not talking about money. There are usually—"

"Oh, them." He pulled a satchel from under the driver's seat of the wagon and retrieved the two letters, handing them to Piran. "Now let's get this unloaded so's I can leave."

"Not so fast, Mister . . ." said Piran. "I don't know what to call you. The archdeacon never told us your name."

"Bolam."

"Well, then, Bolam. You're not leaving before you have my letters to take back to Exeter. Help Jori unload and store these supplies while I go see what's in these . . ." He waved the letters in the air. ". . . and write my replies." Switching to Cornish he added, "Don't let him go anywhere, Jori. I'm not paying for another messenger."

Once in his room, Piran opened Étienne's missive first. It contained little more than the usual pleasantries, admiration for the new polyphonic music Father was introducing into the services at the cathedral, and affirmation that Archdeacon de Northwode was indeed in ill health. Nothing about this driver/messenger or the lightness of Piran's purse. So he turned his attention to de Grandison's missive.

Salutations with the blessings of God and ourselves

My dear Piran

It saddens me deeply that I have no good tidings for you on the subject of your visit to your family. The king has yet to summon Parliament. It has been three long years since he's done so, but, while his need for money may be less while the fighting in France is suspended, there are many matters of the governance of the kingdom that are being neglected. Matters of new laws, judgments of disputes, matters of trade . . . The barons are growing increasingly concerned.

We are hopeful – now that he has negotiated another treaty with the king of France to secure England's gains and set King John's ransom – that Edward will return his attention to the governance of his own kingdom. The treaty agreed last year was roundly rejected by the French États Généraux and one must hope this new one does not meet the same fate. The ransom is an enormous sum – three million écus – more than all the trade and commerce done in France in an entire year. King John is to be freed after a third of it is paid, but even that is an amount almost beyond imagining. England's Treasury will be full for decades to come.

But I know, my dear Piran, that this is not the news you seek. I tell you this only so that you will know why I'm finding it so difficult to get an answer to what must, to you, seem a simple question. I have not forgotten you, my son. And should this peculiar situation persist much longer, I will consider putting my own good reputation with the king at risk by making a unilateral decision on your behalf.

Please know that I feel keenly how disheartened you will be to read these words. I can but pray that you will not fall into the mistaken belief that I have in any way abandoned you.

May God grant you his blessings and the equanimity to endure for just a bit longer.

John de Grandison

Written at our manor of Chudleigh the 15th day of June 1360

You're right, Father, thought Piran. *I'm deeply disheartened. Heartsick might be a better word. But what am I to do?*

Knowing that Jori might be hard-pressed to detain this Bolam character much longer, Piran sat down at his little writing table and hastily wrote two replies. To de Grandison, he tried to temper his disappointment and wrote *I trust you to always have my best interests at heart.* It was to Étienne that he addressed the question about the missing money.

When Piran returned to the waiting cart, Bolam was pacing back and forth under Jori's watchful eye. "Here, Mister Bolam." The driver grabbed the letters from Piran's outstretched hand, hopped up into the driver's seat, and flicked the reins across the pony's rump, urging him to a trot.

"Something's not right about that man," Jori muttered as they watched the cart cross the drawbridge and make its way through the main gate.

"I don't like him either, Jori."

Thoughts of Bolam vanished as soon as his cart disappeared over the horizon. It was time to pay Arthur another visit. During the spring and early summer, the old man only wanted to talk about his family – particularly the ancestors who had shared his name. Once, he had said, "I can't ever forgive Morgana for not naming her son Arthur. If she had, he might still be here today and be custodian of the legend."

"Surely you must find it in your heart to forgive, Arthur. Christ teaches us that forgiveness is the path to inner peace," Piran had replied.

"Oh, don't you mind an old man, boy," said Arthur. "In truth, there was nothing to forgive. 'Twas her husband what put his foot down and said his firstborn son would bear no name but his own. Still, I couldn't help but wish Morgana had tried a little harder. Still wish it. But that's all in the past. And you're here now to write everything down so it isn't lost after all. Maybe God sent you here for that." He paused before adding, with a twinkle in his eye, "Or maybe the spirits of the headland called you here."

Today, though, he wanted to return to the stories of the dark times. "I don't know how many more days I have on this earth, son, so best I don't leave it too late."

"You seem the same as ever to me, Arthur," said Piran.

"And I feel that way in summer, but every winter gets harder and a man never knows when the number of his days will be reached."

Piran smiled inwardly. *Well, at least he doesn't have some mystical vision of his own end.*

"Let's see. Where were we?"

"Gorlois and Uther had just taken their armies and returned home."

"Indeed they had. And for months, Gorlois doted on his young son. But as the boy grew, the father began to notice things. The boy didn't look like him at all. Blue eyes. Yes, Ygraine had blue eyes, but Gorlois's own were dark – almost black – and Gorlois claimed never to have seen a child with blue eyes unless both parents had that color. The boy's hair was light, tending toward ginger. Yes, Ygraine was blonde, but her hair was golden.

"Ygraine tried to reassure him. Sometimes traits skip a generation or two. Maybe our son looks like my grandfather or some cousin of mine. Maybe one of your forebears had blue eyes. Who else's son could he be, Gorlois?"

"Did Ygraine still believe the boy was Gorlois's?"

"She must have been having some doubts by then, but she couldn't figure out how it could have happened. And she knew her son's safety – hers too – depended on Gorlois believing the boy was his.

"One day, it came to Gorlois that he knew only one man with ginger hair, so he confronted his wife, demanding to know when the child was conceived. And that's when Ygraine made a fatal mistake. She told her husband it was when he'd ridden home from the battlefield to lie with her in the middle of the night.

"Gorlois went on the rampage, and in the face of his fury, two sentries finally admitted they'd fallen asleep on duty on the night in question. Gorlois had them killed then gathered his army to march to Ynys Writin to kill Uther."

At that moment, Morgana appeared in the doorway. "You two need a refill on your small ale?"

Arthur picked up his mug and looked at the contents. "Nay, girl. Maybe later." Morgana disappeared without a word. When she'd gone, Arthur said, "Girl sure knows how to interrupt a good story, doesn't she?"

Piran smiled. "And what if that mug had been empty? You'd have been wondering where she was, now, wouldn't you?"

The old man laughed out loud. "Aye, that I would."

"So Gorlois was on his way to kill Uther," Piran prompted.

"Yes, he was. But Merlin let Uther know Gorlois was coming, and then he turned his attention to the boy. It didn't take much for him to convince Ygraine that if Gorlois came back alive, he'd kill her and the boy both. But if she'd let him take the child away, Merlin could hide and protect him for as long as it took for the boy to be safe in the world again. Ygraine resisted at first, but she eventually realized she had no choice. So Merlin smuggled little Arthur out of the fortress and away from Tintagel.

"And when the armies of Gorlois and Uther met in the field just outside Weolingtun, both men knew only one of them would walk away."

Piran could see the old man was tiring. "That's a remarkable story, Arthur. A lot for me to write. Perhaps it's best if we stop there for now and finish on my next visit."

"You just be sure you bring those pages with you."

"Don't I always?" Piran patted Arthur's arm, much as Arthur had done to him on the early visits, then rose to go.

"There's something else you should know, boy. You'll feel it one day. The presence as strong as you've ever known it. And there'll be a great storm, unlike any storm you've ever seen before. The storm of the great battle. You mark my words. It won't be long now."

As he made his way home, Piran couldn't shake the feeling that Arthur's last words were a portent of something. But a portent of what, he had no idea.

XXXV

Tintagel, 1361

It had been a difficult year. Arthur had taken ill during January so Piran had added prayers for the old man's recovery to his daily ritual. It wasn't to be, however, and the old man passed into the next world on St. Wulfric's day. Piran was surprised how much Arthur's death affected him – as much, even, as when his *maam* had left this earth. So his prayers turned to Arthur's soul, hoping to speed his passage into Heaven.

Somehow Piran had managed to make his meager twenty-five shillings last until the middle of March. Quite how, he wasn't certain, though he suspected Jori was paying for more than his half of the supplies. When Piran asked, he'd added, "And don't think you can get away with not telling me the truth."

"You think I'd lie to a priest?" Jori managed to sound indignant. "That wouldn't make sense. Say I lied. If I did, then I'd have to confess it to you so I could receive the sacrament, right? And then you'd know. So what would be the point of lying in the first place?"

"I don't know, Jori. Maybe to spare my feelings for a few days or weeks longer?"

"Wouldn't change what would happen in the end."

Piran shook his head. Jori wasn't about to admit to anything. "Have it your way, then, Jori. But I do have a bit of money left over from when I came back to England. It's not much, but I can still pay my share until summer."

He'd watched his meager funds dwindle over the coming months. Somehow, they never had a shortage of supplies and yet it never cost him as much as it had in previous years. Had Jori been stealing from him – padding the amounts – for more than a decade? Piran laughed at himself for even considering that. By Jori's logic, that wouldn't make sense either since he'd never once in all these years confessed to the sin of stealing. *I'll just have to find some way to make things up to him. Maybe Étienne will come this summer and I can ask for the rest of last year's salary to finally be paid.*

But summer arrived and Étienne didn't. Neither did the archdeacon. Nor that peculiar driver. Not even a messenger from the bishop.

At first, Piran worried about his friends and prayed for them. Had the plague returned? Had some other dreadful disease men had never seen before come to the kingdom? Even if there was no sickness, Father was growing older. Had he gone to be with God and no one thought to send the news?

It rained on St. Swithun's Day. That put even Jori in the dumps. "Forty more days of this," he lamented. "Garden's going to get too much water and we'll be lucky if we get any harvest at all."

"You really put stock in that?" Piran asked.

"A saint being angry that his grave was moved? That's nothing to scoff at. If the saints can help us when we need them, why shouldn't we believe they could punish us if we offend them? Mark my words. We won't see the sun reliably again until St. Bregwin's Day."

Whether it was the saint's vexation or just the vagaries of the weather, Jori's words proved prescient. For weeks, they awoke to grey skies, often to rain. Now and then, the sun would break through for an hour or two in the afternoon, but the clouds and the rain always returned. The gloomy weather did nothing to help Piran's mood.

Jori was right about the garden too. By mid-August, almost every plant had yellowing leaves. When they pulled the first carrots at the beginning of September, almost all of them were mushy and inedible. Same with the parsnips and onions. They got a few radishes and some green beans, but unlike previous years when the beans were so plentiful they could share with the villagers, this year's crop only lasted them a couple of weeks. They'd have to wait until October to see if the neaps survived, but it didn't look hopeful. Which meant they'd have to buy more this year. Which meant a greater strain on Piran's purse.

As late summer yielded to the cooler winds of autumn, Piran grew increasingly despondent. He celebrated mass for the duke every day. But each time he removed his vestments was an opportunity to look around the little chapel and take stock of his situation. No matter how much he prayed to see things differently, he couldn't help feeling abandoned. It cut deep into his soul that those who meant the most to him in the world – who he trusted the most – loved the most – could turn their backs on him without even a word of explanation.

With no way to understand why, he was left with only questions. *What do I owe to those who protected me and kept me safe? Who made sure I could thrive when others sought to prevent that? Has the debt been paid? Is such a debt ever paid? Or is it even a debt? Were they put here on earth for that very purpose?*

And what do I owe to the king? Certainly, I had an obligation when I was being paid. But is he even still paying? Has he ceased his commission? Is that why no one comes any longer? How am I to know, isolated out here on this headland? Do I really owe the king anything at all? He doesn't know who I am. All he ever wanted was a priest – any priest – to pray for his son.

And what do I do when my money runs out? Which it will. Long before next summer. Where could I go – who could I ask – for a place in this world?

He contemplated writing to Étienne then asked himself, *Why hasn't **he** written to me?*

As October prepared to give way to November, there was a new chill in the air that presaged the coming winter. Piran once again had that strange sensation of another presence here on the headland. It had been a while since he'd felt it, but this time, it seemed stronger than ever.

The morning of St. Elizabeth's Day was the warmest they'd known in weeks. But the air was sultry, portending storms. Jori spent the day making the rounds of both courtyards, meticulously securing anything that might blow about in a strong wind. Then he and Piran brought the horses in from the paddock to the little stable. Piran had never seen the animals so skittish. "They feel it too," said Jori. "There'll be a big blow afore the night's over. I just hope all the roofs stay on."

When they left the kitchen after supper, the temperature had dropped considerably. "I'll just go check the horses one more time," Jori told Piran. "You bring your mattress and blankets down to my room so you can sleep there tonight. It'll be safer if anything happens to the roof or things start blowing around and crashing through windows."

In all the time he'd been here, Piran had never seen Jori show such concern about the weather. So when he collected his mattress, he also collected his oiled-wool cloak, his purse, and the red velvet pouch that held de Grandison's mother's rosary.

When Jori returned carrying an armload of firewood – "We'll need plenty that's dry if we want a fire tomorrow," he said – the wind howled through the open door. And by the time they banked the fire and crawled into their beds it was a raging gale and the rain had begun pelting the windows and the sides of the building. Piran had almost fallen asleep when the thunder and lightning jarred him back to wakefulness. *Is this Arthur's great storm?* Piran couldn't help but wonder. Lightning streaking from the heavens to the ground over and over and over again. Sheets of lightning illuminating the skies as brightly as the sun. Thunder so loud it sounded as if a giant stone mason was trying to cleave the earth with a massive chisel. And the wind screamed and the rain poured and the two men huddled in their beds, praying to be spared from the wrath of the storm.

When they rose the next morning, the worst of the storm had passed. It was still windy and raining, but at least not with the ferocity of the previous night. Thanks to Jori's foresight, they soon had a fire going though they shivered for a bit until the flames started to break the chill in the room.

"Best I go check for damage," said Jori, reaching for his cloak on the peg by the door.

"I'll come with you," said Piran.

"Nay, you stay dry for now. You'll get soaked soon enough going to the chapel."

While Jori was gone, Piran took stock. They'd made it through the night, but the severity of the storm was just one more reminder of how isolated they were here on the headland – and how alone he was in the world now. He opened his purse. Two gold florins left. He had a decision to make.

It wasn't long before Jori was back, his cloak dripping water as he hung it on the peg. "Not too bad," he reported. "A couple of slates off the roof of the buttery. I'll have to put them back in place once the sun comes out." He crossed to stand in front of the fire, rubbing his hands together to warm them. "But the storeroom's dry. And no broken windows as far as I can tell. Didn't go across the bridge. That side will just have to wait."

When it came time for him to say mass, Piran donned his cloak, pulled the hood over his head, and trudged through the rain toward the chapel, keeping his head lowered against the ceaseless wind. As always when it rained in late autumn and winter, the chapel was cold and damp. But he donned his vestments and prepared to commune with God. The mass complete, he stood for a long time contemplating the crucifix above the altar. His suffering was as nothing compared to Christ's. But in a moment of clarity, he realized that, unlike Jesus, he had it within his power to do something about his own. And in that moment, he felt at peace.

Throwing his cloak on over his vestments, he stepped out into the rain and closed the door behind him. As he started back toward the castle gate, he happened to glance toward the little garden and the pear tree. The tree he had nurtured and enjoyed its fruit for so many years. Something in the storm had cleaved it in half, and one half lay, sad and forlorn, on the ground. The other, though, stood tall, brave and resilient against the worst ravages of nature.

Piran made his decision. He took one last look at the little chapel. And the next morning, when the sun shone once again in a brilliant blue sky, he packed his belongings, said farewell to Jori, and walked away.

XXXVI

Chudleigh, 2nd week of Advent, 1361

"He's gone, Father," Étienne stood in the door to de Grandison's study, his heavy cloak dusted with the falling snow he'd ridden in for the last hour of his journey.

The alarm on the bishop's face as he looked up from his reading was unmistakable, but he kept his voice calm. "Shed those snowy clothes, Étienne, and come warm yourself by the fire. And tell me everything."

They had known something was wrong. Otherwise, Étienne would not have made the journey to Tintagel so late in the year. It had been a year and a half since either of them had heard from Piran. Every June, when the king's purse was delivered, de Grandison sent a letter – most years, Étienne did as well – and every year Piran's replies were full of cheer and invariably included some new insight he had about life in a remote corner of the world. Two years ago they'd worried when the archdeacon returned emptyhanded, and the bishop chastised him for being remiss in his obligations. When Piran's replies arrived in mid-July, it seemed as if all was well once again. But then last year, his letters were rather more perfunctory. To Étienne, he'd even posed the question *Why is my salary so low?* Knowing it was the king who made that determination – and thinking Piran might only be having a moment of self-doubt – Étienne hadn't mentioned it to de Grandison, who couldn't do anything about it anyway.

These days, Étienne saw himself as something of a protector for the man who'd given him a home and a purpose after he'd left the Holy See. De Grandison was sixty-nine now, and though his mind was as sharp as ever, the wrinkles at the corners of his eyes had deepened and his once brown hair was now mostly grey. He'd inherited his family's titles and estates three years ago when his elder brother died, so he now represented both the spiritual and the temporal in Parliament.

They'd expected an exuberant reply to the news de Grandison had sent in June – that the king had wholeheartedly endorsed Piran's wish to visit his family. It had taken much longer to secure the permission than anyone would have wished. Piran had somehow managed to restrain his impatience. Perhaps, having finally received an answer, he'd simply gone to his family straightaway and postponed sending a reply. But as the weeks turned to months, they'd become increasingly concerned.

Étienne gave his outer garments to a servant then poured himself a draught of brandy from the elaborately decorated glass bottle on the sideboard – to warm himself from the inside while the fire did its work from the outside. "Father?" He held up the bottle, offering to pour some for the bishop.

"No, thank you. Just come sit here and tell me what you've learned."

Settled opposite de Grandison and with his first swallow having its desired effect, Étienne recounted what he'd been told. "I really don't know much. The caretaker . . . the one I've told you about before who's been there since Piran arrived . . . Jori's his name. Anyway, he said Chegwin returned from saying mass one miserably rainy day in early November and just started packing up his things. When Jori asked him why, Piran said, 'It's been long enough, so it seems my commission is finished. Time to move on.'"

"Did this Jori ask what he meant by that?"

Étienne took another sip of brandy. "He's not the type. But he did ask Piran where he was going, and Piran wouldn't say. Actually, what Jori said was that Piran said he didn't know yet, but he was sure it would be someplace where he would be content and could bring God's comfort to ordinary people."

De Grandison rested his chin on steepled fingers. "That's what he always said was his dream for his life."

"The caretaker said one other thing that I'm not sure what to make of. He said no one brought the money this year. He *might* have meant his money for the upkeep of the castle, but it struck me that he was talking about Piran's money." Étienne paused for another sip of brandy. "Jori said something else that troubled me. He said Piran mumbled something about being abandoned by all the people who once loved him. Jori thought Piran meant his family. But I pondered that a lot on the ride home. Father, I don't think our last letters ever reached him."

De Grandison's pensive mood disappeared in an instant. "How could that be?"

"In truth, I don't know."

The bishop sat forward in his chair. "Get to the bottom of this, Bonfils. I want to know exactly what happened and who's responsible. In the meantime, I'll try to come up with some way to find Piran."

The problem of trying to find Piran brought back for de Grandison memories of his quest years ago to locate de Villiers. At least this time he was seeking someone within the Church and not some rogue who could be anywhere. But there were thousands of parishes in England so, as with the earlier search for de Villiers, the question was where to start. Cornwall was the obvious place, of course, and the easiest. His archdeacon, Philip de Beauchamp, should be able to discover quickly if Chegwin was there.

But Piran's remark about feeling abandoned troubled de Grandison deeply. Not only did it break his heart that Piran would ever feel thus, but it probably also meant he would seek solace somewhere other than those places where he'd once found contentment. Which brought de Grandison back to the problem of thousands of parishes.

Until inspiration dawned. He rose from his writing table and took a book down from the shelves beside the fireplace. The work he'd assembled on the lives of the saints. The work Piran and Étienne had both contributed to. It didn't take long to find the pages he was looking for – and to confirm that his memory wasn't failing him. Yes, St. Piran had come to Cornwall from Ireland. Chegwin would remember that. And that's almost certainly where he would follow his heart.

The bishop returned to his writing table, removed a clean page from the drawer, dipped his quill in the ink pot, and began.

In nomine Patris et Filii et Spiritus Sancti

May God's blessings be with you my dear Archbishop

I write to seek your help in locating the current whereabouts of a priest who was for many years my protégé, Father Piran Chegwin. I have reason to believe he may have come to Ireland when he departed his most recent post, which happened rather abruptly and is the reason I've lost track of him.

Knowing the size of my own diocese and the number of parishes within it, I realize this is no trivial request. But if you should already have or be able to discover any information as to Chegwin's whereabouts, I would be grateful for the knowledge so that I might resume our correspondence of many years' duration and bring him news of his family still in Cornwall.

With my most humble gratitude

John de Grandison, Bishop of Exeter

Written at our manor of Chudleigh this 6th day of December 1361

He made a second copy of the letter and addressed one to the Archbishop of Dublin and the other to the Archbishop of Armagh. There would be more letters to send in the coming days, to his fellow English bishops. But something deep in his soul told him these two missives were his best hopes, so he went in search of his steward that they might be dispatched without delay.

"You're not going to like this, Father," said Étienne when he returned to Chudleigh three days later.

De Grandison chuckled. "A very good friend of mine once told me that if you have a distasteful task to complete, it's best to just squeeze your nose and get on with it."

Étienne pinched his nose briefly. "Does your friend say the same applies if you're about to learn something distasteful?"

"I'm not sure he ever mentioned that, but anything that led to Piran's departure is unlikely to improve my mood."

"Very well." Étienne pinched his nose again then released it. "It goes back about three years, to the time when your nephew, Otto, was archdeacon. In his last couple of years, it seems he was . . . how shall I put this? . . . inconsistent, shall we say, in some of his duties. Preferred to spend his time in Devon and somewhat neglected Cornwall. After he made the journey to Tintagel to deliver Piran's money in 1359, he decided that was just too far, so he hired a messenger to carry his letters to the Cornish parishes and, of course—"

"Piran's money and our letters." De Grandison finished the sentence.

"It gets worse."

"I assumed it would."

"When Pempel arrived, he kept the messenger on and simply assumed that his predecessor's latest practices in Cornwall were approved."

De Grandison wrinkled his nose. "I never did like that man. Maybe he's better suited to his new role as dean of a chapter. What does Philip have to say about all this? And have you managed to find this messenger?"

"Father de Beauchamp inherited the messenger when he became archdeacon. Says the man seemed reliable enough, so he just kept him on. But he's just as appalled as you're going to be by what we've learned."

"Do go on, Étienne. Don't keep me on tenterhooks."

"I think you should hear it from the man himself. The archdeacon and the messenger are waiting in the entry hall. Let me just fetch them."

"Yes, yes . . . get them in here."

In less than a minute, Étienne was back with the others. De Beauchamp crossed the room straightaway to sit opposite the bishop. "I had no idea, Uncle. How could my predecessors have let something like this happen?"

"All in good time, Philip. Let's hear what the man has to say."

The man in question lingered by the door, cap in hand, clearly uncertain what was expected of him. When Étienne beckoned, he walked tentatively toward the group of priests. "Get over here, Bolam," Étienne admonished. "Time for you to tell the bishop what you told me. And start at the beginning – how you came to be in Exeter in the first place."

"Well . . ." Bolam looked around, hesitating. "Well, I . . . I got this letter, see, from Martin who said he needed my help, and he said what he needed—"

De Grandison held up a hand to interrupt. "Martin, you say. Does this Martin have any other names?"

"De Villiers, Father. Martin de Villiers. The one what hired me for that business in Oxford all those years back."

A dark shadow settled on de Grandison's face. Étienne knew the bishop could imagine what was coming next. "Go on, Bolam," said Étienne.

"So I got this letter from Martin and he said as how it was time to finish what went wrong back in Oxford and he needed my help to do it seeing as how I was the only one what nobody had seen my face or knew who I was. But first we had to find the Cornish pig." He stopped as all three priests glared at him. "Sorry, Father . . . Fathers. Those were Martin's words, not mine."

"Why don't we call him Chegwin from now on?" de Beauchamp said.

"So first we had to find Chegwin," Bolam went on. "But Martin had an idea where he might be, so he said I was to go to Exeter and find out. I started doing little errands and odd jobs for the cathedral and asking around and found out the p . . . Chegwin was off at some castle at the far ends of Cornwall. And I also found out the only one who ever visited out there was the archdeacon. Not you, Father." He nodded to de Beauchamp. "Not even the one afore you but the one afore him.

"Anyway, folks said this Chegwin got paid to say prayers for the king's son, and it must be working on account of how he won that great battle and captured the French king. So I wrote to Martin and told him. And a couple of months later, he writes back and says I'm to get myself hired by this archdeacon and prove myself a reliable messenger and find a way to be the one to carry the money to the . . . to Chegwin. And that's what I did."

"Tell the bishop what year this was, Bolam," said Étienne.

"Was in the spring, almost three years ago now. Be three years come this next spring."

Bolam stood quietly, apparently waiting for another question or to be told what to do. "Get back to your story," Étienne prompted.

"Well, anyway, that's what I did. I got myself all cleaned up and presentable-like and the archdeacon, he said he'd try me out and I could go with him on his rounds that year. And that's when I saw this Chegwin for the first time and got to see the money and the letters delivered. And then the archdeacon said mayhap I could do this for him the next summer. So I wrote to Martin again and told him everything.

"It were autumn afore he wrote back, but he told me exactly what to do. And he said he'd pay me and I could even take some of the p . . . some of Chegwin's money too."

Once again, de Grandison interrupted. "Something's puzzling me . . . Bolam, is it?"

"Aye, Father."

"You don't speak like an educated man and yet you claim to have carried on this correspondence with de Villiers. How can that be?"

"Well, I was supposed to be educated, see? My uncle was going to pay for me and his son to go to Oxford together, so he had our parish priest teach us to read and write and cipher when we were just littl'uns. And he was starting to teach us Latin too. And then, when I was about eleven or twelve, my uncle just fell over dead one morning. After all his debts were settled, there was no money left. His widow had to go live with her brother and my cousin and me had to go to work. My cousin apprenticed with a blacksmith and eventually got the smithy in Marsh Baldon. But the blacksmith didn't need two apprentices, so I wound up doing odd jobs in the taverns. Mostly sweeping up and that kind of thing until I got older and strong enough to help with shifting the barrels and such. That's where Martin found me – in The Stag."

"Alright, Bolam. That satisfies my curiosity. Now back to your story. What was it Martin told you to do?"

"He said I was to make everything look more or less normal the first year, but I could take some of Chegwin's money for my trouble – not all of it though. That summer I kept half for myself and gave Chegwin the other half. He looked at me kind of funny and asked 'Where's the rest?' but I just told him that was all they gave me.

"Then the archdeacon died and a new one came and it looked like everything was going to go wrong again. But I told Father Pempel about my arrangement with Father de Northwode and he said that sounded like a fine idea to him, so I didn't have to write to Martin and get him all upset because I couldn't do what he wanted. That was a weight off my shoulders for sure.

"Last summer was when I was supposed to finish things so Martin would pay me what he promised."

"And did you?" asked de Grandison.

"When it came right down to it, Father, I couldn't. See, I was supposed to do away with Chegwin . . . and that caretaker too, so no one would be the wiser. But by the time I got to Bodmin, I knew I couldn't do it. So I got drunk and bought myself a woman." Bolam suddenly stopped short. "Sorry, Father," he nodded toward de Grandison. "You wouldn't know about such things."

"I'm quite familiar with the carnal appetites of men, Bolam. Now finish your story."

"There's nothing more to tell. The next morning, I turned around and came home. I figured I could tell Martin I'd done the deed and he'd be none the wiser, being as how he's off in France. And I could keep the money and tell Father Pempel I'd delivered it like I was supposed to."

"What about our letters to Chegwin?" asked Étienne.

"Tossed them in a pigsty at a farm on the way back. I figured if I told Martin I'd done that, it would make him happy."

"And how is it you come to still be here, Bolam?" asked de Grandison. "It seems to me you'd have wanted to be as far away from here as possible when we started asking questions."

"A man's got to work, doesn't he? And I had good work at the cathedral."

"You can lay the blame for that at my feet, Uncle," said de Beauchamp. "I listened to the dean, who said Bolam had always been reliable enough."

"Actually, what I choose to lay at your feet, Philip, is credit. If you hadn't kept this man around, we'd never have gotten to the bottom of this. Now, Bolam, it seems to me you have no idea what a parlous state you find yourself in. You've stolen seventy-five shillings of the king's money, and he'll want it back."

"But, Father, it was the p . . . Chegwin's money," Bolam protested.

"It wasn't Father Chegwin's money until it was delivered into his hands. Until then, it was the king's money, entrusted to you to deliver on his behalf. So I repeat, you've taken seventy-five shillings of the king's money. Now . . ." De Grandison paused for effect. "The simplest solution is for you to simply give me the money, which I will return to the king, and we'll say no more about this, since you made the uncommonly good decision not to carry out de Villiers's instructions."

Bolam hung his head. At long last, his voice almost a whisper, he said, "I don't have it, Father."

"None of it?"

"None of it."

"What's happened to it?"

"Spent, sir. Last year was only twenty-five and that went really fast."

"This year was fifty. What did you spend it on?"

"Drink . . . and women . . . and . . ." Bolam's voice trailed off.

"Fifty shillings in five months? That's a lot of women, Bolam." Fidgeting with his cap, Bolam didn't notice the smirks on the faces of Philip and Étienne, but de Grandison did and had to struggle mightily to keep his own expression stern.

"'Tweren't all women, Father. I had debts, see. For my lodgings and stabling my horse and at the taverns."

This man is a living testament to the Proverbs about fools and wealth, thought de Grandison. *But it's time for him to learn a hard lesson.* "And now you have a sizable debt to the king. How to you propose to repay it?"

"I have to write to Martin – might even be better to go see him in person – and get what he promised to pay me. That would be enough."

"Bolam," said the bishop, "you're a fool if you thought Martin de Villiers ever intended to pay you a penny." *And a bigger fool if you think I'm going to let you out of my sight for even a moment.*

"So what am I to do, Father?" As the truth closed in on him, Bolam's tone became increasingly plaintive.

"As I see it, there are two possibilities. I can turn you over to the authorities to face the king's justice. And if I recall correctly, the penalty for theft of an amount like this is prison until such time as restitution is made. That could be the rest of your life unless someone in your family pays back the money for you."

"And the other?"

"I will repay the king on your behalf. But to work off that debt, you'll work as a gardener for the monks at Launceston Priory. I'll pay you two pennies a day – which is more than the job is worth – but I'll keep your wages until they add up to seventy-five shillings. Let's see . . ." He paused to do the mental calculation. "That's nine hundred pennies. Which means you'll owe me four hundred fifty days, after which you'll be free to get on with your life."

"What am I to do for money in the meantime, Father?"

"You won't be needing any. The monks will provide your lodging and your meals. And I'm told they brew a very fine ale."

"But what about . . ." Bolam whined.

Philip and Étienne struggled to keep their amusement in check. De Grandison didn't dare look their way lest he lose control. "There are some, Bolam, who believe that a period of abstinence is good for a man. It's less than a year and a half. It would be far longer than that in the king's prison unless your blacksmith cousin could be persuaded to pay your debt."

Totally defeated, Bolam slumped forward and gazed at the floor, still fidgeting with his cap. "Perhaps next time, Bolam," said de Grandison, "you'll think more carefully about what sort of man you choose to tie your destiny to. Now which is it to be – the king's justice or mine?"

"Yours, Father," Bolam mumbled.

"Very well. I think you've chosen wisely." De Grandison finally turned his gaze toward de Beauchamp. "Philip, can I count on you to take him to Launceston yourself and give the prior my instructions?"

"Without question, Uncle."

"And Bolam, don't even think for a moment about trying to escape from the archdeacon or the priory. If you disappear, I'll have every sheriff in Devon and Cornwall and all the south of England looking for your sorry hide."

When the others had left, de Grandison sat for a long while, gazing into the fire. It was as bad as he'd feared. In its essence, it was what he'd expected. Were it not for a simple man's momentary pang of conscience, it could have been much worse. But that didn't absolve de Villiers from the evil of his intentions.

At long last, de Grandison rose and went to his writing table. There was another letter that needed to be sent without delay.

Salutations and may the blessings of God be upon you in this most holy season

To Cardinal Élie Talleyrand de Périgord

He paused and studied the words he'd just written. *Ah, Pierre, if only you'd lived to see this day. I think you would approve.* Cardinal des Près had gone to meet his maker on the feast day of St. Jerome, leaving Talleyrand as the new Dean of the Sacred College of Cardinals – and the keeper of the secrets of de Villiers's sins.

The time has finally come, Eminence. There is now a position within my purview to grant that is a fitting earthly penance for the sins, past and present, of Father Martin de Villiers. The ones past, you know. His inordinate pride, you know. His most recent exhortation, from within the Holy See, for a man to commit murder on his behalf will be news to you, as it was to me today. Thanks to God's grace, the deed was not done, but the man who was supposed to carry it out has, of his own free will, revealed all to me, Archdeacon de Beauchamp, and Father Bonfils.

So I ask you now to send de Villiers to me. Tell him only that there is a position waiting for him that permits him to serve both Crown and Church. Appeal to his vanity if need be. He's to present himself to the dean of the collegiate church at Ottery St. Mary.

Two things I ask especially. Make no mention of my name as that would scare him into flight. And send someone utterly reliable to accompany him, to be absolutely certain that he doesn't decide to go elsewhere.

My gratitude to you for accepting responsibility for this rogue knows no bounds. And I am glad to be able to relieve you of the burden.

John de Grandison

Written at our manor of Chudleigh this 9th day of December 1361

XXXVII

Ottery St. Mary, February 1st, 1362

When the dean of the chapter announced that his visitors had finally arrived, de Grandison was surprised to find the Bishop of Salisbury waiting for him in the chancel. "You were not who I was expecting, Wyvil, but I'm pleased to see you nonetheless."

"Your good fortune, my friend, that I just happened to be ready to return from Avignon when Talleyrand needed a minder for that rather unpleasant man I left waiting in the Lady Chapel. What on *earth* do you want with him?"

"It's a long story, Wyvil."

"Perhaps you'll tell me one day over a glass of wine after a session of Parliament."

De Grandison chuckled. "It would probably require two or three pitchers full, but if the wine's good, it might be an enjoyable way to spend an evening. Now, take me to this miscreant." Wyvil raised an eyebrow but didn't comment.

They found de Villiers pacing back and forth in front of the chapel's altar. He stopped at the sight of Bishop Wyvil and then screwed up his face as he studied de Grandison. "Do I know you?"

"Yes, Martin. It's been many years, but you do. Or should I call you Martinus?"

The expression on de Villiers's face as realization dawned might have amused de Grandison in other circumstances. "Holy Mother of God! You're that archdeacon . . . the one who ruined my life in Oxford."

"Bishop of Exeter now. And the only one who ever ruined your life, de Villiers, was you."

"I should have known. I should have figured this out long before we got to this place." De Villiers's tone and manner were pure defiance.

Wyvil, who'd been watching the exchange with curiosity, couldn't resist chiming in. "You were too besotted with traveling in my company to think of anything but how important that made you." It was all de Grandison could do to keep from laughing out loud. Wyvil certainly had the measure of his charge. "But my task is finished," he continued, "so I'll leave you here and continue my journey."

"And you, de Villiers," said de Grandison, "will come with me. My carriage should be waiting for us by now."

Martin planted his feet wide apart and crossed his arms over his chest. "I'm not going anywhere with you, bishop or not."

"Yes, you are," Wyvil took Martin's arm and propelled him forward. "Orders of Cardinal Talleyrand."

Bonfils and de Beauchamp were waiting in the carriage when Wyvil shoved de Villiers inside. "I trust you'll be safe, John?" Wyvil asked.

"Quite . . . now that he sees he's outnumbered."

Wyvil shook his head. "Now I *really* can't wait to hear this story – and especially how it ends."

Finally, de Grandison could laugh. "All in good time, my friend. For now, Godspeed and fair weather for the rest of your journey."

They made straight for Exeter Cathedral. De Grandison had no wish to befoul his favorite residence with de Villiers's ignominy.

De Villiers sat in glum silence throughout the journey. Observing him, de Grandison was confident he knew what was happening inside that head. *Trying to work out how to extricate yourself from this current predicament, Martin? Scheme all you like. This time, your usual tricks will get you nowhere.*

When the carriage drew to a halt in the cathedral close, Bonfils and de Beauchamp walked closely on either side of de Villiers – ready to grab an arm if he gave any sign of running – as they all followed de Grandison into the episcopal palace. Even before they'd taken their seats in the bishop's study, de Villiers's attitude was on display. "I'm having no part of any of this. The cardinal lied to me. There's no position here, so there's no reason for me to stay. But have your say. Let's get it over with, and then I'll be on my way."

"Oh, there's a position." De Grandison's tone was muted – soothing almost. "Cardinal Talleyrand doesn't traffic in lies. Nor do I. The position is exactly as he represented it – a chance to serve both Crown and Church. And you are correct, Father de Villiers. You will be at liberty to decide for yourself whether or not to accept it. But before we come to that, perhaps we should revisit what's brought us to this point."

As de Grandison spoke, Martin began walking circuits about the room. De Grandison was unconcerned. There were two canons outside the door ready to prevent any premature attempt at departure.

"Revisit," Martin sneered. "What you mean is you want to tell your side of the story to those two."

"They already know the truth, Martin. What I want is for you to reflect on the past before making a decision about your future."

"Revisit to your heart's content. I don't have to listen."

"You remember Oxford, I'm sure. Your thwarted plot and the midnight attack gone wrong. You're still wanted by the authorities for the murder of that young man, you know."

"So turn me over to them. That's what *you've* wanted from the beginning."

"All in good time, de Villiers. I can't even imagine how you managed to achieve such a lofty degree from the University of Bologna, but I doubt very seriously that it involved either honesty or hard work on your part."

De Villiers cackled. "I'd been cheated out of my degree at Oxford by that Cornish pig, so what I got in Bologna was no more than I deserved."

"Which brings us to your next malfeasance." De Grandison could see that his own calm demeanor and the steady enumeration of past sins was having the desired effect. "Rumors and innuendo meant to discredit Father

Chegwin within the Holy See. Lies that ruined a promising career. And with the goal of advancing your *own* career."

"*Quid pro quo*, Bishop. An eye for an eye."

"And most recently, procuring the theft of the king's money. And procuring the death of not one but two fellow human beings."

"You have no proof of that." De Villiers was so defiant that de Grandison was certain the man didn't know his instructions hadn't been carried out.

"To the contrary. You see, the man you ordered to do your bidding is both stupid and possessed of a Christian conscience. A flawed one, to be sure, but a conscience nonetheless. He could bring himself to steal but not to kill. And he was foolish enough not to flee after he'd stolen. Bolam was quite forthcoming. Told us everything."

De Villiers stopped in his tracks, obviously taken by surprise. But the hesitation was a mere hiccup. The arrogance and the pacing were back in an instant. "Well, as you yourself said he was stupid, why would you believe a word the man says? And why would you think I would even know such a character?"

"He told Father Bonfils far too much about the incident in Oxford for there to be any doubt. Including the fact that you and your gang hid out in his cousin's smithy for the first few days after the fight. And as I said, de Villiers, Bolam has something of a conscience, which I'm not sure you do."

"So what did you do with him? Turn him over to the sheriff?"

"I gave him the same choice I'm going to give you. Justice at the hands of the authorities or restitution of the money and atonement for his sins. He chose the latter and is now working and living at a priory until his debt is paid. I wonder how you'll choose, Martin."

Martin had stopped walking about. "You haven't told me yet what my choices are."

"Indeed I haven't. Although I'm sure you know one of them is that I hand you over to the authorities for both your deeds in Oxford and your recent attempts at crime."

"And the other one?"

"The path of atonement. The king has commissioned daily masses and prayers for his son, the Duke of Cornwall. That position is now open and is in my power to give. It will never lead to a bishop's mitre, but it will keep you alive and out of the king's prisons."

The three priests watched as de Villiers's brow furrowed and he looked quizzically from one to another of them. "And how did this position become available?"

"When I was there last," said Étienne, "I found that the previous occupant had left his post because he hadn't been paid."

Finally, recognition dawned. His tone almost one of defeat, de Villiers said, "You're talking about Chegwin's job, aren't you, Bishop?"

"It is his no longer. It's your job if you choose to take it. But you're free to choose the path of the king's justice."

"And for how long do I have to do this?"

"Until the king withdraws the commission or until you can repent sincerely, show contrition and acceptance of God's teachings, confess to and atone for the sin of pride, and make restitution to the family of the young man you killed in Oxford." De Grandison paused. "Whichever comes first."

Some of the bravado returned. De Grandison was sure that was because Martin was already calculating how soon he would be able to convince the bishop that his claim to be penitent was genuine. "Then I accept your position, Bishop."

"Very well, de Villiers. Archdeacon de Beauchamp and Father Bonfils will accompany you to Tintagel. You will under no circumstances inflict any harm on the castle's caretaker but will treat him with dignity and respect. And I promise you that if I learn anything to the contrary, I will immediately turn you over to the authorities. The archdeacon will deliver your salary each year, and both he and Father Bonfils will visit when you least expect it to make sure you're behaving yourself. Know that the caretaker is in our confidence and will not hesitate to report any failure to carry out your duties. You're pledged to the king and to God to say mass every day and invoke God's protection for the prince. Is that clear?"

"As you say, Bishop."

De Grandison knew better than to believe him. But he also knew that the caretaker was now employed by the diocese and that the parish priests in Tintagel and Bodmin all knew what was coming into their midst and what their bishop expected of them. He also knew that the coachman who would take them west and the footman who would accompany them had both served in the king's armies in France and would have no qualms about keeping de Villiers in line.

"Very well." De Grandison rose. "You depart in the morning." He paused at the door. "There's just one more thing I'd like you to explain, de Villiers. Why do you harbor such animosity to Father Chegwin?"

"Isn't it clear, Bishop? He's a Cornishman. Unfit to be admitted to the priesthood. For Christ's sake, we don't even allow *women* to be priests! And as inferior as they are, they're *far* superior to a Cornish pig."

"Then may God have mercy on you, de Villiers, since you're to be surrounded by Cornishmen for the rest of your days."

"Wait! What do you mean the rest of—"

De Grandison turned his back and walked out the door.

XXXVIII

Chudleigh, 1362

Whitsuntide was approaching when de Grandison finally received a reply to his inquiries to Ireland about Piran's whereabouts. He sat at his writing table for a full quarter hour just looking at the sealed letter on the tabletop. What if it held bad news? Did he really want to know?

At long last, he picked up the letter and walked outside to the walled garden where he always sought solace when things were troubling him. When he'd first come to Chudleigh, the space was overgrown from years of neglect by his predecessors. He'd had it cleaned out and replanted. Shrubs and hedges to give a softer look against the hard stone walls. And abundant flowers, so that from the first snowdrops of late winter until the autumn crocuses shivered in the November winds there were colorful blooms with ample nectar for the creatures that fed on them. Opposite the long stone bench under the ancient oak tree in the southwest corner he'd placed a statue of the Blessed Virgin cradling her baby son in her arms – the same image that adorned his bishop's ring.

Now, as June began, the garden was awash in color as roses, poppies, peonies, lupins, sweetpeas, and more vied for the attention of the butterflies and bees flitting from bloom to bloom. Here, a man could feel the miracle of God's creation and commune with that creation in a way that wasn't possible inside the walls of a church, hallowed though that space might be.

Carrying the still unopened letter, de Grandison walked every path, pausing now and then when a butterfly lit on his arm or the scent of a particular rose demanded that one deeply inhale its sweetness. Eventually, he made his way to the giant oak and settled on the bench. *Holy Mary, let this letter not bring sadness but joy and hope.* He turned the missive over and over in his hands and finally broke the seal.

In nomine Patris et Filii et Spiritus Sancti

To Bishop John de Grandison

You are no doubt wondering why I have delayed so long in replying to your letter. The truth is that I have been of two minds about my response. As you were not particularly forthcoming with your reasons for wanting to reestablish contact with your former protégé, I had to weigh whether or not such contact would be welcome. I have, at long last, come to the conclusion that I should leave this in God's hands and give you the answer you seek.

Father Chegwin is indeed with us here in Ireland as a parish priest in Ballycomeen. I am given to understand that he is beloved by his parishioners, who would be quite bereft were he to leave them. I am also given to understand that Chegwin is a good priest and as devoted to his flock as they are to him. And now, perhaps, you will comprehend my hesitancy in answering your inquiry.

There was one peculiar thing that his bishop mentioned. It seems that, on Christmas Eve, Father Chegwin followed an order of service that is somewhat different from our normal practice here. When asked about it, Chegwin replied that it was in memory of someone he cared deeply about who had somehow become lost to him. His bishop and I have decided we have no reason to interfere.

May God's blessings be with you, sir, and may this information give you some comfort. May God also guide you to the right choice for peace for yourself and for Father Chegwin.

John de St. Paul, Archbishop of Dublin

May 12th in the year of our lord 1362

De Grandison's eyes welled with tears and he made no effort to stop the flow. Tears of joy that Piran was alive. Tears of sadness that he thought he'd been abandoned. Tears of love that no matter what, he still remembered. *Blessed Mary, guide me now. Give me the wisdom to know what to do.*

An hour later, Étienne found him still sitting on the bench, holding the letter in his hand, the streaks on his cheeks revealing the tears that had been shed. Wordlessly, Étienne sat beside him. Wordlessly, de Grandison handed Étienne the letter. When he'd finished reading, Étienne folded the page and returned it to his dear friend.

They sat in silence in the warmth of the summer sun as a light breeze rustled the leaves of the giant oak. At long last, Étienne asked, "What are you going to do?"

"He's happy. He's living the life he always dreamed about." De Grandison paused for a very long moment. "We're going to leave him be."

Epilogue

Dublin, Ireland, July 1369

He'd never been summoned by the archbishop before, so Piran was filled with curiosity as he waited in the entry hall of the bishop's palace while the canon who had admitted him went to announce his arrival. That curiosity was piqued even further when it was Archbishop Minot himself who returned to the hall. "Father Chegwin, I presume?"

"Yes, Father." Piran bent and kissed the proffered ring.

"It's a fine day. Shall we talk in the garden?"

"As you wish."

Minot led the way to some benches opposite a grove of young trees. "Two days ago, Father Chegwin, I received a letter from Exeter, from a Father Bonfils. Someone you once knew, perhaps?"

"Aye, Father. We were once the best of friends."

"From what I've been able to learn, Chegwin, it appears you came to us at a time when you were leaving the past behind and that you've been quite content here in Ballycomeen. All of which leaves me uncertain if you would want to know what Bonfils has written or if that would cause distress you would prefer to avoid."

"I've made peace with the past, Father. If Étienne is sending word to me now, he must believe it's something I should know."

From beneath the sash of his cassock, Minot retrieved a folded page. "Then I'll leave you to read this." He handed the letter to Piran. "And if you decide you wish to take a brief leave from your duties here, you need only let one of my canons know and we will see that your parishioners are cared for during your absence." He rose to leave. "God be with you, my son."

Piran waited until Minot was out of sight before opening the letter.

In nomine Patris et Filii et Spiritus Sancti

To the most reverend Thomas Minot, Archbishop of Dublin

It is with a heavy heart that I write to tell you that our dearly beloved Bishop of Exeter, John de Grandison, went to be with God yesterday as the bells tolled for Vespers. We grieve his passing even as we know he will be welcomed into Heaven.

There is one other who, if he is yet alive, will, I think, be saddened by this news. If Father Piran Chegwin is still within one of your parishes, I would be most grateful if you would convey the news to him. You may tell him also that I have long missed his company and would be comforted should he choose to join me, no matter how briefly, to mourn the man who was such a dear friend to us both.

Yours in Christ,

Father Étienne Bonfils

Written at Chudleigh on the 17th day of July 1369

Piran folded the letter and went in search of a canon. There was no question about what he wanted to do.

Exeter, August 2nd, 1369

The cathedral was as beautiful as Piran remembered. He made his way down the long nave, through the elaborately carved screen, and past the stalls of the choir to kneel before the altar. When he finished his brief devotion and stood, a voice from behind him said quietly, "May I be of any assistance, Father?"

He turned to find one of the canons of the cathedral chapter standing beside the nearest stall. "Perhaps you can. Is Father Bonfils here?"

"Let me fetch him."

Étienne found Piran standing beside Bishop Branscombe's beautifully carved and painted tomb. They embraced for a very long time, as if trying to bridge the years that had separated them. When at long last they stood apart, Étienne said quietly, "I was so in hopes you'd come."

They went out into the cloister and found a quiet place to sit and talk. "Tell me everything, Étienne," said Piran. "What went so wrong?"

Étienne recounted the whole sad tale of de Villiers's last crimes and his reckoning at de Grandison's hands then continued, "Father searched for you, Piran. Wrote dozens of letters to anyone he could think of who might know your whereabouts. It was six months before we heard from Archbishop St. Paul, who told us where you were and that you were fulfilled and content. Father made the heart-wrenching decision that the kindest thing he could do for you was to leave you in peace. He grieved your loss, Piran, but wanted you to be happy."

"Tell me about his last years . . . about how he died."

"He was actually in robust good health until this spring, and even then, he wasn't really ill – just slowing down considerably. When we got the news shortly before Midsummer's Day that de Villiers had died, he started to decline more rapidly. I think perhaps the knowledge that there could never be another threat against you allowed him to accept that his work here on earth was done. He was fully at peace when he left us."

They sat together in silence for a very long time. Eventually, Piran said, "As I walked about the cathedral, I didn't see anything underway for his tomb."

"That's the way he wanted it. When the west front of the cathedral was being finished, he had a small chantry chapel built there, just to the south of the main entrance. 'A simple resting place for a simple bishop,' he once told me."

"Take me to him, Étienne."

They made their way back through the cathedral and out the entrance. Turning to the left, Étienne said, "Just there." A small arched door in the stonework might easily be overlooked if one was admiring the grandeur of the west front. The inset painted red, it was adorned with a simple lattice of wood with carved quatrefoils. Étienne opened the door and the two men stepped inside. A plain stone sarcophagus bore a metal plaque that read "Piteous bishop, most piteous servant of the Mother of Mercy."

"Exactly as he wanted." Étienne's voice was almost a whisper. After a long silence, he added, "The last thing he said to me was, 'If you ever see Piran again, tell him he was the son God sent me because I could never have one of my own.'"

As Étienne quietly left the small chapel, Piran knelt beside the tomb, laid the red velvet pouch containing de Grandison's mother's rosary on top of it, and let the tears flow freely down his cheeks.

Author's Notes

To be honest, I'd never thought about writing a book about a medieval priest. But when a friend sent me a photo of the plaque at Tintagel's ruined chapel, the first two lines just took hold of my imagination. How had that priest come to be there in the first place? And how did he become so disillusioned that he decided to just walk away?

I also never thought I'd set out to write a book that spanned forty-three years. But as the trajectory of Piran's life took shape in my head, it just turned out that way. In large part, it was shaped by known events in the lives of the historical figures Piran encounters, most particularly John de Grandison.

Originally, de Grandison was intended to be primarily a catalyst who propelled Piran in one direction or another. But the more I learned about him, the clearer it became that he would be a central figure in the evolution of the narrative. In various sources, his name is given as de Grandison, de Grandisson, Grandison, or Grandisson. These days, he's generally referred to as Bishop Grandison. In the 14th century, however, surnames of the nobility in many languages often included "of" either to denote a person's place of origin or to link them to an important or powerful family. The bishop's family originated in a French-speaking area of Switzerland and the English branch of the family would almost certainly have spoken Norman

French as their first language. For that reason, I've chosen to refer to him as "de Grandison."

Unlike many other bishops of the time, de Grandison does not seem to have been particularly ambitious. He never sought a government position nor did he appear to have any interest in becoming an archbishop or cardinal. He preferred his work on formalizing and documenting the many orders of service for Exeter Cathedral and on documenting the lives of the saints (both mentioned in this narrative). His humility was also evident in his choice of a final resting place. Sadly, his chantry chapel was ransacked during the Reformation and is no longer open to the public. But the little door is still there if you know to look for it.

Historical Figures

This novel is more heavily populated with actual historical figures than some of my previous stories, so it seemed worthwhile to document them here. While their names may be incidental to the plot, their roles are essential and, since the names of the individuals in those positions are well known, it would have made no sense to create a fictional character. Whatever else you may think of the Roman Catholic Church, one thing they excel at is record-keeping, even in an era where records of other institutions, such as the great universities, may be incomplete or lost. And much of that information is available online, either directly from Church sources or from reliably documented secondary sources.

The personalities, dialogue, and actions of historical figures who appear in this narrative are all products of my imagination. In the case of Cardinal Robert, it wasn't my intent to impugn his legacy by having him associated with someone of de Villiers's ilk. It was simply a matter of his being in the right place at the right time. I needed to get de Villiers to the papal court with some connection to the Chancery if he was to continue his mischief, and the timing of Robert's elevation to Cardinal and his appointment as a notary were a perfect fit.

Dates given below are the dates during which the individual held the position indicated.

John de Grandison, Bishop of Exeter 1327-1369

To this day, the longest serving Bishop of Exeter in both the Roman Catholic Church and the Church of England

Archdeacon of Nottingham prior to his episcopate

Inherited his family title and estates in 1358 upon the death of his elder brother without a direct heir

Studied civil law briefly at Oxford in 1306

Studied theology under Jacques Fournier (later, Pope Benedict XII) at the University of Paris 1313-1317

Protégé and friend of Pope John XXII (Jacques Duèze) for whom he conducted diplomatic missions

Completed the reconstruction of Exeter Cathedral, founded a collegiate chapter at Ottery St. Mary, and rebuilt the church there

A well-known bibliophile who assembled a substantial library, including some books that went back to Bishop Leofric in the mid-11th century; famous for making notes in the margins of his books

Created formal specifications for the liturgy and services at Exeter Cathedral; his service for Christmas Eve (known today as the Grandison Service) was discontinued for a time but recently revived and is now the formal Christmas Eve service at Exeter Cathedral

A devotee of the Virgin Mary, his bishop's ring, found in the ruins of his tomb after it was desecrated during the Reformation, has a carving of the Madonna and Child which is believed to have been enameled, as a few bits of the enamel still remain

In Avignon

Pope John XXII (Jacques Duèze), 1316-1334

Selected, at the age of 67, by the highly contentious Conclave that lasted from 1314 to 1316; longest reigning of the Avignon popes

Chosen largely because it was believed he wouldn't live long and wouldn't have much effect on the Church or the institution of the papacy; he proved everyone wrong by living to the age of 87 and instituting significant reforms in the Church

Canonized Thomas Aquinas (among others)

Expanded and decorated the former episcopal palace in Avignon to become a lavish papal residence; the Papal Palace seen today in Avignon is a newer edifice built by later popes on the same location as John XXII's palace

Pope Benedict XII (Jacques Fournier), 1334-1342

Elected when one faction of the Italians (who wanted the Holy See returned to Rome) joined the French (who wanted to remain in Avignon) because of a feud with another Italian faction

Began construction of the Papal Palace we see today, demolishing John XXII's palace in the process

Pope Clement VI (Pierre Roger), 1342-1352

Reigned during the first occurrence of the Black Death in Europe, which devastated the town of Avignon

Added the "New Palace" wing onto the construction begun by his predecessor

Cardinal Pierre des Près

Vice-Chancellor of the Holy Roman Church, 1325-1361

Dean of the Sacred College of Cardinals, 1336-1361

Known to be a friend of John de Grandison

Built the collegiate Church of St. Pierre in Avignon (very near the Papal Palace)

Cardinal Bertrand de Montfavez

Protonotary Apostolic

Cardinal Imbert Dupuis (sometimes spelled Du Puy)

    Protonotary Apostolic

    Camerlengo of the Sacred College of Cardinals, 1340-1348

Cardinal Adhémar Robert

    Notary Apostolic

    Related to Clement VI (either cousin or nephew) on his mother's side

    Named a cardinal by Clement VI in the consistory of 1342

    Died in 1352, five days before Clement VI

Cardinal Élie Talleyrand de Périgord

    Succeeded Pierre des Près as Dean of the Sacred College of Cardinals

Archbishop Gasbert de Valle

    Camerlengo of the Holy Roman Church, 1319-1347

In England and Ireland

King Edward III

Richard de Braylegh, Dean of Exeter Cathedral, 1335-1352

Henry de Seton, Master of Balliol College, 1324-1328

Katherine de Grandison

    Younger sister of John de Grandison

    Married William Montagu, close friend of Edward III who helped overthrow Roger Mortimer and later became the 1st Earl of Salisbury

John Droxford, Bishop of Bath and Wells, 1309-1329

William Melton, Archbishop of York, 1315-1340

John Langton, Bishop of Chichester, 1305-1337

Otto de Northwode, Archdeacon of Exeter, 1345-1360

Stephen de Pempel, Archdeacon of Exeter, 1360-1361

Philip de Beauchamp, Archdeacon of Exeter, 1361-1371
    Great-nephew of John de Grandison

John de St. Paul, Archbishop of Dublin, 1349-1362

Thomas Minot, Archbishop of Dublin, 1363-1375

Robert Wyvil, Bishop of Salisbury, 1330-1375

Officials of the Holy See

Readers not familiar with the operations of the papal court may appreciate some guidance as to the responsibilities of the various departments and the offices therein. It can be confusing when different titles are used at different times for exactly the same office, so I have tried to provide some clarity here.

Chancery

The department within the Holy See responsible for administration and records

In addition to the notaries, there were *scritores* (scribes who prepared final documents), *abbreviatores* (who drafted documents), and *lectores* (who read documents during the process of listening to the material and recommending final revisions; *lectores* were usually *scritores* doing the reading)

Chancellor of the Holy Roman Church, Vice-Chancellor of the Holy Roman Church

Different titles used at various times for the same office

Head of the Chancery

Typically, a cardinal

Protonotary Apostolic, Notary Apostolic, Papal Notary

Different titles used at various times for the same office

The senior clerics in the Chancery and responsible for the documents produced by and documentation of the transactions of the Holy See

There were seven notaries within the Chancery

At various points in history, only cardinals were eligible to be notaries; at other times, there was no such requirement

Camerlengo

From the Italian that means "chamberlain"

Responsible for administering property and finances – much like a Chief Financial Officer in today's business world

The Camerlengo of the Holy Roman Church is responsible for the finances of the Holy See

The Camerlengo of the Sacred College of Cardinals holds similar responsibilities for the separate finances of the College of Cardinals

Dean of the Sacred College of Cardinals

The most senior of the cardinals, leader of the college

At various times through history, this was either an elected position or was occupied by whoever was the longest-serving cardinal at the time

Among other responsibilities, convenes and leads the Conclave to select a new Pope

Place Names

As in previous books, I've used the names of places as they were known at the time of the story. In some cases, different names appear on modern maps.

- *Aquae Sulis* was the Roman name for the city of Bath
- **Ballycomeen** in Ireland is known today as Blessington
- **Grope Lane** in Oxford is now known as Magpie Lane. Its depiction in the story is authentic for the period. I didn't include it for fun or sensationalism, though it is atmospheric. If you look at very old maps of Oxford – I found one from 1440 – it's clearly the fastest route from most of the High Street to the priory church.
- **Mor Havren** was the ancient Cornish name for the Bristol Channel
- The **Swindlestock Tavern** was a fixture in Oxford from 1270 until 1709 and was the site of the St. Scholastica Day riot in February, 1355. It was located at the intersection of High Street and Fish Street (today called St. Aldate's Street) at what is now Abbey House, the home of Bank Santander.
- **Trevelgi** is the Cornish name for Trevelga
- **Weolingtun** was the medieval name for Wellington in Devonshire
- **Ynys Witrin** was the ancient name of the lake that once surrounded Glastonbury Tor

Tintagel

Many people know Tintagel's link to the King Arthur legends, and there *are* early medieval ruins on the headland. What some might not know is that there was also a late medieval castle on the site. Built in the 13th century, it was unusual in that half the castle was on the mainland and the other half on the headland, which were, at some point connected by a narrow land bridge. Each half of the castle had a courtyard and significant structures.

Time and the constant pounding of the sea have deepened the ravine and collapsed some of the cliff walls so that the headland is now essentially an island. That erosion had begun even in the 14th century. The new visitors' bridge (opened in 2019) is in the same location as the ancient land bridge (and the later man-made bridge) that connected the two courtyards. There are some quite dramatic photos online that show the two halves of the castle, now separated by a deep ravine.

At the time of this story, the late medieval castle belonged to Edward of Woodstock, Prince of Wales and Duke of Cornwall – Edward III's heir, later known as the Black Prince. Through neglect and lack of maintenance, it was already falling into disrepair. The roof over the main dining hall had been pulled down as it was in danger of collapse. But the buildings in the courtyard on the headland were still intact. It's said that the duke never visited this castle. That assertion is quite plausible since, from the time he was about sixteen, the prince was actively engaged in his father's wars in France, and after the Treaty of Brétigny was signed in October 1360, he was made Prince of Aquitaine and spent most of the rest of his life there administering that territory for England.

Dates & Days of the Week

Because the world still used the Julian calendar in the 14th century, I've used that for determining any days of the week mentioned in the story. I've also done my best to get the dates of Easter correct for the period. That said, because Easter is a complex calculation based on the occurrence of the vernal equinox and the full moon, many sources claim that accurate dates for Easter at the time are difficult or impossible to calculate. I did, however, find two distinct sources that agreed on the most likely dates and have used those in the narrative.

The dates of Edward III's parliaments are historically accurate. The rationale for the big gap between 1357 and 1361 is entirely my speculation.

I've mentioned in the Author's Notes of previous novels that serendipity often comes to the writer's rescue, and there's an instance of that in this book. There were a number of constraints involved in the timing of the knife fight in chapter IX. I was working both forward from Easter and backward from when Piran would receive his degree. There needed to be a few weeks of de Villiers's absence prior to the fight and then, of course, sufficient time for Piran's injuries to heal. To complicate things further, I wanted the fight to occur on a moonless night – and on a Friday so that de Grandison would be walking home from his usual Friday supper with Bertran. Quite a daunting task – or so it seemed. I got lucky. I found a source for the moon phases in 1326, showing a new moon on 1 June, which would have been a Sunday. Back up two days to Friday, and the moon would have risen at approximately 4:00 a.m. So it would have been a moonless night on May 30th when Piran and his mates left the Swindlestock.

The Arthurian Legend

Geoffrey of Monmouth's *The History of the Kings of Britain* – one of the earliest written works to give structure to the King Arthur legends – was written about 1136, so it would have been known in the 14th century. As an educated man, Piran might have been aware of the work. But it seems to me that ordinary villagers on the far western coast of Cornwall would not – they would've had only whatever oral traditions had evolved in the area.

One choice I could have made would have been to have Piran bring the oral tradition and written work together through recounting Geoffrey's version of the tales to the villagers, but I quickly discarded that as boring. Piran is already a spiritual person. Using his connection to the spiritual and the effects of isolation on the human psyche as a bridge between legend and reality – in a place where the two naturally converge – offered a much richer opportunity for storytelling.

Miscellaneous

The plaque at the chapel ruins at Tintagel states that the chapel was dedicated to St. Hulanus. Other sources say it was dedicated to St. Julitta or St. Juliot. Those sources indicate that St. Julitta and St. Juliot are likely the same person. Whether or not St. Hulanus actually existed appears to be open for debate. I chose to use Julitta, as that appears to be the Cornish form of Juliot.

In the 14th century, the Catholic dioceses of England were divided into two provinces, one overseen by the Archbishop of Canterbury, the other by the Archbishop of York. While in later years, Nottingham was within the diocese of Lincoln (and therefore subject to the Archbishop of Canterbury), at the time of this story, Nottingham came under the supervision of the Archbishop of York.

After the departure of the Romans from Britain, the territory we know today as Wales was organized into a number of separate kingdoms, with the number, size, and organization of those kingdoms shifting a lot over time. Deheubarth wasn't formed until around 920 CE, which is a little late for the Arthurian legend, but I've taken a bit of artistic license by using the name to represent tribes along the northern shore of the Bristol Channel (southern coast of what is now Wales).

The word "Mister" as the generic honorific for a man came into the language somewhat later than this story. In the 14th century, that honorific would have been "Master." But then there's the problem that the "chief academic officer" of a Hall or College at Oxford is referred to as Master. To avoid confusing my readers, I've used the anachronistic "Mister" for ordinary folk in this narrative.

There being no formal postal service at the time, the only means of sending letters was to hire a messenger or courier. But that didn't stop people sending letters, even several centuries before this tale. Perhaps one of the most famous couriers of the fourteenth century was someone not generally known for his role as a letter-carrier – Geoffrey Chaucer. Wikipedia reports that, in October 1360, Chaucer was paid nine shillings by Lionel of Antwerp (third son and second surviving son of Edward III) to carry letters from France to England. A messenger's fee varied greatly depending on the pre-eminence of the individual hiring him and the distance between sender and recipient.

The medieval remedy for a man who's been badly beaten (at the end of chapter XI) comes from the book *Revolting Remedies from the Middle Ages*. This fascinating little book was compiled by Daniel Wakelin, Jeremy Griffiths Professor of Medieval English Palaeography in the Faculty of English, University of Oxford, and several students in his Master's course on handling and reading old manuscripts, specifically from the 7th to the 16th century.

You can listen to a performance of "Hush-a-bye My Little Crumb" by a British folk singer at:
https://www.youtube.com/watch?v=-K337urH_v4&t=0s.

ACKNOWLEDGMENTS

Doing the research for this book was as much of a joy as actually writing it. In retrospect, I wish I'd had more time while in the UK to immerse myself in the places that figure in the narrative, but I suppose that's always the case. After all, when one sets out to research a story, it's impossible to know what you don't know and how that will shape the narrative – and it's equally impossible to know how the evolving narrative will shape what you might need to know.

I can't say enough about the wonderful people who, despite my highly compressed schedule, gave generously of their time and knowledge to help bring this story to life. If I've gotten anything wrong, the fault is entirely mine and not theirs.

Even before I left on the trip, I had a very helpful e-mail exchange with Dr. Robin Darwall-Smith, who, among other roles, is Archivist at University College, Oxford. Thanks to his suggestion of *English University Life in The Middle Ages* by Alan Cobban, I had some background reading for the flight that gave me a grounding in what student life at Oxford University would have been like in the 14th century.

Miranda Hockliffe, Volunteer and Visitor Coordinator at Christ Church Cathedral, kindly organized my visit there. David Allen provided a richly detailed tour that focused on what the cathedral would have been like in 1326 when it was still the priory church of St. Frideswide's Priory. Christ

Church College Archivist Judith Curthoys, was a wealth of information both about the cathedral and about life in Oxford in the 1320's. Her generous gift of a copy of her book, *The King's Cathedral: The Ancient Heart of Christ Church, Oxford*, was invaluable as I wrote of the time Piran spent in Oxford.

I was supposed to meet Lizzie Casey, Choir Manager at Merton College Chapel, early in the afternoon on the day of my arrival in the UK. So naturally, my flight was delayed three-and-a-half hours, during which time I had no way to let her know the situation. It was my great good fortune that her patience and her work schedule for the day allowed us time to visit after all. Even though the chapel didn't end up making it into this book, I've no doubt the time she spent showing me around will prove valuable at some future time.

In Exeter, my visit with the cathedral's archivist, Ellie Jones, was nothing short of spectacular. In addition to the resource materials she provided for later reference, her personal knowledge about Bishop de Grandison gave me insight into his life and work that informed how I developed his character in the book. Among the many highlights of my visit with her was the opportunity to view two books from the period – working texts for the cathedral clergy – one of which had a margin notation in de Grandison's own handwriting. She also showed me the bishop's ring and wax seal, which were not on public display at the time of my visit.

Thanks also go to Professor Adrian Freeman for his particularly informative cathedral tour that clearly delineated what parts of the cathedral were complete when de Grandison arrived and what was completed during his episcopate. He also made sure I didn't miss seeing the entrance to de Grandison's chantry chapel.

None of this would have been possible without the wonderful Sara Thornton, who cared for my Corgis while I was away. Maggi and Tay both love Sara. And knowing she was looking after them allowed me to focus on the research without having to fret about their welfare.

Behind every good author, there's always a good editor, and I'm fortunate to have Linda Kirwin in my court. Thank you, Linda, for everything you do.

Thanks, as always, to my publisher, Black Rose Writing, for your continued support.

And thank *you*, dear readers, for bringing these stories into your lives. I hope you've had as much pleasure reading or listening to them as I've had in bringing them to life.

ABOUT THE AUTHOR

Pamela Taylor's "trip of a lifetime" may have been the one where she got to touch a 700-year-old book and examine the account rolls for the construction of a gothic cathedral. A self-professed history-geek, she finds the past offers rich sources of character, ambiance, and story that allow readers to escape into a world totally unlike their daily lives.

"Weaving a narrative around gaps or exploring contradictions in the historical record is fertile ground for the novelist," she says. "And just as intriguing as imagining the lives of actual historical figures."

Pamela shares her home with two Pembroke Welsh Corgis who frequently remind her that a dog walk is the best inspiration for that next chapter.

NOTE FROM PAMELA TAYLOR

Word-of-mouth is crucial for any author to succeed. If you enjoyed *The Last Priest of Tintagel*, please leave a review online—anywhere you are able. Even if it's just a sentence or two. It would make all the difference and would be very much appreciated.

Thanks!
Pamela Taylor

We hope you enjoyed reading this title from:

www.blackrosewriting.com

Subscribe to our mailing list – *The Rosevine* – and receive **FREE** books, daily deals, and stay current with news about upcoming releases and our hottest authors.
Scan the QR code below to sign up.

Already a subscriber? Please accept a sincere thank you for being a fan of Black Rose Writing authors.

View other Black Rose Writing titles at www.blackrosewriting.com/books and use promo code **PRINT** to receive a **20% discount** when purchasing.